dixie OWENS

dixie OWENS

Bonneville Books
Springville, Utah

This is a work of fiction. The characters, names, incidents, places, and dialogue are products of the author's imagination, and are not to be construed as real.

ISBN 13: 978-1-59955-402-0

Published by Bonneville, an imprint of Cedar Fort, Inc., 2373 W. 700 S., Springville, UT 84663
Distributed by Cedar Fort, Inc., www.cedarfort.com

LIBRARY OF CONGRESS CATALOGING-IN-PUBLICATION DATA

Owens, Dixie, 1943-
Becoming Kate / Dixie Owens.
p. cm.
ISBN 978-1-59955-402-0 (alk. paper)
1. Traffic accident victims--Fiction. 2. Brain--Transplantation--Patients--Fiction.
3. Multiple personality--Fiction. I. Title.
PS3615.W448B43 2010
813'.6--dc22

2010005517

Cover design by Tanya Quinlan
Cover design © 2010 by Lyle Mortimer
Edited and typeset by Heidi Doxey

Printed in Canada

10 9 8 7 6 5 4 3 2 1

Printed on acid-free paper

Dedicated to
my good friend and pen pal,
Diana Howell

prologue

Saturday, September 15, 8:12 AM—Hayward, California

Liz had no idea that today would be the last day of her life. It started like any other Saturday. She wore the same jeans she wore every weekend, applied the same color lipstick, grabbed the keys to the same Honda she'd been driving for six years, and slung her same old purse over her shoulder. There was too much to do and not enough time. She had an hour to grocery shop before she had to take Mark to his karate lessons, eat lunch, and then shuttle Megan and her friend, Alicia to gymnastics. Then later that evening she was hosting friends for dinner followed by card games for the adults and video games for the kids.

Liz stuffed the grocery list into her jeans, planted a quick peck on Mark and Megan's cheeks and called back as she hustled out the door, "Don't forget to make your beds, put your cereal bowls in the dishwasher, and Megan, put the milk in the fridge."

Outside, her husband, Bruce, was washing the Blazer while Algae, the family dog, was successfully attacking the squirting hose. It was a game they played each week, weather permitting. Both were thoroughly soaked and joyful.

Algae, a large black Lab with soulful eyes and a playful spirit, trotted over to Liz and tried to place a wet paw on her leg. But she jumped back and shook her head. Liz was amused when Algae turned, tail wagging, and trotted back to Bruce.

Six years Liz's senior, Bruce stood over six feet tall, had black curly hair, dark sensuous eyes, and deep cut smile lines. After ten years of marriage, and even in a pair of tattered jeans and a wet T-shirt, he still looked mighty good to her.

Jumping into her Honda, she shouted above the noise of the hose, "I'll be back in less than an hour. Mark's karate outfit is on top of his dresser. Don't let him get it dirty before his lesson."

She slowed as she drove over the familiar speed bump in front of her small two-story track home. Every other house on the street was a clone except for the different paint colors and various attempts at landscaping. She tried to erase the sorry images, accelerated, and steadied the wheel. She popped a CD into the player and sang along—slightly off-key.

She jumped as the alarm on her cell phone beeped twice. Grabbing her purse from the floor, she pulled the phone from the outer pocket. The screen read: "Maria's birthday tomorrow." Liz gasped.

How could she forget her friend's birthday? She silenced the CD player, pressed the voice activation button on the phone, and clearly enunciated, "Maria." She glanced up and down the street to check for cops. The last thing she needed was to be pulled over for talking on her cell while driving. After six rings, the familiar recording came on: "We screen all incoming calls. If we're not answering, it's because we don't want to talk to you."

Liz laughed and waited for the tone. "Pick up, Maria. It's Liz. Just want to find out your plans for tomorrow. Call when you have a chance, and we'll celebrate your birthday." Liz ended the call. Frustration filled her. There was too much to do—too much to think about. She was stretched to the limits.

She slowed to stop at the next intersection, muttering a curse as she eyed the temporary wall that blocked her right view. This had always been her route to the grocery store, at least until two weeks ago when construction had rendered it a blind intersection.

Her eyes shifted left to right. With no pedestrians or traffic in sight, she turned right onto Mission Boulevard.

Screeching. Blaring horn. Her eyes widened as the grill of an eighteen-wheeler skidded directly toward her. For a split second, she froze. Then she stomped her foot on the brake and turned the wheel wildly. She stiffened as the world moved in slow motion.

In detached wonder, Liz watched her car pirouette in a smooth arc. The leaves on the trees near the curb were clear and shining. She could almost count them. She smelled lilies, felt the warm sun, noticed billowy clouds that made pictures of people and animals. Oddly, she realized she hadn't looked at clouds this way for years. One clump of clouds reminded her of her husband, Bruce, who was at home performing his weekly tradition of washing the Blazer with Algae, their dog. By now both would be wet and enjoying each other. She imagined seeing her nine-year-old daughter, Megan, dressed in a leotard, about to try a new gymnastics trick. Then other clouds formed into her son, seven-year-old Mark. She saw him practicing karate chops in his oversized white pants.

The truck danced nearer. She saw the insignia on the hood of the green truck—a small scratch on the fender.

Liz studied the face of the man behind the wheel, sure that he had brown hair. *Why does he seem so frightened?* Or maybe he was just concerned.

She felt amazingly calm . . . almost euphoric.

chapter one

Tuesday, September 18, 2:18 PM

Liz felt as if her soul had been ripped from her body and sucked back in. *Probably been dreaming.* In a moment or two, she'd snap out of her trance and come to.

Pungent antiseptic odors assaulted her, made her grimace. The scent permeated the air—a familiar odor, but not home. Steady beeping noises, mingled with whispers, caught her attention. The words weren't clear, but she could hear concern. Yet, unlike the odor, the voices weren't familiar.

Sharp pains shot through her head. She gasped.

As she opened her eyes, a surge of vertigo struck her. She was falling backward, tumbling. A hundred feet, two hundred feet—the descent continued, reeling downward. Pain racked her body, contorting it.

"Bruce," she called. But what came out was just a groan.

Voices became louder. They were saying, "Kate, Kate . . ."

The room was still out of focus, and a bright, unpleasant light blinded her.

Shivering and moaning, she lifted a free hand and rubbed her eyes as she turned her head toward the sounds. Someone was patting her other hand. Liz looked into the teary-eyed face of a well-groomed, middle-aged woman.

She tried to speak, but something was different—her tongue, her throat, even her lungs felt strange. Her teeth didn't fit the same.

No. Oh no. I must be paralyzed.

As another groan escaped her lips, she found her voice and rasped, "Who are you?"

"Oh my goodness," the woman said, tears streaming down her face. "You're awake! It's me, Kate. It's your mother!"

Liz blinked at the stranger. "No, no, you're wrong," she mumbled.

This had to be a dream. She closed her eyes, sure that when she reopened them she'd be home.

But no, the dark-haired woman with hazel eyes and porcelain skin was still there, murmuring kind phrases.

"Kate . . . our miracle child," quavered a male voice. Next to the woman stood a tall, handsome man, shaking his head as though in disbelief.

Liz looked around. She was in an unfamiliar room with windows that allowed people from the hallway to see in. *How did I get here?*

Still in pain, she turned toward the incessant beeping and sighed when she saw the vital signs monitor.

Bruce, get me out of here.

She glanced at her left hand and saw an intravenous feed-tube dripping life-saving fluids, but her hands were wrong. The nails weren't hers. The fingers weren't the long, self-manicured fingers she knew so well. Instead, they were small and thin with knobby knuckles. And where was her wedding band?

As Liz lifted her other hand to her hair, she gasped. Where was her long reddish-blonde hair? Frantic now, she looked down at her body. Gone were the womanly curves. Panic seizing her, she pulled up the covers and looked down at two short white bony legs.

Was someone playing a cruel game? Was she crazy? Still dreaming?

She ripped the tubes from her hand, pushed the "mother" woman away, and tried to get out of bed. But bedrails were up. As she fought to escape, buzzers went off, followed by the sound of footfalls in the hallway. Despite pain and an uncharacteristic lack of strength, Liz rose to her knees. Just before collapsing, she saw her reflection in the window—a bald, bewildered pre-pubescent female.

Blackness enveloped her.

7:40 PM

As Liz drifted in and out of consciousness, bold colors and kaleidoscope designs flashed across the backs of her eyelids. When she neared consciousness, she caught a few nonsensical phrases: "transplant . . . organ rejection . . . memories erased . . . physical therapy . . . body memories . . ."

Once again she opened her eyes. The pain had subsided, and the petite woman, her so-called mom, was talking with a doctor in the hallway. At Liz's left, a nurse was changing a bag of IV liquid.

Panicked, Liz tried to move, but her arms were tethered. They had put her in restraints. Desperate, she began to sob. For a moment, she thought she would drown in her tears.

When she could finally make sense of the scene, it was as though she was peering through gauze.

"Where am I?" she demanded between sobs. "And what have you done to me?"

The nurse came to her bedside and put a hand to Liz's cheek. "Mrs. Craig, she's awake," the nurse said, directing her comments to the woman in the hall.

Liz honed in on the nurse's badge. It was emblazoned with the words "Stanford Hospital—Margaret Schlickter, R.N."

Mrs. Craig interrupted her conversation with the doctor and walked to Liz's bedside. She cooed gently, "It's all right, Kate. You're going to be just fine. Momma loves you." Her words were choked with happiness.

Liz shut her eyes tight and tried to remember. What was the last thing that happened before waking here?

Suddenly there was a flash. She relived the truck bearing down on her and the slow-motion ballet between car and truck. After that, she recalled sounds . . . no physical feelings . . . no visuals. She remembered crinkling metal, sirens, loud voices, wheels turning, doors shushing open and closed. She recalled her husband's voice and someone remarking about her driver's license . . . an organ donor stamp on the back. And she remembered that, for a moment, she had thought that she had seen her mother bending over her and smiling.

But that was impossible. Her mother had died nine years earlier.

Then she recalled a bright light. A light so warm and inviting that she had risen up to meet it. Then there was no sound, no consciousness—just a void.

"Oh, no!" Liz cried out as the middle-aged woman came to her side.

"Kate, darling, don't cry. Momma's here," the "mother" said as she stroked Liz's cheek.

Not real . . . not real . . . Liz closed her eyes tight and shut out the world.

9:00 PM

Liz saw two men and a woman, all in doctor's jackets, walking toward her room. One man was tall, slender, and graying; the other was a bit shorter, Asian, with dark, horn-rimmed glasses. The woman appeared to be African-American, in her mid-thirties, with short black hair and a slight limp.

Liz feigned sleep, afraid to move. As the doctors entered her room, she heard the female say, "I'm so glad the surgery went well, Dr. Jamison. The results are amazing."

Liz frowned. *What surgery is she talking about?*

"I'm very pleased, Dr. Johnson," Dr. Jamison replied. "Ready for this, Dr. Yamaguchi?"

"Sure," Dr. Yamaguchi said, "just want to check the restraints first. I heard that the patient woke up disoriented and was difficult to handle today."

The female doctor gently touched Liz's wrists and arms. Then, as Liz struggled to maintain control, she heard the doctors discuss her chart and the readings from the monitor.

Liz sneaked a peek and saw that Dr. Jamison, a tall man, was obviously the "leader" of the pack. His body language was unmistakable; he called the shots. He was the one who had been talking with her "mother."

"Deborah, Felix," Jamison said to his colleagues, "yesterday we made medical history."

Medical history? What was he talking about? Liz frowned but remained still, listening. She wanted answers, and she wanted them soon.

"I'm amazed at our success," Johnson said. "Kate is not only alive but spoke this morning and displayed an alertness—beyond all expectations."

Johnson touched Liz's forehead. There was something gentle, caring, in the touch. She hadn't referred to her as "the patient." Instead, she had called her "Kate."

"Yes, but as you know, the road to recovery will be tough. It's been two and a half days, but we still have a lot of hurdles to overcome, like swelling and organ rejection," Dr. Yamaguchi said.

Organ rejection?

She felt the man's breath as he touched parts of her head. Some areas felt soft—as though sections of her head were missing.

What kind of freak am I?

"And later, when the swelling goes down," Yamaguchi continued, "we'll need to conduct the plastic skull replacements."

"Tomorrow I want to start her on a program of physical therapy with Marcy Ames. The patient's body was partially affected by the brain deterioration. She needs muscle build-up and may need to relearn how to send and receive messages to control her movements," Jamison said.

"You're right; she needs physical therapy and social interaction. Marcy's a good listener—works wonders with young people. Great choice."

Liz's mind raced. What did they mean by "brain deterioration"? She wanted to ask, but she knew they'd think she was crazy, so she waited, praying they'd let her out of the restraints if she could show them she wouldn't do anything rash.

Lord, help me, she prayed, even though she wasn't a deeply religious person. She was a Unitarian Universalist—a woman of the "thinking person's" faith, not any of the other religions *de jour.* Yet here she was, looking for answers—ready to place her life in the hands of a higher power. But whose hands? Her world had gone topsy-turvy, and she couldn't breathe.

Now what? Angry and sad, she wanted to throw something, or cry. Most of all, she wanted to see her husband and children.

"Well," Dr. Jamison said, "we've performed the first successful brain transplant. Now all we can do is wait. She either lives, or she dies. If she lives, we have to hope that by erasing the donor's personal memories, we haven't disrupted her other rudimentary skills. And, like the first heart patient, if the organ is rejected, it will happen in the first few weeks."

Weeks!

A wave of knowing filled her. Brain transplant! It was still her brain—her memories—just not her body. They didn't know. *What will happen if I tell them I still have my memories? Will they order a second surgery and do it right next time?*

Her heart sank. In her twenty-nine years, she had handled many crises, but she didn't have any experience to draw upon for this situation. Would she ever see her family again? Could she survive in this young body?

She flashed back to thirteen years ago, when she was with her mother in a doctor's office. "You have advanced breast cancer," the doctor told Liz's mother. "Even with chemotherapy you probably have only a few months."

Her mother had winked at Liz and then turned to the doctor and said, "Do you think I can cancel my dentist appointment?" Her mom always tried to find something positive in every situation. She'd lived another three years, and passed away days after holding her first grandchild.

Liz focused on this scene and called upon her mother's image to give her renewed strength. *Yes,* she decided, *I want to live. I'll take life however I can get it.*

Re-energized by her decision, she could feel her body's immune system growing stronger. She shook off depression and replaced it with the sheer wonder of "being."

She opened her eyes. *I'm Liz, I'm Kate—Kate—and I'm alive!*

She saw the three doctors' heads snap up in sync as her life signs on the monitor registered a stronger, regular heartbeat; a healthy blood pressure; and steadier, deeper breathing. As hope rushed through her veins, she felt her unfamiliar lips form a small smile. The three doctors laughed and gave each other the "thumbs up" sign.

Now she just had to make it past the next few weeks . . . and then find her family.

9:00 PM

Bruce tucked Megan and Mark into bed and kissed them good night. They wanted the night-light on, and he couldn't blame them. He needed one too.

Exhausted, he went downstairs and let Algae inside. He then grabbed a beer and popped the tab. He gulped down a long draft, wiped his mouth with his sweatshirt sleeve, and slumped into one of the straight-back chairs at the kitchen table. With elbows on the table, he cradled his head in his hands. His eyes felt swollen. He ran one hand through his unkempt hair. *Why did you go to that corner? You knew the right-hand view was blind.* He finished the beer, crushed the can with one hand, and tossed it in the recycle bin. "Two points!"

He'd had only brief naps since the police officers had arrived at his home on Saturday morning. He had just emptied the wash bucket, shooed Algae into the backyard, and was rolling up the hose when they pulled up.

"Are you Mr. Lindsay?" an officer had asked him. Bruce nodded. Then he saw both Megan and Mark peeking out the door. "We need to talk with you," the officer said. Bruce's first thought was that Liz had done something stupid—like driving too fast.

"Mark, Megan, go upstairs to your rooms," he yelled to them. "I'll be there in a minute, kids—this is adult business." Mark and Megan's eyes widened, but they were obedient—not a word of dissent.

From there the sequence of events was jumbled in his mind: neighbors watched the kids; he drove to the hospital; he saw her lifeless body—so bloody, so contorted. He felt as though he'd fallen down the rabbit's hole. She had placed a stamp on the back of her driver's license giving permission to use her undamaged organs. Bruce recalled a discussion with a doctor, but he filed it under "nightmare" and pushed it from his consciousness.

Now she was gone . . . his beautiful Liz. He choked back tears. *How can I handle the house and the kids without you? How could you leave us?*

He couldn't tell the kids. He'd called his sister, Maxine, in Oakland to come out and stay—gave her the tough job of explaining what had happened. When she told them, Megan sobbed and threw herself on her bed; Mark just stood there white-faced. Then Mark ran to Bruce, grabbed him, and hung on for over an hour until he was exhausted from grief. That day and the next, neither would speak to their Auntie Max. Bruce wondered how long it would be before they would forgive her for being the messenger of death.

Tomorrow would be his last day to make arrangements and to figure out how to move on. There was no life insurance on Liz, just on him. She had been housewife, college student, taxi driver, and mother. He never dreamed that such a thing would happen to her. On the other hand, *he* had plenty of life insurance. Bruce grimaced. *This is not the way things were supposed to happen.*

His X-ray technician contract at Kaiser provided him with three days paid leave for "family bereavement." He thumped the table with his fist. *Three days for ten years of marriage—for what was supposed to be "happily ever after."*

Helpful neighbors pitched in. But he had so much to work out and no familiarity with funerals, internments, or cremations. There were household accounts that needed to be changed, death certificates to get—and details—so many details.

His sister had gone home earlier that day, promising to return tomorrow to help. He furrowed his brow. *I need lots of help.*

He stood, pushed himself from the table, and trudged upstairs. Algae followed, head down and tail tucked, as though sensing the tragedy. He entered their bedroom and stood there for a moment in total bewilderment. Algae curled up on the floor at the foot of the bed and let out a small whimper.

Bruce felt a tear run down his face. He stared at the massive king-size bed—too big for just one. Memories of Liz sent Bruce into a jumble of contradictory emotions—loving embraces, quiet moments, and a dark abyss of despair and anger at Liz for not being careful.

The covers and sheets were in a tangle, and the throw pillows that Liz had bought just last week were on the floor. Making the bed had been a shared activity. *Guess I'm still waiting for you.*

Lovingly he touched the small jewelry music box he'd given her on their first anniversary. It played the theme from an old flick, *Love Story.* He opened it gently. When the music began to play, he picked up a charm bracelet. Hand shaking, he reached into his jean pocket and pulled out the engagement and wedding rings the hospital staff had handed him. He noted the small solitaire diamond—at the time it was all he could afford. He carefully placed the rings in the box and left the lid open so that the music continued to play.

He gasped in anguish, face contorted, and shook his head, hoping to clear it. No good. He began to shake violently, so violently that his shoulders heaved between sobs. *Get these thoughts out of my mind!* He closed the lid and pushed the box further back on the dresser.

As if in a trance, Bruce walked to the closet and opened it. Liz's clothes seemed to jump out at him. They took up four-fifths of the space. As the doors opened wider, he caught a whiff of her perfume, Youth Dew. The scent lingered on her red woolen sweater. He breathed it in, tears rimming his eyes.

Stumbling into their bathroom, he opened drawers. He stared into them and noted that as with the closet, her things took up most of the space. And there were all those "female things"—her make-up, shower gel, and something called toner. Through blurry eyes, he smiled. *Love you.*

He ran from the room. Liz seemed to be in every square inch of it. He flew down the stairs, rushed into the family room, and plopped down in his recliner. But when he looked up, Liz's trophies from her high school swim competitions stared back at him. Her *People* magazines were on the coffee table, and her slippers were lying on the floor in front of the sofa.

He closed his eyes tightly. *Why did you have to leave?*

chapter two

Wednesday, September 19, 9:30 AM

Fifteen-year-old Josh Craig stepped out of his family's Mercedes and turned off his iPhone. Reluctantly, he dragged himself into Stanford Hospital. His mom made him wear the tie and jacket—his shirt collar was too tight. He'd had just about as much of this media circus surrounding his sister, Kate, as he could stand.

"Hey, young man, you're Kate Craig's brother, aren't you?" said a reporter, jerking a microphone toward Josh's face. Josh scanned the KROX press badge. It read "Charles Rubenstein." "What's your reaction to this miracle surgery?" Rubenstein asked.

Josh felt a surge of heat crawl up his face as he pushed the reporter and cameraman aside. *First Mom and Dad—now the whole world. How long will my sister be the center of attention?*

The first five years had been bad enough, sharing his parents' affections. But when they learned about Kate's brain, his parents had become obsessed with finding a cure. But there hadn't been one—until now.

He walked behind his parents to the dais. News crews gathered close. The third press conference regarding his sister was about to commence.

Josh stewed as the cameras flashed—but his parents glowed. When Dr. Jamison pushed his way to the forefront, Josh stepped back into the shadows—his place.

From this vantage point, Josh measured the "miracle" doctor: mid-fifties, silver-haired, tall, with an air of superiority. But Josh noted that the man walked with a slight stoop, as though he carried a heavy weight. He reminded Josh of a muppet, right down to the bushy eyebrows and the mole on his cheek. Jamison was front and center for everything. He did all the talking.

Josh saw that the pushy reporter, Charles Rubenstein, had wormed his way into the front row. He was shouting out questions to Dr. Jamison and Josh's parents. "How do you feel now that the surgery is over? How does she look? Will she fully recover from the surgery, or will there be complications?" His parents tried to get out a few responses, but Jamison quickly interrupted.

"I can't emphasize enough that it has only been four days since the surgery, and we are still in a very critical period. With each passing minute, her chances for survival improve. Yes, it was a successful surgery—the brain is functioning—and I am happy to report that she gained consciousness yesterday afternoon and again this morning."

Josh wondered at this statement. What did he mean "consciousness?" Could Kate talk? He remembered how large her vocabulary had been when she was five. At that time their relationship was okay. He'd enjoyed the role of being big brother. But by the time the operation was conducted, she was nearly a vegetable; she hadn't spoken a single word for over two years.

Josh drew his attention back to the media circus.

"Dr. Jamison," a woman reporter shouted, "in layman's terms, tell us, how did you find a match for the brain transplant?"

"There were many factors taken into consideration. Of course blood type and organ size, and, unlike other transplants, we felt matching sex was important too. With these, and other more complicated factors, we had as good a match as possible."

"What are her chances for really surviving? You know, walking and talking?" asked one of the reporters.

"It's too soon to say. She will be on drugs to help reduce the chance of rejection. Recovery will be long and arduous. We will do everything humanly possible to provide her with whatever . . ."

Josh zoned out, fantasizing about Melissa Arnett. He liked the way she walked—no swayed—down the halls at Castro Valley High. He got the impression she liked him too.

Josh was jerked from his reveries when sometime later his mother touched his arm and motioned for him to move toward the hall.

He'd avoided seeing Kate until today—after all, school was back in session. But today his parents had insisted that he come with them, and he was stuck.

"Time to go see our little girl," his mother said.

"Don't you mean little ghoul?"

10:15 AM

The moment the conference was over, Charles Rubenstein, his camera operator, and four other reporters tried to follow the family to get a few exclusive words. Charles noted that Mr. and Mrs. Craig were walking hand-in-hand toward the bank of elevators and that the boy, Josh, walked a few steps ahead of them, dodging reporters and their questions.

As they reached the elevators, Charles held a microphone up to the father. "Mr. Craig, how soon do you think your daughter can come home?" he asked.

"Don't know," he responded as he pushed the "up" button. "It depends on her recovery. But we've been told if everything goes well, she could come home in maybe two months. Now please leave us alone. We just want to see our daughter."

Charles noted a sharp glance from Kate's brother, Josh. The kid seemed to have some anger issues.

"Mrs. Craig, when did you first note that something was wrong with your daughter?" Charles asked.

"I'm not . . ."

John Craig broke in, "That's enough. No more questions. That's what the press conference was for."

Charles and the rest of the press tried to get onto the elevator but were stopped by security. "No one except immediate family and attending staff permitted."

Charles Rubenstein wanted—no, needed—an exclusive, and this was the best shot he'd had in his four years as a reporter. He needed the money that success would bring—money to pay for his mother's mounting medical bills.

He could be persistent, and he would be. His dad had been wrong about him. Maybe he hadn't finished law school. But that didn't make him a loser.

"Go back to the office," he told his cameraman. "I'll stay for a few minutes."

He sauntered over to the hospital cafeteria, paid for a cup of coffee, and sat down in the far corner. He wanted a smoke, but it was forbidden inside the hospital, and right now his plan of attack was more important than his nicotine habit.

Seven targets. He wrote their names: Kate Craig, Donna Craig, John Craig, Josh Craig, Dr. Deborah Johnson, Dr. Felix Yamaguchi, and Dr. Donald Jamison.

It would be tough to get to Kate. But he'd find ways—both while she was in the hospital and afterward—if she survived. He jotted notes: *2nd floor . . . therapies . . .*

The mother seemed ready to respond to questions. But she followed her husband's lead. "Remote possibility," he wrote. More notes: *Castro Valley . . . Does Donna Craig work?*

The father was another story. Probably wouldn't cooperate. It was hard to get men to talk—to really open up—unless there was something in it for them. He put a question mark next to John's name, and then added *occupation?*

The boy was belligerent, but maybe that was good. Maybe he had something to get off his chest. A story from the perspective of the older brother. Now *that* could be really good. He wrote: *Castro Valley—School? . . . Girlfriend?*

Doctors Johnson and Yamaguchi were possibilities—couldn't overlook anyone—but they were minor players. Still, they could give technical aspects and maybe prognoses on her day-to-day recovery. Worth a try.

Ah, but Jamison—good possibility. He seemed to crave attention, glory. If Charles played this right, he could have a win-win. He placed asterisks next to Jamison's name. *Must plan—insist on seeing the doctor. I'll ask for an exclusive. Tell him his name will stay on the front of newspapers and on the evening news.*

He put his pencil down and took another sip of coffee. It was tepid.

A thought struck him. *Maybe there's an eighth target. What about the donor's family?* He jotted quickly: *Who has info about the donor? Who was she? How did she die?* He quickly looked at his notes and saw the information—female, probably young. What was Kate's blood type? The death had to be recent if a brain's viability was similar to that of other organs.

Heart racing, he scribbled down his thoughts. He knew that his first stop had to be Dr. Jamison. He threw his leftover coffee away and walked to the information desk.

10:30 AM

Dr. Jamison entered his office and let out a deep sigh of pleasure. He placed his cup of steaming coffee on his mahogany desk. As he ran his hand over its surface, he smiled and leaned back in the ergonomically correct, well-worn leather chair. This was where he was supposed to be. His hospital was world-renowned for transplants and neurosurgery—and here he was, the champion of both.

He had fought so hard to get here. He was one of those great exceptions to life's harsh rules. Not only was he the first in his family to graduate from high school, but now he was Professor Jamison, MD, PhD.

His father had been so proud of him when he'd graduated—with highest honors—from Springdale High School. And when the full scholarship came for Stanford, Clyde Jamison went door-to-door telling neighbors, "My boy's off to Stanford!"

Jamison dismissed thoughts of his whisky-breathed mother. She'd been gone since the winter he turned six. She ran off with a truck driver. But when spring came, he and his dad shared their melancholy and decided they were better off. They'd always had each other to hunt with, fish with, and talk to about life.

Despite his father's lack of formal education, Jamison respected the man. A carpenter by trade, he was a hard worker who helped build additions to the University of Arkansas in Fayetteville. His dad was a lifetime Razorback fan. Even when money was short, he'd find ways to pay for the tickets to home games.

Making a living had been tough. Work was seasonal. Most years they lived for months on unemployment insurance and the cash from odd jobs. Jamison recalled one year when his dad was unemployed for seven months. The benefits ran out after six months, and they borrowed from the market to buy food. He wondered if there were still markets that let people pay when they could.

Jamison knew that this moment was due to his father. How many times had his dad said, "Be someone, Donald. Go to school."? And sometimes, when he took the easy way out, his dad had chided, "Ah, come on. You don't have to be a brain surgeon to do that!" Maybe that's what did it.

On second thought, it was more likely his dad's untimely death—the brain aneurysm that took him at age fifty-three, two weeks before the final exams in Jamison's first year of medical school.

If only I'd been with him that day. If only I'd known then what I know now! I could have saved him.

If Dad were alive today, he'd be going door-to-door, boasting about his "brilliant son."

Jamison smiled to himself. Now, after eight years of higher education, twelve in internship, and two decades in the operating room, he had finally "arrived."

He logged onto his computer and watched as the Stanford Hospital website opened up. He grinned when he saw both the US News insignia, naming Stanford as one of "America's Best Hospitals," and the announcement of the successful brain transplant by Dr. Donald Jamison. There was talk of a Nobel Prize next year and being named *Time* magazine's "Man of the Year." Who would have ever thought that he, a man from Fayetteville, Arkansas, could become a brain surgeon?

He had everything. His wife, Inna, a Russian beauty fifteen years his junior, was a boon to his career. She looked the part of doctor's wife and played it too. Her leadership and service on a dozen socially important committees had solidified his career.

He licked his lips at the thought of his tall, willowy Inna—always coiffed, always beautiful, and always accomplished at spending his money on all the right accoutrements. She looked good on his arm, and he couldn't help but walk a little taller when he was around her. He adored her, and she seemed to reciprocate.

He was glad that when they married, they agreed not to have children. Unlike his father, he didn't have the patience, time, or commitment to raise a brood. Fortunately Inna felt the same.

As a result, his home was a showpiece nestled on a little over an acre in Atherton, a spacious place with marble floors, crystal chandeliers, and a four-car garage, which wasn't really necessary for just the two of them. But it housed his black BMW and his wife's white Corvette—two of his joys. They deserved these symbols of success.

He thought about Kate Craig and remembered that the first heart transplant patient had lived only eighteen days. Nonetheless, the achievement was still celebrated to this day, and the chief surgeon continued to hold a place in history. *I want more—at least three months.*

Jamison pecked at the keyboard, entered his password, and opened the file "Craig, Katherine S." He entered a series of check marks to prescribe treatments, tests, and staff coordination. Then he wrote instructions: review immunosuppressant drug prescriptions; if alert, begin psychotherapy a week from Friday; diagnostic tests—daily pulmonary tests; every other day run CT scans, MRIs, and blood tests; twice weekly test visual field and nerve connection; review physical therapist's findings and recommendations; review recommendations from critical care medicine specialists.

He stopped occasionally to take a sip of his Starbucks. *The problem is, how do I keep the momentum?* He had to keep Kate alive, for his sake as well as hers, and he needed Kate to be available to him—probably for the rest of her life, no matter how long that might be.

He stared at the screen for a moment. The parents could become a problem. If she were to survive for any significant period, they would want to take her home. Castro Valley was a long way from Palo Alto. He furled his brow . . . *can't let that happen.* There was still so much to learn.

He looked in the computer file at the scanned copy of the papers Kate's parents had signed permitting the surgery. It was marked "experimental" and gave him certain limited access to her.

He typed in orders for additional tests and therapies for Kate. As long as he kept her days filled, he could ensure that the Craigs had limited access. *I can extend this indefinitely—and I must.*

There was a sharp rap on the door. Jamison put down his pen. "Yes?"

Beatrice, his secretary, peeked her head around the door. "Sorry to bother you, Dr. Jamison," she said, "but there's a young newsman from KROX—a Mr. Charles Rubenstein—who says he won't go until he can interview you. I told him to leave his card, but he refuses to go. What would you like me to do?"

10:35 AM

Liz saw Kate's mom and dad coming down the hallway. A tall, lanky, teenage boy was with them. He was handsome and looked a lot like the man who claimed to be her father. But she could see that the boy was still in the throes of growth and development—his arms and legs didn't seem to belong to him. The teenager grimaced at her as he entered the room.

Kate cringed. She knew in an instant that this kid resented her—or rather, he resented Kate. Or was he just taken aback by her horrible appearance?

"How are you doing today?" the mother asked while scurrying over to Liz's side. Kate's father stood next to the woman and looked on in anticipation.

"I'm okay," she replied, playing along.

The young man flinched as if shocked.

"Josh, come over here and say something to your sister." The mother beckoned to him. "It's been a long time since the two of you had a conversation."

Josh stood stiffly at the foot of the bed, looking as if he wished he were anywhere but here. "How ya doin'?" He shifted his weight from one foot to the other. His hands tightened over the foot railing.

Liz/Kate nodded in acknowledgment and smiled. Although she'd learned a lot since last night, she hadn't known that there was a "brother" until now. It was obvious to her that whatever the issues between them, they ran deep.

Thankfully Dr. Johnson had removed the restraints this morning after she'd demonstrated a willingness to cooperate. But to her horror, the woman had also told her that her head was very fragile and any head injury could cause swelling. Although the word was never spoken, Liz realized that any head trauma could lead to sudden death. Dr. Johnson had also advised her that when she was able to get up, she would need to wear a helmet—at least until skull replacement surgery was performed.

But she figured if she ever wanted to see her "real" family again, she would not only need to recover, but also to gain some measure of trust from both her new family and those in charge at the hospital.

So she spoke in short phrases and played the role.

Liz/Kate turned to Josh and said, "Hi."

"You see, Josh?" his father said. "It's all coming back to her. She's going to be fine!"

Josh crossed his arms and took two steps back from the bed, his body language making it clear how he felt. His right eye displayed an almost imperceptible tic.

She expelled a small sigh when a nurse's assistant entered and advised Kate's family that the physical therapist would be in soon and that they would need to leave when she arrived.

Josh looked visibly relieved.

Unfortunately the next few minutes seemed to take an hour. With every kind word from her "parents," Josh appeared more restless. Liz thought he needed attention, but not from her.

When the therapist came in, "Kate" kissed her parents good-bye. She tried to say something to Josh, but the words that came out didn't make any sense. She hoped it was just because she was stressed.

10:50 AM

Marcy Ames felt a thrill run through her at her next assignment: she was to treat the celebrity girl. Her one-inch sensible heels clicked, echoing as she walked down the hall and turned the corner toward ICU room 4. She glanced again at Katherine "Kate" Craig's chart.

Marcy loved working with kids. They were so much more honest—so much easier to work with than adults. By and large they did the exercises she asked them to do and looked at her through those innocent, trusting eyes. And the results of her therapy treatments were almost always rewarding.

Eleven years as a physical therapist, eight of those here at Stanford, had given Marcy a comfortable living and a fulfilling career. She had been married—once—to an army officer, a career man. Although her marriage to Earl didn't work out, their nine-year-old daughter, Adriana, was a love they shared.

Even with Earl's long absences to Germany, South Korea, the Persian Gulf, Baghdad, and Turkey, he kept in touch with his daughter, and whenever he was in the States, he spent time with Adriana. He was a good father—just a lousy husband.

Marcy had reviewed the chart several times and knew that her new patient was two years older than her daughter—to the day. They were both born on Valentine's Day.

She couldn't imagine the strain the Craig family had endured over the years, and now, with the phenomenon of Kate's rebirth. She smiled at the wonder of it all.

When Marcy reached the doorway, she paused out of respect to let the family say their good-byes to their miracle child.

She withheld a gasp when the parents moved aside and she got her first glimpse of the girl. Although she had seen scores of brain surgery patients over the years, she was taken aback at the sight of this hollow-eyed, bald girl with her stitch lines extending from ear to ear just above what had been her hairline. The sunken-in areas around her head—where a skull used to be—and the shunt sticking up from the middle of her head for drainage made the little girl look grotesque. *Oh, poor child.*

Trying to appear calm, Marcy smiled. "Mr. and Mrs. Craig, hi, I'm Marcy Ames," she said in an overly cheerful voice. She shifted the chart to her left arm and extended her free hand to the father.

"The name is John—John Craig. I'm pleased to meet you," he said as they shook hands.

Marcy noted his height—something she automatically did with men. Looking up, she realized that he must be about six-foot-one-or-two—a good two, maybe three, inches taller than she. She liked standing next to tall men. It made her feel feminine.

Small smile-creases appeared around his deep blue eyes. His tanned face was uncommonly good-looking. The thought crossed her mind that he was probably a golfer—one who belonged to a country club.

John turned toward his wife. "And this is Donna," he said with obvious pride.

Mrs. Craig, a petite brunette, was dressed in a smart gray-and-black-striped pantsuit. Her complexion was flawless—like a China doll. But it was her feet that drew Marcy's attention—they were so small. Blushing, Marcy thought of her own size eleven, AAA shoes and tried to conceal them by standing close to the bed.

She nodded to Donna. "I'll be Kate's physical therapist. I want to assure you that I will provide daily reports on her progress and do what I can to speed her recovery to get her back home to you soon."

"Thank you, Marcy," Mr. Craig said. "Josh, come on over here and meet Marcy." He motioned to the teenage boy. "Marcy, this is our son, Josh."

Josh took a step toward Marcy, and she quarter-turned to meet him with her hand extended, "How you holdin' up with all this excitement?"

The boy gave her a wry smile and shook her hand. "Fine . . . just fine," he replied, but Marcy thought she detected a note of irony and wondered how he was really feeling.

Marcy turned back to Mr. Craig as he spoke again. "We appreciate everything your staff here at Stanford is doing for our daughter. We were informed earlier today that the CT scans and MRIs have shown good signs. We couldn't be more pleased."

Marcy saw the teenage boy stiffen slightly. She was a master at observing reactions—after all, it was her job—and Josh was obviously uncomfortable.

Must be hard on him. He's at that difficult age.

"We better let you ladies get busy with your therapy." Mr. Craig bent down and pecked Kate on the cheek.

"Thanks, Mom and Dad. I'm glad you came." She leaned forward and tried to say something to Josh, but it came out as gibberish.

Marcy frowned, surprised that she was articulate so soon after surgery. And Kate's hand and eye coordination seemed almost perfect. But why had she changed so dramatically when speaking to her brother? Maybe just stress . . . maybe brain-body disconnect. Marcy made mental note on the Kate-Josh reaction. She thought there might need to be a psychiatrist involved at some point and, if so, she would pass on the observation.

After the door was shut, Marcy closed the blinds and approached Kate's bedside. She lowered herself into the visitor's chair and leaned forward. "Since you and I will be a team for the next several weeks, I think we should get to know one another." Marcy smiled pleasantly at Kate.

The girl returned the smile. "I heard the doctors talking about you. They say you're good."

Marcy smiled at Kate and spoke in simple terms so the girl would understand. "I know that Dr. Johnson told you about the top of your head—how soft it is. You and I must be very careful when doing exercises, so that you never bump your head. Do you understand?"

Kate nodded.

"Good. So tell me, Kate, how do you feel?"

"Well, I have a bad headache and some vertigo," Kate responded.

"Vertigo?"

"Yes."

Marcy reviewed Kate's chart again . . . meningitis at age five . . . near-fatal episode followed by a severe case of acquired hydrocephalus . . . multiple surgeries at Stanford to implant shunts . . . series of seizures and short periods of coma . . . complications.

Marcy shook her head. It didn't seem possible, even with full recovery, that Kate could have such a vocabulary. "Vertigo, huh? Where did you learn that word?"

"Uh . . ." Kate appeared flustered, her face flushed. "I don't remember." She looked up, blinking rapidly.

Marcy needed time to gather her thoughts. Quickly changing the subject, she said, "I'm going to test your physical reactions—your strength, range of motion, and coordination levels—and I need you to help me out here. Can you do that, Kate?" She raised her eyebrows.

The girl sat up straight and adjusted her covers. "I'll try."

Marcy began her initial evaluation and entered notations on her therapy charts. She checked the girl's ability to follow her hand with her eyes and the strength in arms, hands, feet, and legs. There were some problems with balance and eyesight, but that was to be expected. She checked reflexes, muscle tone, sensation, and range of motion by having Kate move her arms forward, backward, up, and down.

Jotting notes after each test, she considered a daily therapy treatment that would help Kate strengthen her muscles and improve her coordination.

"You're doing well, Kate," Marcy said. "I'm so proud of you. You'll be up and out of bed in no time."

Observing every movement, Marcy saw Kate grit her teeth.

"What's wrong, Kate?"

The girl shook her head. "It's nothing."

A tear trickled down Kate's cheek, and she lowered her head as though trying to hide her face.

"Did the exercises hurt? Did I do something that caused you pain?"

"No, it's not that. I'm sorry, Ms. Ames." Kate's face screwed up, and she shook her head violently.

"Something's wrong. Tell me," Marcy said.

"I can't tell you . . . can't tell anyone."

Marcy put her hands under Kate's chin, cupped it, and drew the little girl's face up close to hers. "Kate, you can trust me. I want to be your friend. Tell me what's wrong."

"If I tell you, they'll kill me," Kate blurted out in a sob.

"No, Kate. That's not true. No one is going to kill you. Everyone wants you to live." Marcy looked straight into Kate's troubled eyes. "Listen to me. I won't let anyone hurt you. I promise."

Kate shook her head and bit her lip.

"How can I help you if you don't talk to me? Look, Kate, I have a daughter who's almost your age. I know how hard it is to talk to an adult, but I promise that whatever you tell me will stay between us. Scout's honor." She held up two fingers and wondered if she should have held up three.

Kate's shoulders went limp. She expelled a loud breath and whispered between trembling lips. "Well, to start with, my name isn't Kate—it's Liz—Elizabeth Ann Lindsay. I'm twenty-nine years old, and I have two children and a husband. My dog's name is Algae. Donna Craig isn't my mother. My mother died nine years ago of breast cancer." Tears rolled down the girl's face, and she sniffed, anguish further marring her features.

Marcy dropped the clipboard and chart on the floor. Dry mouthed, she shook her head and said, "I don't understand. What's going on here?"

"You tell me," her patient replied. "One day I'm getting ready for my son's karate lesson and heading off to do the weekly shopping, and the next day I'm here. And you—and everyone else—are calling me 'Kate.' I want to go home to my husband and kids and to my house in Hayward."

Marcy all but collapsed in the chair next to Kate. She put her hand to her mouth and bit her lip. Feeling dazed, she sat in stunned silence and then got up and went into the bathroom. She took a paper cup from the wall dispenser and filled it with water, gulped it down in two swallows, poured another, downed that, and then came back to the chair.

"This is unreal," she said. "But it's true, isn't it? You're the first successful human brain transplant, and you're telling me your brain's personal memories—your donor's memories. This wasn't supposed to happen!"

Marcy felt the armrest for support. "What did the doctors say when you told them? How did they react? They were so certain that a form of irreversible amnesia would erase personal memory. They said if the transplant was successful, you would retain simple acquired language and other life skills. What did they say when you told them?" Her voice raised an octave.

Kate hushed her and whispered, "I didn't tell the doctors. I didn't tell anyone. You're the first person I've told. When I woke up here, I thought I was having a nightmare. Later, when I saw my image in the mirror, I freaked—and passed out. When I woke up the second time, I was in restraints, and I heard the doctors talking. They thought my memory was erased. I knew they had made a mistake, and I was terrified."

Kate covered her eyes with a hand and pressed her eyebrows together. "Help me. Please help me!" she begged. Fresh tears ran down her pale cheeks.

Thoughts raced through Marcy's head. What should she do? She had promised Kate she wouldn't say anything, but this was big . . . very big. Taking Kate's small hand in hers she said, "You were right not to tell anyone else. Don't say anything to anyone—yet," she whispered. "Give me a chance to think about this, and I'll see what I can do."

Marcy moved closer to Kate. "I'm going to be here every day for the next several days, and we can talk. We can work things out. In the meantime, I'm so sorry . . . so terribly sorry."

Marcy sat forward and put her arms out to the girl. She gently cradled Kate's distorted head and rocked her, cooing. "It'll be all right. I'm here. I'll be your friend. You can trust me."

Marcy felt Kate—or was it Liz?—begin to shake uncontrollably, tears flowing. It was as though the floodgates had opened wide, draining her of every drop of emotion. Marcy could feel the child's body releasing its terrible load.

What a burden. What an awful, awful burden . . .

"You can count on me. You're going to be okay," Marcy whispered.

Kate kept clearing her throat as though trying to speak. Finally, after what seemed minutes, in a low choking voice, Kate murmured, "Please . . . promise me something else—check on my family. I need to know how my daughter and son are doing—how my husband, Bruce, is doing. I need to know. Please. Look them up. Promise me." Kate choked back another shudder and pushed Marcy away. She stared directly into Marcy's eyes. "Promise me."

"I promise," Marcy said, the added burden weighing heavy on her heart.

chapter three

Thursday, September 20, 8:00 AM

There was so much to think about and do. Food was Liz's last concern; besides, they had that drip fluid flowing into her veins. But the matronly nurse implored her to eat the light breakfast on her tray.

Just by running her free hand over her extremities and ribs, Liz could feel how terribly thin and frail she was. She had overheard conversations between the doctors and her mother about her weight loss, which was the result of chronic nausea—a side effect of a condition called hydrocephalus. A nurse practitioner had referred to hydrocephalus as "water on the brain." Liz had heard of this condition but had no idea what it was—or what it meant.

One thing she knew for certain; she had to regain her strength. So she nodded at the nurse and said, "I'll try."

"Good girl. I'll come back and check on you later," the nurse said as she turned and left.

Although Kate was alone in the room, she felt as though she were in a goldfish bowl. Everyone who walked by could see her, and she knew she looked horrible. She had avoided looking at herself. She—that stranger in the glass—was so ugly. The image wouldn't go away—that mutilated pale head. She had seen pictures of Nazi concentration camp victims. She looked worse. It would be some time before she would willingly look at her image again—if she ever did.

She chased those morbid thoughts from her mind. Her task was to get well. She sipped the cranberry juice and enjoyed the coolness in her throat. She tried small bites of cereal—chewed ever so slowly, swallowed, and ran her tongue over the unfamiliar teeth. What the—there was a small gap between her front teeth. Her tongue worked it for a minute. Then, determined to get through this meal and quit stalling, she lifted a spoonful of cereal to her mouth again and felt a wave of nausea. Willing herself to keep it down, she held the spoon tight in her hand, shut her eyes, and leaned back.

Just then she heard the door open and turned to see Marcy quietly enter the room. Marcy closed the blinds like she had the day before. "How are you feeling today?" she asked as she walked to Liz's side.

Liz put the spoon down, pushed the tray away, and looked up. "Terrible, except for the fact that you're here," she sighed.

"Sorry to hear that. Is it the headache?" Marcy inquired sympathetically.

"Yes, that—and trying to figure out how you can visit my family without letting them know what's happened to me."

Marcy cleared her throat, hesitated a moment, and murmured, "I know I promised I'd help, but I didn't think you meant for me to visit them. I just thought you wanted me to call your house or find out from one of your friends how your family is doing. But visit?" Marcy held up her hands. "No, I can't do that."

Liz's hopes faded. "Please, Marcy. I need to know how my family's doing. It'll be easy. You can pretend we were friends—that you read about the accident and you just 'stopped by' to pay respects." Liz clutched at Marcy. "Can't you do that for me?" she begged.

Marcy's eyes went wide. "How can I? I'm a terrible liar. They would see right through me."

Liz held onto Marcy's hand and squeezed as tight as her feeble hands would permit. "No they won't. I'll help—I'll feed you information. You can do it." She looked up, imploring her. "All we have to do is to figure out how you and I might have connected before the accident, how we might have known each other."

Marcy was silent. Liz could see that she needed to say something that would push her over the edge—make her feel compelled to help. "Can you imagine what it's like—unable to see my kids? No one in this whole world to help me, except one person? And that's you. I-I don't know if I can go on like this," Liz sobbed and held Marcy's hand to her wet face. "I need to know that my kids are okay."

Marcy pulled her hand free. Her mouth became a straight line, and her lower lip twitched. "Let's talk while I manipulate your arms and legs. Your muscles need to be worked. And I think better when I'm working," Marcy said, her voice tense.

Marcy began gently bending Liz's legs and applying pressure. "How could we be connected? You said yesterday that you were twenty-nine. Well, I'm thirty-three years old—four years older than you. So we couldn't have been school friends. I live in San Mateo. You live in Castro Valley."

"No, I don't. That's Kate. I live—lived in Hayward," Liz explained, choking on her words.

Marcy appeared momentarily flummoxed but continued the therapy. "Hayward and San Mateo are at least 25 miles apart. I still don't see how we could have known each other."

Kate/Liz's voice trembled as she spoke. "Well, maybe we could say we met at college—some class we took. She closed her eyes to help her think. "I've been going to Cal State East Bay for the last two years. I was just starting my senior year—studying marketing."

"I graduated eleven years ago from Long Beach State. No connection there."

Marcy furled her brow as she massaged Liz's other leg. "I took computer classes a couple of years ago, but that was local—won't work."

"Maybe it will!" Liz countered. "I took classes in Excel, Word, and PowerPoint. What did you take?"

"I took two three-day training classes, one in Word and one in PowerPoint," Marcy said.

"Great! You can say you came to Hayward two years ago in October . . . I think that's when I was there—to take . . . uh . . . PowerPoint. You needed it to make presentations. And that's where we met. No one will doubt you," Liz declared.

"So? How does taking a class make us friends? That's not reasonable. There were lots of people in my training sessions, and I can't name a single one of them."

Sucking air in between her teeth, Liz asked, "Do you have any hobbies, special interests?"

Marcy half-closed her eyes and thought for a moment. "I like to spend time with my daughter."

"You have a daughter? How old is she? What's her name?"

She's nine. Her name is Adriana. And she's the love of my life."

Liz noted a twinkle in Marcy's eyes.

"Nine . . . that's the same age as my daughter, Megan," Liz said. "She's my little gymnast . . . light as a feather. She's a smart little thing too . . . loves to hear herself talk. Gets it from me, I guess. And what about your husband?" Liz asked.

"You mean 'was-band.'" Marcy laughed. "I was married . . . didn't work out. It's a long story. I'll tell you some other time."

Liz sat in deep concentration as Marcy pulled gently on her left arm and rotated her shoulder. "I don't have many hobbies—too busy," Liz said. "I used to be quite a swimmer—girls' swimming champ of Hayward High. But that was more than a decade ago. Now I'm a soccer mom—for my son, Mark—and a taxi driver for my daughter's gymnastic class. What else interests you?" Liz prodded, pulling them both back to the critical task.

Marcy massaged Liz's right arm and rotated her wrist. "Well, I love to read . . . like to travel. And I sing in a community chorale."

"You sing? I tried to sing—took some lessons too, but I never had much of a voice. What kind of music do you sing?" Liz felt a burning in her muscles. She moaned.

"A variety—renaissance, Broadway tunes, a little Mozart, Bach, Brahms, Palestrina, and the like. We perform twice a year . . . nothing big, but the music I love most is opera. I can't sing it, but I enjoy listening."

Liz fought to contain herself. "That's it! That's a second connection. I love opera, but I can't afford it. Each August I go to the free opera in the park though—at Stern Grove. I went the weekend before the accident and heard Patricia Racette and James Lalenti."

Marcy's mouth dropped open. "You're kidding! So did I."

"That's it. That's another connection," Liz said.

"But there were thousands of people there. I don't see how that will work."

"This *will* work," Liz said. "First, you tell Bruce that we met at the October PowerPoint class two years ago, that we sat together—two at a station." She could feel a small grin form on her still unfamiliar face. "Tell him that we went to eat afterward, talked about our families, exchanged email addresses. Then say we communicated with each other a few times after that, until we ran into each other again at the free opera last year. Then we shared our picnic and figured it was fate—so we became email buddies."

Marcy listened but responded only with a tilt of her head and a lifting of one eyebrow.

"Look, this will work. I promise you." Liz let out a gasp as a particularly sharp pain ran down her leg. She recovered quickly. "Tell him we've stayed in touch, sharing stuff about our families. I'll fill you in on stories I've sent to friends about the crazy things my kids and husband have done. Then, if they ask, you'll have answers. What do you say?" Liz asked.

"I don't know." Marcy frowned as she lowered Liz's leg and moved forward. "How did I learn about your death? There was nothing about it in my local paper."

"Umm . . . say you were taking BART to some event in the city, and someone left a copy of *The Hayward Review* on the seat. You were reading it and saw the article about the accident. There had to be one—Google it. You can bring up the article and read it."

Liz didn't mean for it to come out like a whine, but it did. "Ple-e-e-e-ase go this Sunday afternoon. They'll be at church in the morning, and even if they're doing things that day, they'll be home by five. School's the next day.

"Tell you what," Liz added, "I'll give you a recipe for their favorite cookies. You can bake them and take them over. Tell them I sent you the recipe and told you it was their favorite."

Marcy shifted toward the head of the bed. "I want you to try to hold your right arm up as I press down," Marcy commanded. "Come on. We have to keep the exercises going, or all this plotting will be for nothing."

Liz took in a deep breath, winced, and pressed as hard as she could. "I'll do everything you say. Just tell me you'll do this. Please."

She could see that Marcy was giving in—her eyes gave her away.

Marcy moaned. "Okay. Okay," she conceded. "I'll do it. Now tell me something I should know about you. Keep it simple. Like I said, I'm a lousy liar." Marcy came around the bed to Liz's left side and repeated the exercise.

The rest of the hour went quickly. Liz told Marcy half a dozen stories. Marcy repeated them to check for accuracy.

Liz was elated. They had worked out a plan that was, in her opinion, believable. And they still had tomorrow to perfect the ruse.

"See you tomorrow, same time, same station," Liz said. "And Marcy," she added, "thanks for being my friend."

Marcy merely nodded before opening the blinds and quietly exiting.

Relieved that Marcy was going to help her, Liz rubbed her sore muscles. She could feel the improved blood flow through her gaunt extremities. Looking for a more comfortable position, she leaned back heavily into the pillow, but before she could get comfortable, she heard a crash and someone shouting. It sounded like an army coming her way.

She sat frozen, her gaze fixed on the paunchy young man who had just entered her room. His face was red and contorted.

With a jolt, Liz sat upright. "What's going on?" she screamed as he rushed toward her.

Click . . . flash . . .click . . . flash . . . click . . . flash. She tried to cover her face, but she was too late.

"Security! Get that man out of here!" Dr. Jamison shouted as he ran into the room. "How did he get in here? Throw him out," he directed the guard. "And watch the door more carefully."

Hurrying to her side, Jamison asked, "Are you all right?" He lifted her wrist, checked her pulse, and ordered something from the nurse that Liz didn't understand. "We need to calm her."

"I'm okay. I . . . I . . ." Liz stuttered.

Marcy swung around the door, almost falling as she gaped at the needle being plunged into Liz's arm. "No! Oh, no. What happened?"

Just then Liz felt a numbness surge through her body, and her vision faded. She heard the doctor say, "Sleep now." But it seemed so far away, as if from inside an echo chamber. Liz tried to focus on Marcy's image. It was vibrating—glowing. Then Marcy's face floated away.

10:30 AM

Patience was not one of Charles Rubenstein's virtues. He drummed the table with his fingers as he waited for his breakfast. He wanted Bob, his cameraman, to deliver the pictures pronto.

He was pleased at how easy it had been to convince Jamison that a picture of the patient would ensure major coverage on the evening news. With the good doctor's help, he'd been able to direct Bob to remain hidden in the back stairwell, which was farthest from the guard and near Kate's ICU room. Bob had been instructed to stay there until the physical therapist left. He was to be quick and quiet and to stop for no one until he had taken as many pictures of the girl as possible.

"Here's your breakfast, sir," said the chipper young waitress. "I'll be right back with more coffee."

Charles watched her bounce to the coffee station and return with a fresh pot. As she poured, she splashed a few drops on the table, then whipped out a dishcloth from her apron to clean the mess. "Will there be anything else?"

Charles thought about her question for a moment and then drove any lascivious thoughts from his mind. "Maybe later," he answered as he flashed his sexiest smile at her.

Feeling satisfied, Charles lifted the mug to his lips and sipped the hot brew. He took a bite of his eggs and reviewed his notes from yesterday's meeting with Jamison. Charles was fidgety. He could barely wait for the three-o'clock exclusive on-camera interview he had arranged. He and Jamison had worked out the questions and even determined which camera angles would give Jamison the most flattering poses. There would be a few charts and those exclusive pictures of the patient. But mainly they'd talk about Jamison's lifetime achievements. Jamison's payout would be high-profile coverage. And Charles would have exclusive rights to interviews and detailed information from Jamison—a win-win.

As he popped a bite of sausage into his mouth, Charles saw Bob enter the restaurant. Bob was panting and sweating, but by the grin on his face, Charles knew in an instant that the pictures were a go.

"Did ya get 'em?" Charles asked.

Bob nodded as he scooted into the booth facing him, his belly touching the table. Still grinning, Bob reached out to hand Charles the manila envelope.

The flap wasn't sealed, so Charles lifted it and let the three pictures slide onto the table. He sat up straight. *Whoa! She's such a mess!*

He could tell at a glance that these were going to be sensational. They would evoke audience empathy and curiosity—but mainly parents would secretly be glad it wasn't their kid.

He'd give one picture to the station to use in conjunction with this afternoon's interview and sell the two most stunning images to a tabloid for thousands.

Not just Jamison . . . but me too. We'll both be famous!

"You did great, Bob. Seriously great!" Charles said as he reached into his pocket and pulled out a money clip. "Here's the hundred and fifty I promised you. Don't spend it all in one place," Charles teased. "Now, let me buy you a Coke. Whadda ya say to that?"

Bob placed the money in his shirt pocket and smiled even wider. "Sounds good to me."

Charles smiled back. "What would I do without you?"

chapter four

Sunday, September 23, 4:00 PM

Anger was an emotion Marcy tried to avoid. She knew what it did to her blood pressure. But as she drove through midtown traffic, she couldn't understand how Dr. Jamison would participate in an interview with a station that had bought that horrible picture.

She wondered if Jamison had known that KROX had the picture when the interview took place.

Frustrated, she hit the steering wheel with her fist. Her Volvo responded with a short, loud beep—ooops! Not good.

She gathered her thoughts. She had a promise to keep, and she always kept her word.

The printout with directions to the Lindsay home was lying on the passenger seat. Marcy picked it up and glanced at it for the third time. It was silly to review it again since she had already memorized it, but she felt so insecure about this whole lying thing.

Bumping across asphalt that was undergoing repair was enough to upset Marcy. But the broadcast with that picture, and now the deception she was about to engage in, gave her cramps. She took in a calming breath and looked at the old fruitcake tin. It held the Lindsay family's favorite cookies. They were called "Mother's Surprise."

She had never been much of a baker, but these were special, and Liz's directions had been easy to follow. Her daughter had relished the couple she'd eaten and begged Marcy to leave a dozen more at home.

Since Marcy's ex was in the area and wanted to visit with Adriana, Marcy was free to fulfill her promise to Liz. She felt guilty that she had extended the lie to her own family, telling them that a friend of hers had died in a tragic accident and she wanted to visit the family.

Maybe it wasn't a lie. *Liz is my friend—sort of—and she did die.* Yet it was also true that she was still very much alive.

Marcy marveled at the intricacy of Liz's deliberations. Liz had covered every possible pitfall in their story. Marcy hadn't thought of it, but Liz had been alert enough to give Marcy her email address and password, "unbeldi," and to ask that she add her email address into Liz's Yahoo contact list. That way if Bruce ever went into Liz's email, he would see proof that Marcy was, indeed, an email buddy.

Liz's password was a reference to her favorite operatic aria, "Un Bel Di" from Puccini's *Madam Butterfly.* Funny, Marcy thought, it was one of her favorites too.

Arriving at the Lindsay home sooner than she had expected, Marcy reviewed the stories Liz had shared. There'd been so many. Marcy felt as though she already knew Bruce and the kids—and Algae.

A Blazer was parked in the driveway, so Marcy was pretty sure that the family was home. A quick glance in the visor mirror convinced her that she looked distraught enough to persuade the family that she was genuinely upset over a friend's death.

She took off her driving shoes and put on a pair of black Mary Jane–style Sketchers, picked up her purse and the cookie tin, and walked hesitantly to the door. The gold-toned knocker was engraved "The Lindsays." Marcy gently rapped three times.

She heard the sound of heavy footsteps coming toward the door and the voice of a young child in the distance. She braced herself and thought about what she would say as the door opened.

She stood there speechless for a moment. Liz was right. Bruce was good-looking, except that his eyes appeared vacant.

"Mr. Lindsay, I . . . I'm Marcy Ames. I was a friend of Liz's, and I just came by to pay my respects."

"Have we met before?" Bruce asked, with a puzzled expression.

"No. But Liz and I were friends. I . . . I read about the accident.

I'm so very sorry. I thought the least I could do was to bring you and the kids your favorite cookies—from a recipe that Liz emailed me."

Bruce tilted his head to one side. A dog—*must be Algae*—came to his side and replicated the pose. Mouth pursed, Bruce hesitated. Then he opened the door wide and said, "Ah, well, won't you come in?"

She was surprised to see a neat living room. Cards and flowers were arranged artistically on the coffee table and mantle. Perhaps Bruce was like her and cleaned with a vengeance whenever he was upset.

As she brushed past him, she noticed that he was slightly taller than she, maybe by an inch or two at most. He had a thick head of dark hair and the darkest eyes she had ever seen. She cast her eyes away from him.

"Kids! Come down here. I want you to meet someone," Bruce said.

Marcy's heart melted as she saw the tow-headed boy and pony-tailed girl descend the stairs. Their demure manner didn't fit the raucous stories Liz had related. But then, they had just lost their mother little more than a week ago.

"You must be Megan," Marcy said as the girl reached the landing. "And you must be Mark," she said to the boy. "My name is Marcy, and I was a friend of your mother's. She told me so much about you two."

Throwing a suspicious glance her way, Megan said, "Well, she never told me about you."

"Do you live near us?" Mark asked.

"Whoa now! Where are your manners?" Bruce scolded. "This nice lady brought us some cookies. Let's be polite. Okay?"

"Ms. Ames, won't you please have a seat?" Bruce offered.

Marcy sat in a small chair next to the sofa and placed the tin on the coffee table. She cleared her throat and tried to relate the story that she and Liz had practiced about how they met—the computer class, the opera, and their emails. But it was when she opened the tin and offered them Liz's special cookies—the ones with the chocolate kiss in the middle—that they finally appeared to accept that she and Liz had, indeed, been friends.

"You know, Liz always said those cookies would make friends wherever she went. You can't go wrong with those!" Bruce gave

Marcy a sad smile that warmed her heart.

Mark came closer and looked up to her with trusting eyes. Marcy tousled his hair. "Your mom told me about a time when you were about three years old and your Grandma and Grandpa Lindsay took you to their church." Slowly she unraveled the story about how Mark had needed to sit still for a long time and how hard it was for him. In a loud voice, he'd asked his grandma for something to draw with, but she'd hushed him, saying, "You're in God's house."

"And you asked her, 'What's the matter? Is God asleep?' Everyone got quite a chuckle out of that, according to your mom."

Bruce sat back and laughed out loud, no doubt for the first time since Liz had died. "Not only that," Bruce said. "Mark also announced that he 'hadn't come to stay all day.' And a woman in the row behind told my parents that she felt the same."

Marcy giggled, enjoying the exchange and relieved that things weren't as strained as she thought they might be. "And you, Megan, your mom said that at your kindergarten parent-teacher conference the teacher shook her head and said, 'That girl of yours runs the class—won't let the other kids out for recess unless they're wearing their sweaters. However, I'm sure that if I ever fall down, Megan will call 911 and give me mouth-to-mouth resuscitation until help arrives.' "

Bruce smiled. "She is self-sufficient—and was even at five years old."

"What else did Mom say?" Megan asked. "Did she tell you about Algae?"

"Only how he got his name," Marcy said as the kids dug into the cookies and handed her one. "She told me that the day your dad bought him, you all went to the beach and Algae ran to the edge of the incoming tide."

"And brought back a big piece of seaweed," Megan offered.

"She said that at first you guys thought about naming him Seaweed, but then decided on Algae."

"Algae is Liz's dog," Bruce said, clearing his throat. "Sorry. I—it's hard for me to talk about her in the past tense. She's still alive to me." His voice trailed off.

Marcy could see tears well up in Megan's and Mark's eyes as their dad tried to hold in his pain. They both ran to him and hugged him. He held them close and kissed the tops of their heads. Then he bent down, took them each by a shoulder, and made them look into his eyes.

Lips trembling, he said, "It's going to be okay, Megan . . . Mark." He choked on the words. "We're sad now, but we still have each other. And I won't ever, ever leave you."

Deeply moved, Marcy joined in their grief. A tear ran down the side of her face as she reached out and touched Bruce's shoulder. "I'm so sorry. I know this is very difficult. Please, I just want you to know that you can call me if you need help." She blurted the last statement out before she could censor herself.

"Thanks," Bruce murmured. He looked with compassion at his children and rubbed his hand over his face. Then he turned to Marcy. "There's something you could do. Come to Liz's celebration of life. It's on Saturday, October sixth at the Starr King Unitarian Church here in Hayward. I'll write down the address and give you directions. Maybe you can say something about her. No one else shared her love of the opera. That would be nice—I'd like to hear more from you."

Startled, Marcy stared at him for what seemed like an eternity. "I'm not sure." She looked at Megan and then back to Bruce. "Let me think about it. I'll . . . I'll call you and let you know."

A knock at the door broke the tension. Bruce walked over, looked through the peephole, and then opened the door.

"Hi, Howard. Come on in." Bruce gestured for the elderly gentleman to enter. "I can't thank you enough for putting me in touch with your attorney," he said as he shook the man's hand. "You were right. The trucking company was at fault."

"Are they going to make a respectable offer?" Howard asked.

"Yes. We've agreed to settle out of court. They offered enough to take care of final expenses, Megan's and Mark's care, college, that sort of thing. It takes a big burden off my mind." As if just remembering Marcy, he turned and said, "Oh, excuse me. Let me introduce you. Howard, this is Marcy Ames, a friend of Liz's. She just stopped by to pay her respects. Marcy, this is Howard Thayer, my good friend and neighbor."

Marcy liked the kindness on Howard's face. He was about her height with a full head of white hair and a neatly trimmed snow-white beard. She calculated that he was somewhere in his late-seventies. He reminded her of a cross between Santa Claus and Sean Connery.

"I'm happy to make your acquaintance," Marcy said. "But I was

Marcy walked to the other side of the bed and resumed the routine. She lowered her voice. "Asking me to go is one thing, but I won't even listen to you talk about going yourself. So put a sock in it." She rotated Liz's shoulder a little too roughly.

"All right already! Uncle!" Liz rubbed her shoulder. "We'll just talk about you going, and what you might say—if you agree to participate. Is that okay?" Liz asked.

Marcy looked pensive. "If I do this, you've gotta know it's not for you, but for Bruce and the kids. Maybe your life has been turned upside down, but theirs have been too. They need to find closure as much as you do."

Liz bit her lip, tears coming unheeded. "You're right. Forget what I said. That was really stupid of me. I don't want my family to suffer any more."

Marcy visibly relaxed. "Well, maybe you're right. Maybe I should go. I know you care about your family," Marcy said as she patted Liz's shoulder. "I could talk about our 'opera' experiences."

Liz felt a huge measure of gratitude to Marcy and carefully followed Marcy's directions as Marcy manipulated Liz's left arm and checked for range of motion.

"I see some real improvement in your coordination, and your muscle strength is much better," Marcy said.

"Every day I do exactly what you say. You know, I really do want to get out of this room. At least get outside, see the sun." She pointed at the exterior wall window. "I'm in a north-facing wing. I never see the sun." Liz could see by the expression on Marcy's face that she was lightening up.

"I'll tell you what. On Friday, when you're moved out of the ICU, we can change the routine. You'll be moved to the Lucille Packard Children's wing, and I'll come get you in a wheelchair. We'll go out to the garden, take a little walk, and start doing your therapy there. We can add some on-your-feet exercises."

Elated, Liz sat up in the bed. "Good. I've only been out of this bed once or twice a day in the last three days—to sit in that chair," she motioned to the visitor's chair, "while they change my bedding or wheel me around for tests."

"You'll have to wear a helmet whenever you're up walking," Marcy said. "Any color preference?"

"No preference. I just want to be mobile. I don't know if you know this, but Kate's mom comes every day. She shows amazing strength. I think she could help me walk—assist me." She smiled at the thought of this new "mother."

Liz watched as Marcy flipped through the chart. Tipping her head, Marcy reported, "So, if all continues to go well, on Friday they'll move you to a private room. There's still an order for a guard to protect you from the paparazzi. You know, they hound your parents and keep pestering the staff for a chance to get a picture or story about you. You're a celebrity now."

"Yeah. We have to figure out how to deal with that. I'll talk with . . . my mom." Liz hesitated at the words, then quickly recovered, saying, "She may have some ideas." Liz found that interesting. She was beginning to think of Donna as "Mom." She wondered if this was a natural progression in their relationship or something else. Liz refocused. "Forget the paparazzi for now. Let's talk about the celebration. I'm going to have to give you something plausible to say."

"Fine. Fill me in. But if I do speak at the event, I won't talk for more than three or four minutes. That should be plenty . . ." Marcy trailed off.

For the next few minutes, they shared their love of the opera. Liz was exhilarated by the energy she felt just by talking about it—her favorite arias, tenors, sopranos, baritones, and basses. She loved the Italian operas.

As they shared experiences, Liz found that the lilt in her young, high-pitched voice amused her. She played on it for effect. She had the sudden inspiration that maybe someday these new vocal cords could sing opera. *Wouldn't that be a kick?*

Then another thought struck her. "I have an idea. I was working on a poem about nature and the interconnectivity of all life. I remember some of the lines, and I'll change it to fit the circumstances. You can read it at the celebration—just pretend you wrote it."

With hands on her hips and arms akimbo, Marcy said, "So, first I lie, and now I plagiarize your poetry? I don't think so! Just give me the essence of what you want to say and I'll do the writing. I'm pretty good. That way there'll be something—no matter how small—that's genuine about me."

"Yes, you be the bard. But bring me a pencil and pad. I'll sketch out some ideas. Then you can write the poem. I could have my ideas ready for you tomorrow when you come."

No problem."

When Marcy finished the therapy session, Liz needed a nap. But now she couldn't sleep. Her imagination was working overtime. She had to find a way to go to the celebration. Nothing could keep her away. *With or without Marcy's help, I'll be there.*

11:30 AM

Despite her attempts to figure out how she could get from the hospital to Hayward, Liz dozed off. When she awoke, she sensed a loving presence mingled with the faint, sweet smell of jasmine. She opened her eyes slowly, but she knew before she saw her. It was her mom, Donna.

"Hello, pumpkin," Donna said in a soothing voice. "How's my girl today?"

Liz felt an emotion that had lain dormant for many years. When Donna touched her, it felt as though she had always been there. This was so confusing, so deep, and yet so wonderful.

"I'm better, Mom. I'm so glad you're here."

As the woman bent down to kiss her, Liz/Kate lifted her hand, gently touched the woman's face, and offered her lips in a child's kiss to her mother. In that moment, something in Liz shifted. It was as if all of the pain and anguish she had been holding in had somehow transformed into a love that was so powerful and so deep that it had no words. She knew, as surely as if the words had been spoken, that Kate was taking over her body. And soon there would be no Liz.

chapter six

Friday, September 28, 8:55 AM

Marcy carried the helmet and pushed the empty wheelchair down the hall toward Liz's new room. She couldn't help but smile as she remembered the call from Bruce. Although she and Liz had rehearsed what Marcy would say if she agreed to participate in Liz's memorial, Marcy didn't really believe that Bruce had been sincere about the invitation—until last night.

She kept reliving the call. There was something about his voice. She had been tempted to accept immediately, but she'd put Bruce off. "I may have to work," she'd told him. "I'll see if I can get the time off. . . . I'll call you back."

She wondered why she had done that. Then she realized she wanted to talk with him again. She knew she could get Chet, the relief therapist, to cover her shift. She could easily go to the life celebration and satisfy Liz's request. But there was something else. Bruce's eyes—they kept haunting her. And Mark and Megan, they seemed so needy.

As she entered the door, Marcy noticed that Liz/Kate was slumped over, even though the hospital bed was upright.

Pushing the vision of Bruce and the kids from her thoughts and centering her attention on her friend, Marcy smiled and said, "Good morning, Kate. How do you like your new room?" But as she drew nearer, she noticed that Kate's eyes were red rimmed and her face was ashen.

Kate looked up. Panic was inscribed on her small, sallow face. "Marcy, thank goodness you're here. I have to get outside," she croaked. She motioned toward the doorway. "I've been cooped up in the ICU until today and I—" She slapped at the bedrail. "I don't know how much more of this I can take. Sometimes I just want to close my eyes and melt into the darkness."

"Has something new happened? Are you all right?" she asked as she came to the bedside.

Kate pulled back the blanket and shouted, "Just help me out of this bed."

Surprised by her sudden aggressiveness, Marcy drew back a step. She was shocked at the change in Kate's appearance.

Kate . . . no, it was Liz . . . pulled in a sob and then reached out and grabbed for Marcy's hand. "I don't know why I'm so upset. I—I woke up this way. I think it's knowing that I may never see Bruce again . . . or Megan . . . or Mark. I can't let that happen. You understand, don't you?"

Marcy looked at the frail young body and breathed deeply to keep her own tears from brimming over. She nodded in response. "This is the helmet you need to wear. It's been modified to allow for the shunt." She cautiously placed it over Liz's head and then helped the small child into the chair. Kate's body was so light.

"Let's get you into the garden . . . into that fresh air," Marcy said as she masked the fear in her own voice. After adjusting the footrests, Marcy stepped silently behind the wheelchair and rolled it toward the doorway. Looking for words of comfort, she whispered, "I heard from Bruce last night. He really wants me to speak at your memorial. I . . . I guess I'm going to do it."

Liz twisted in the chair, pursed her mouth, and stared up at her. Marcy felt unnerved. She knew Liz was trying to say something. Then, with that high-pitched, little girl voice, Liz stammered, "Th-thanks. You know, it means a lot to me." She held her chest and coughed. "B-but I need to tell you something." She was shaking her head. "Whether you approve or not, I'm going to the celebration too." She paused. "With or without your help."

A fierce look of determination erased any semblance of an eleven-year-old in Kate's features. "I'll tie the sheets together and go out the window—hitchhike if I have to," Liz said. "This is so unfair. I've done nothing to deserve being held prisoner. I'm not a felon."

The elevator opened, and for a moment Marcy wanted to leave Liz there and run, but she knew this was part of the grieving process—the anger phase. "Shush! Please don't talk 'til we get to the garden . . . or someplace where we have some privacy." Marcy rolled the chair into the elevator, pushed the button, and stood silent until the door shut. *How did I get myself into this mess?* She cleared her throat. "You have neither the strength nor the means to attend the memorial. You're not thinking rationally."

"What is rational? I'm living between two worlds. I need to find my way—and I don't know how," Liz moaned. "I . . ." She stopped speaking as the elevator doors opened. An elderly couple, the man using a walker, slowly stepped into the small space. Marcy saw them both look down at Kate, their eyes filled with undisguised pity.

Putting on her best casual smile, Marcy nodded at the couple, hoping they would stop staring and find their manners. The woman caught on first and looked at Kate as though she were a normal girl. "Hi, dear, what's your name?" she asked kindly.

Liz/Kate looked up and cried out, "I don't know—I don't know anymore!"

Marcy took a short step between the couple and the wheelchair, forced an uncomfortable smile, and said, "This is Kate. She's a little confused today. But thank you so much for asking."

As the doors swished open, Marcy wheeled Kate out. She couldn't move fast enough.

She pushed the disabled button that automatically opened the double doors and rushed out to the garden. Unfortunately, the head housekeeper was seated on a bench, probably taking a break. She looked up as they entered. It was as though she sensed their need for confidentiality because she nodded at them both and then stood and left the garden.

The scents of fall filled the air. Mother Earth was changing her garments again. Gratefully, Marcy inhaled the luscious, crisp fragrances and noted that some fall-blooming crocuses, Rose Blush

Chrysanthemums, and other late summer and early fall flowers were reveling in the morning sun. She shared these observations with Liz, hoping they could find a new topic to discuss. She didn't know how many times she had sat in this garden or why until today she had overlooked the beautiful bronze statue of a mother playfully whirling her young daughter through the air. She wished she'd noticed it some other time because today it was the symbolic antithesis of her current situation. She was in the presence of a woman—a girl—who wanted to be with her daughter and son, and not only couldn't swing them around, she couldn't even see them.

As soon as they were out of earshot, Liz was back on track. "I know how we can do it. I know how I can go with you. Please, at least listen to me."

Marcy felt conflicted. Maybe she should let the doctors know about Kate's brain memories. They could erase them. After all, they thought they had. She could point out their error—get it "fixed." Maybe everyone would be better off. But could she betray Liz? She jerked herself back to the conversation and shook her head. "I've told you before. It's not possible."

"Just listen. Please!" Liz pleaded as she turned the wheelchair to face Marcy.

"I'll tell you what," Marcy told Liz. "I'll listen to your far-fetched schemes, but only while we walk. That's why we came here—for your physical exercise. Got it? I'm not promising you anything more than my ear." She glared down at Liz. "And if you don't get up and walk, I'll just take you back to your room—now—and we can go through the bed routine again."

Marcy squared her shoulders and lowered her voice, "And another thing. In our conversations, from this point on, I will only refer to you as Kate. And I'm going to *think* of you as Kate, and you need to do the same."

Kate's nostrils flared and she sat stone still for several seconds. Then, with a silent nod, she began pushing at the footrests with her feet. Marcy quickly bent to adjust them and then helped Kate to her feet.

Kate reeled for a moment and held onto Marcy for support. But her despondency morphed into determination as they walked and talked. Kate seemed to grow stronger with each sentence.

In self-defense, Marcy responded with shrugs and "uh-huhs" unless Kate asked her for a commitment, in which case she shook her head no.

Liz/Kate had the outline of a plan as she put it. *Such subterfuge.* At one low point in the conversation Kate cried, but she kept up the steady pace. Her face seemed thinner and longer. "I realize that I'll never be Bruce's wife again—just in my memories. And my kids won't accept me as their mother—I'm only two years older than my daughter and four years older than my son." She half laughed and half cried. "But I can't stop caring about them. I still have a responsibility. It was born in me when I felt their first kicks inside my womb." She touched her small abdomen.

Marcy closed her eyes and tried to close her ears, but she heard every word.

After ten minutes of walking and twenty-five minutes in the garden, Marcy wheeled Kate back to her room and continued the therapy.

As Kate climbed back into the bed, she looked up at Marcy and said, "You know, you're my hero. I couldn't make it without you." She smiled briefly at Marcy. "Please let me go with you, Marcy. It's my last request."

Marcy cupped her hand over her eyes, and sighed. "Kate, you're not in physical shape to do half of what you're planning. It's a harsh reality, but you need to face it."

Kate sat up straight and began repeating some of the exercises, working her range of motion and flexing her muscles while staring steadily at Marcy.

Marcy took a deep breath, turned, and wheeled the chair from the room, her shoes clicking as she walked. *No way. No way.*

12:05 PM

Leaning against the outside wall of his high school gym with one leg bent and his foot against the wall, Josh waited for Ron. What could Ron give him that his best buddies couldn't? He wasn't sure. But he was about to find out. Ron was a junior at Castro Valley High, a year older than Josh and about as tall. Girls liked him, gawked at him. He was cool—had an almost new Mazda RX-8 and was always laid-back. He'd hinted that he could set Josh up with some "good times." *I could use some good times.*

Although school wasn't difficult for Josh, he was bored. He didn't study, didn't turn in homework, and skipped classes. He knew his grades would suffer, and he would probably be kicked off the JV football team, but he didn't care. He was done trying to please his parents.

Ashlyn walked by. "Hi, Josh. Watcha doin'?"

He shrugged. "Nothin." He lowered his head, hoping she would take the hint and walk on by. Luckily, she harrumphed and strutted off as Ron came into view.

"Hey, Josh!" Ron greeted. "Watcha been up to, pal?"

Josh pushed himself away from the wall. "Same ol'. Same ol'," he replied.

"I got an idea. Let's go off campus for lunch. We can take my car—grab a burger and fries. Then we can go to my house. I got some stash," Ron said.

"Sounds good to me."

Josh followed his new friend through the student parking lot and watched as Ron pressed a button on a small remote. The car beeped, then unlocked. After a few seconds, the motor started. *The man knows how to live.*

4:00 PM

Charles Rubenstein had arrived at his desk early that morning and leafed through the pages of recently recorded deaths of young females. The KROX research section had given him the list after Penny, his news manager, had requested it on his behalf.

He focused on his quest to identify Kate Craig's brain donor. He was pleased that Penny had approved the assignment. She thought it would be a great human-interest story.

Charles relished the fact that he was riding high at the station. Everyone had stopped to congratulate him on his exclusive interviews with Dr. Jamison. And, with his special "in" with the head surgeon, he was KROX's star reporter on Kate's daily prognosis. Jamison had been helpful but couldn't give him the name of the donor—he said he didn't have access to that information, and that organ donations remained anonymous unless the next of kin released the information. The best he could offer was the matching factors. The rest would be up to him and KROX.

Charles needed the name of the family. He wanted to cover the donor side of the story before anyone else worked that angle.

The research department had already contacted organ transplant coordination organizations and had the list of donors whose kin had given permission to release information to both the recipient and media. The list was short, and the brain organ wasn't among those listed, since this was a new procedure.

Charles would have to contact donor families and find out whether they'd be willing to release information to the press if their loved one had been "the one."

Charles looked at the national listing of deaths. It was daunting. With computer coordination and air transportation, the brain could have come from almost any metropolitan area.

In his research he'd learned that until last year, transplants had to occur within four hours of harvesting. But with new technology, most harvested organs could be maintained in viable condition for up to ten days—and the brain, according to Jamison, could remain viable for up to seven days.

Charles felt he could eliminate most rural deaths, especially those who died several miles from a hospital. The organs couldn't have been harvested in time. He also eliminated deaths from fires, cancer, drug overdose, and infectious diseases.

He studied the list. Over 2,400 young women between the ages of ten and thirty had died in accidents, complications of childbirth, or other causes that could leave the brain unaffected, and, of those, 2,200 had died in metropolitan areas in the week before the transplant. He knew that sifting through these would take time, but until he tried, he had no idea just how long and how tedious the job would be.

After more than six hours of calling, he learned that some families didn't want to know the identity of the recipients . . . others did. So far he had tried to contact sixty donor-families. It was a regular workday, but he figured that with a recent death, family members might be home making arrangements. Out of the list, only eighteen answered the phone. Of those eighteen, only four of the deceased women had been transplant donors. Three of the four knew which organs had been harvested—heart, liver, corneas, but not the brain. The family of the fourth woman refused to talk with him after the briefest of conversations.

Charles looked at the notes on the others he had called that day. He'd left voice messages with thirty-eight potential donor-families. So far, only three had returned his calls, and none had been organ donors. Four of the sixty either had no immediate family members listed or had moved. Whole families could have perished and he'd never know.

Charles shifted uncomfortably in his desk chair. He breathed in between his teeth, making a *shhing* sound, and then bit his nails. There must be an easier way. At this rate, there could be a second or a third brain transplant before he had the donor information—then who'd care? Would his story even hit page three?

An idea struck him. He rose from his chair and walked briskly to the manager's office. *Why didn't I think of this sooner?* He rapped twice on the glass door.

"Come in, Chuck," Penny said. "What is it?"

He fumbled for a moment. "Finding the donor is harder than I thought. If we want info on the donor while it's still news, I need six staff assigned to me for a week to make calls," he implored her. "Is that possible?"

Penny wrinkled her nose. "I have all but one staff member currently assigned to other stories or research. And most are putting in overtime. I can give you Giovanni, but other than him, I don't have anyone. Sorry."

Charles ran a hand over his left temple and down his cheek. He cupped his chin. "Would you approve hiring four or five temps for a week? I could give them a script and supervise them. How about it?"

She gave him a look that made him feel queasy. Then she relaxed. "Oh, all right. But only one week. I'll call human resources and let them know what we're doing. The temps will have to report there first."

Charles gave her a quick grin and a salute.

He returned to his desk and quickly wrote out the script for the callers. Then he divided the list of names and numbers into six lists. By Wednesday or Thursday he would have the name, or at least a short list that he could work from himself. And tomorrow, once he got the callers started, he had an appointment at noon to meet with Josh Craig at the bowling alley in Castro Valley to get another perspective from the older brother. *Poor guy. Seems a bit unhinged by all this.*

5:46 PM

As Bruce pulled into the driveway, Megan and Mark came running out of the Thayers' home to greet him. He marveled that they were smiling and giggling. *How quickly children adjust.*

As he opened the door, he couldn't help smiling. Both were doing what he called the "excited jiggles"—jumping up and down. At the same time he heard Algae in the backyard, barking a welcome home.

"Daddy, Daddy, I got an A in spelling," Mark shouted.

Megan pulled on her dad's arm as he climbed out of the Blazer. "And, Daddy, Auntie Bea helped me, and now I can do a flip-flop. Watch this!" Megan let go of his arm and ran to the center of the lawn. She glanced back to make sure he was watching and jumped backwards to her hands then flipped over to her feet. As she landed, she slipped on the wet grass and fell on her bum. "Did ya see? I did it without any help. Auntie Bea says I'm really good," Megan boasted.

"Watch me," Mark shouted. "I can do a one-elbow cartwheel."

Before Bruce could react, Mark arched through the air, landed on his elbow, and rolled across the wet lawn.

"Are you all right?" Bruce asked as he took two long strides over to help Mark up. He could tell at a glance that Mark was fine. Bruce laughed and gave him a noggin rub.

"Hey, guys, you're both great. But, Mark, you stick to karate and soccer, okay? We don't need any broken bones. However, I will say that was the best one-elbow cartwheel I've ever seen. And Megan, your flip-flop was terrific."

Just then Bea opened her front screen door and came out with a casserole in hand. "It's just macaroni and tuna. The kids say they like it—I used one of Liz's recipes. Thought you'd like this with a little salad tonight." Compassion and caring was written all over her, and her voice was soothing.

Overcome with gratitude, Bruce sighed. The Thayers were filling in and doing many of the duties that Liz had done. He met Bea halfway and swallowed back his emotions. He thought she might have seen his Adam's apple bob, and he felt a flash of embarrassment. He wasn't normally this emotional, but these neighbors had really come through for him. He was learning quickly what was most important in life.

"What you and Howard do—caring for the kids after school, taking Megan to her gymnastics—it means the world to me. You two are angels in my book, and we," Bruce motioned toward the kids, "we're just so fortunate to have you both. I don't know how I can ever repay you. Just know that if you're ever in need, I'll be there."

"Oh, hush," she said. "We enjoy Megan and Mark. They're like the grandkids we never had. Caring for them has given our lives new meaning. We should be thanking you for letting us be part of your family."

Algae barked. He obviously wanted to join them. Mark and Megan raced to the gate at the same time and opened it. Algae leaped out, hair flying. He slathered Mark with three quick licks and then turned to Megan, tail wagging, and gave her an equal number. Then he leaped across the lawn and pranced around Bruce. Bruce balanced the casserole in one hand as he gave Algae the reward he knew the dog wanted—a pat on the head.

"Well, I need to get back in and tend to my laundry," Bea said as she turned and waved. "See you tomorrow."

"Thanks again," Bruce said as he waved back.

Bruce pushed open the front door, cradling the casserole under one arm. He bent to gather the mail on the floor with his free hand. "Gotta attach a box under that mail slot," he thought for the hundredth time.

As soon as they walked through the door, they all looked up at the family picture hanging on the entry wall. Bruce noticed that the mood instantly changed. It was like a pall hung over them. His kids' smiles transformed into somber expressions, and they trudged up the stairs and disappeared into their rooms.

Bruce walked into the kitchen, Algae following close behind. He sighed as he sorted through the mail. He'd already developed a new routine. Up until two weeks ago, Liz had taken care of the mail. He would just get a report on important items, and she would share personal cards and letters. He hadn't realized how many little things she had tended to.

Now, almost unconsciously, he stepped to the kitchen counter and pushed the button on the answering machine: "You have two messages. To listen to your messages, press one," the familiar female voice said.

The first message was from Maria, Liz's best friend, wanting to know what else she could do to help out. Bruce liked Maria and her husband and their four kids. Victor, their seven-year-old, took karate lessons with Mark, and the two were signed up to play on the same soccer team when the season started. Their teams was the Wildcats. The name fit them well.

"We'll pick up Mark and Megan tomorrow about half an hour before the karate lesson," Maria's message said. "And we'll have them back after the traditional stop for pizza. We know you have lots of things to tend to before next weekend, so don't worry about them."

Bruce marveled at Maria's energy. She was a pediatric nurse, a devoted mom, and a volunteer savior of baby seals and other marine life. Liz sure knew how to pick friends.

He played the second message. "Hi, this is Marcy Ames. I was just calling to let you know that I found a sub for the sixth . . . so I'll be at the celebration. One-thirty, right? Umm, I need directions to the church, so I was hoping you'd call me back, area code six five oh, and then four, three, three, nine, four, four, nine. Or an easy way to remember it—the area code and G-E-E W-H-I-Z. It's kinda silly, I know. I like making phone numbers into words when possible. Anyway, call me when you have time."

Bruce raised his eyebrows and felt his somber mood fade. He picked up the phone and dialed six, five, oh, GEE WHIZ.

6:00 PM

Liz swallowed a spoonful of applesauce and forced herself to focus on getting better. The things she planned to do would be impossible unless she regained her strength. Walking and sitting upright for two hours were still enormous challenges.

Oh, God, whoever you are, help me! I'll do whatever you want if you let me see my family. She knew she was bargaining with God. But what else could she do? She'd never felt so helpless before. She'd always had such drive, such energy, and such strong physical and mental abilities.

She took a breath then expelled the air, picked up her spoon, and purposefully savored another mouthful. *An apple a day keeps the doctor away.* She let out a high-pitched chortle and almost choked at the thought of keeping the doctor away.

Liz recalled her earlier session with her psychiatrist. Dr.

Manning had asked so many questions. She had feigned confusion during the session, even stupidity. She only answered the simplest questions and said what she thought the woman wanted to hear.

The only part of the session that had really been of interest to Liz was the part about depression. She told the doctor, using her "little girl" vocabulary, that sometimes she felt "very sad." But when Manning asked her why she thought she was sad, she lied and said she didn't know why. Maybe it had to do with being in the hospital, not at home.

She was honest about her feelings toward her "mom." She genuinely loved Donna. It was as though her whole being was connected to her. Somehow the woman managed to be at her side every day for at least two hours. She was phenomenal—always up, always friendly with the staff. Sometimes Liz would try to visualize her real mother's face, but like a slide show, Donna's face would skate into view.

Liz also had warm feelings for John, Kate's father. He was there occasionally, but she could feel his love and concern, some other kind of connection—a spiritual one, maybe. She told Manning that she had "some memories" of him.

When Manning asked about her brother, she told the truth and simply said she didn't remember Josh from before. The psychiatrist nodded and said she understood that there would be no "body memories" of a sibling, not like there would be of a mother. That phrase fascinated Liz. "What is a body memory exactly?" she'd asked.

"There's a theory that, like the brain, the body stores memories—like playing an instrument or knowing how to dance."

Liz merely nodded. But she bit her lip to keep from blurting out her true feelings—the truth about who she was. If she had, Jamison probably would have reacted quickly to erase her memory. Then Liz would truly be dead.

She drew her attention back to her dinner and closed her thoughts on Manning. As soon as she did, another thought made her jerk upright. It was as though she'd found the missing piece to a puzzle. All along it had been right in her pocket. *Marcy knows who I am!*

As soon as this fact sunk in, she knew exactly what she had to do. It would be a mean-spirited thing to do to her friend. And she'd have to put on the performance of her life. But what other choice did she have? She had to see her family.

Yes, Marcy will take me to the celebration. She can't refuse me!

Tomorrow she would give Marcy an ultimatum. She would bargain, and win. Of this she was sure.

Re-energized, she attacked her food with vigor and looked up as her mom walked into the room.

"How ya doin', honey?" Donna asked as she approached Kate's bedside, the fragrance of jasmine accompanying her.

"I couldn't be better, Mom." And she meant it.

chapter seven

Saturday, September 29, 9:05 AM

Preparing herself mentally for what she knew would be her most difficult hours with Marcy, Liz silently went over her lines—what she would say, how she would behave so that Marcy would believe her. She preferred to reason with Marcy and garner agreement, but if that didn't work, she had one last "silver bullet," and she would fire it if she had to.

Liz was in a near trancelike state, thinking about her day, when a student-volunteer, Brandi, came in with the wheelchair. "Looks like you have a long session with Mrs. Ames today. She wants me to take you to the garden. You ready?" asked Brandi.

With a slight body jerk Liz/Kate looked up and nodded. "I am *sooo* ready." Determined to appear lighthearted through all this, she put her nose in the air and pretended she was a princess.

"Ah, a sense of humor. Now I know you're feeling better," Brandi said as she helped place the helmet on Kate's head. Another thing, I can tell you're putting on weight. You now have a dimple when you smile. That's important, you know . . . if you want a boyfriend someday. Boys like girls with dimples."

Liz laughed. The girl was a chatterbox. She obviously wanted

Liz to know everything about her—who she was: cheerleader, good Samaritan, straight-A student, prom queen. Although the girl was self-centered, Liz had to concede that she was fun loving and bubbly—and caring enough to have noticed Kate's weight gain.

Today the only assistance Liz needed to get from bed to wheelchair was for Brandi to put the bedrail down. Sliding off the mattress, she stood erect for a moment and then turned slightly and sank into the seat. She didn't need any help and was tempted to wheel herself to her therapy session. But that would get both Brandi and herself in hot water, so she refrained.

The nonstop chatter continued all the way to the garden. Liz/Kate just nodded and smiled.

"Here we are, your majesty. Will there be anything else or am I dismissed?" Brandi said in a hoity-toity voice, followed by a deep curtsy.

Liz/Kate flicked her hand in a gesture that indicated Brandi could leave. "Go now, my child. Return for me at eleven. It'll be a bit early for tea, but we'll do something very proper."

Liz needed that bit of role-playing to prepare for what lay ahead. She shifted gears. In moments, she would be playing the biggest role of her life. Worse than queen, she would be playing beggar, and if that didn't work, traitor.

I don't want to hurt Marcy, but I may have to. God, forgive me!

The garden was empty of other visitors, and those inside the building were seated facing away from the garden. This gave Liz a feeling of privacy. She hoped they wouldn't be interrupted.

Brandi hadn't noticed Kate's change in expression. She just giggled when she saw Marcy entering through the double glass doors and then left the garden, stopping every few steps to turn and curtsy.

"What's that all about?" Marcy asked, having viewed the spectacle as she entered.

Liz felt a chill run through her, perhaps an omen of things to come. But she had to continue to play the role and try to ease the coming tension, so she swallowed her own self-loathing and continued the charade. "Oh, just having fun with babbling Brandi. She's such a character. She'll probably be a senator someday."

Liz was glad to see Marcy laughing—a positive sign.

"Yes, I know. She is a nonstop talker, isn't she?"

"Boy, I'll say." Liz smiled.

Part of Liz's strategy was to cooperate fully for the first hour of today's two-hour session and not talk about the celebration. For one, she needed a good workout to ensure added strength and flexibility; second, she needed to build her own resolve. She was certain that once she got to the subject, the rest of the session would be stressful. She hoped that her own sense of guilt over her tactics wouldn't show through.

The first hour went so slowly it seemed like three. Liz tried to keep her mind on the therapy. It wasn't until she sneaked a glance at Marcy's watch and saw that it was a few minutes after ten o'clock that she finally brought up the subject. "How are you coming on the poem?" she asked in a nonchalant manner as she tried to walk steadily down the pathway with little assistance.

"Oh, I feel pretty good about it. I'll bring it in on Tuesday and read it to you—see what you think," Marcy said as she sat Kate on a bench and jotted notes on the chart. She nodded in approval at Kate's physical improvement.

"That'll be great. I'll bet you're very creative." Then, in what Liz hoped would appear as a sudden afterthought, she added, "Oh yes, and I thought that perhaps I should tell you about some of the people who will be there. That way, when you meet them, you can say we talked about them. It will add more credibility to the fact that you and I were friends."

"Fine," Marcy said as she moved Kate's right arm out to her side and horizontal to the floor. "Hold your arm out straight and try to keep it up while I press down."

Liz followed Marcy's directions as she began divulging information about her closest relatives and friends. She found it hard to concentrate on the details while her mind was knitting her next lines. She was relieved when Marcy began paraphrasing back most of what she said about each person. Liz believed it might give Marcy an inkling of how many people had been part of her world—the world that had been snatched away from her in one careless moment.

Marcy seemed soft at the moment, so Liz tried a more direct approach while drawing on her "little girl appeal" as much as possible. "You know, I've figured out a way that I can get to the church and no one would even know that you brought me," Liz said.

She noticed Marcy flinch and draw back. "I thought you understood. That isn't going to happen. I don't want to talk about it anymore." Marcy turned slightly and stared at her. There was a hint of sympathy in her eyes that soon shifted to sternness. "Look, Kate, I'm responsible for your well-being when we're together. We have a patient-therapist relationship, and you need to respect that."

Liz retreated from her pursuit for a few minutes to regroup her thoughts. She wanted to demonstrate to Marcy her undivided attention to the therapy, at least for a few minutes.

Less than ten minutes later, Liz revisited the subject. "Listen, Marcy, you know me. I wouldn't even be trying to have this conversation with you if it weren't for my deep love for my family. Please, put yourself in my place. What if you were only twenty-five miles from Adriana and someone told you that you could never see her again? What would you do? You wouldn't take it on the chin. You love Adriana as much as I love my family. I know you would try with every bit of your strength to see her."

A look of dread registered on Marcy's face. This gave Liz the impetus to press on. "It's really simple. If you take me, I won't enter the church with you or sit with you. I'll go to the back of the sanctuary and sit in total silence. You won't even know I'm there. No one will know."

Marcy shook her head. "No. I said no. Now cut it out. I mean it." But she spoke in a whisper, not a shout. Liz could see that Marcy was emotionally exhausted.

Liz needed to keep pressing—but more gently. "Well, you can't say that I'm not persistent—a real thinker. Or would you say a 'little stinker'?"

Marcy dropped her guard for a moment and smiled. "A little stinker, more likely." Liz saw Marcy's shoulders relax.

But every time Liz approached the topic, no matter how reasonable she thought her ideas sounded, Marcy gently rebuked her. She always had some medical reason that she couldn't do it.

Time was running out. The session was coming to a close, and Brandi would be there soon. Liz could see that Marcy was about to wrap things up, so Liz had to act now, had to use her last weapon—the one she'd been hoping to avoid. It would cause friction and pain.

But she owed it to Bruce, Megan, and Mark to try. She needed to see them, needed to know that they were well. She just hoped that somehow, someday, Marcy could forgive her for what she was about to do.

Taking a deep breath, she cleared her throat, and said, "You have to take me, Marcy. Because if you don't," she paused, her insides shaking, "I'll tell Dr. Jamison about my memories. I'll tell him who I am, Elizabeth Ann Lindsay. And I'll tell him that you've known all along, actually conspired with me—visited with my family." She lowered her voice, forcing herself to finish the awful words she'd prepared. "You know, they can check that out. You'll probably lose your job. And Kate's parents, I mean *my* parents, may even file suit against you."

Marcy glared at her, confusion and disbelief written on her expression.

Liz cast her eyes down, unable to look at Marcy, and forced herself to press on. She stood up from the bench as tall and straight as she could and pointed to her distorted head. "Maybe they'll erase my memory, but so what? As far as I'm concerned, I'm already dead." She fought back tears. "Not seeing my children has been worse than death to me. You're a mother. You must understand." Then she slumped her shoulders. "You decide. It's up to you. Will you take me?"

She raised her face in time to see Marcy's eyes widen. Then she saw a knowing frown crawl across Marcy's forehead. Marcy seemed to turn a subtle shade of green. She sat down heavily and put her hands on the bench, her knuckles turning white. For a moment Liz thought Marcy was going to pass out. Then she noted Marcy's jaw clench and what looked like pain cross her face. Marcy slowly nodded in agreement.

Liz knew she had dealt Marcy a terrible blow. Their remaining conversation was sparse, terse, cold, and unyielding—all business. A cloud seemed to form a veil over Marcy's eyes, all sympathy gone.

Marcy laid out two conditions. "You must be able to walk the equivalent of two blocks, and you must be able to sit upright by yourself for more than two hours and then walk another two blocks. If you can't do that," she warned, "then I won't take you. It's too risky."

When Brandi entered, Marcy grabbed the chart and raced from the garden. Looking back over her shoulder, she shot a parting glance at Liz that nearly froze her to the bone.

Liz grasped the awful truth. The price for winning was very dear. She had just lost the one and only friend she had.

11:02 AM

Marcy marched toward her office, clutching Kate's chart to her chest, fighting back tears. She couldn't remember when she had been so angry, so hurt. Her "little patient" had dealt her a powerful blow.

Everything had been wonderful when they started today's therapy. There'd actually been lightness and sweetness in Kate's disposition. Then she'd become a monster. And it had been Marcy's willingness to help Liz that had put her in this impossible position.

What was she thinking to permit Kate—No, that wasn't Kate; it was Liz—to put her in this spot? *This isn't happening. I have to do what she says or lose my job!* Marcy was now a victim of her own kindness.

Pulling a tissue from her pocket, she blew her nose. She should have reported the problem to Dr. Jamison when Liz first confided in her. Now her compassion could be her undoing. The publicity alone would be damaging—would even hurt Adriana. *How could I be such a fool?*

A feeling of dread engulfed her. What if Liz wasn't physically and mentally ready by next weekend? Being responsible for life was the first commandment Marcy lived by. *If she isn't, there's no way I'll meet her demands, even if it ends my career.*

She was still quaking. She shook her head to clear it, picked up the phone, and dialed Chet's extension. She got his answering machine and tried to sound casual as she left a message. "Hi, Chet, this is Marcy. I'd appreciate it if you would handle my therapy appointments next Saturday—all but the first one, Kate Craig's. I can handle that. You'll just need to cover the others. In exchange I'll handle all your Sunday appointments. Please call me back and let me know if this will work for you."

11:05 AM

Liz sat slumped in her bed. She felt terrible. Her conscience was eating away at her heart. Hurting Marcy was the last thing she wanted to do, but she couldn't think of another way to get what she so desperately wanted . . . needed.

Her lips quivered as she thought about her babies. Would she ever be able to really let go? Could she stay out of their lives? Could she stand by, without knowing where they were or what they were doing? *I can't even start to answer those questions. And Marcy!* How could she ever make it up to her? *I would never have told Jamison or anyone else. But she believed me—believed I really would.*

Liz stifled her remorse and got on with her task. As she sat up in her bed, she tightened, held, and released her arm, leg, and stomach muscles over and over again. The next few days would be critical. First she had to do all that she could to be strong, to walk long distances on her own, to sit unattended, to fool everyone. She gripped the side rails, pulled herself up, and then let herself down, slowly, deliberately—flexing and relaxing, flexing and relaxing.

Second, she had to keep Marcy believing her threat and, somehow, she had to find a way to appeal to Marcy's own strong maternal instincts—and win her back. Third, Marcy and Kate had to design a foolproof plan: a way that she could be gone from the hospital for up to four hours without being missed.

11:55 AM

Charles racked up the balls on the pool table. The poolroom was sectioned off from the bowling alley by a glass wall. This way Josh would see Charles when he came in. But Charles had to look twice to confirm that the young man who had just walked through the front door was Josh. He seemed so different—pants hanging from his hips, hair completely tousled. Josh looked the very essence of a rebel—an angry young man with a chip on his shoulder.

"Hey, buddy. How you been?"

Josh just grimaced and after an uncomfortably long pause said, "Okay, I guess."

"Call me Chuck. Now grab a cue stick and help me clear the table." He motioned to the cue rack on the wall and watched with interest as the teenager, transformed by clothes and attitude, sauntered to the rack and selected a cue stick. The boy removed his jacket and threw it under the table. Then he swaggered over to stand next to Charles, self-importance written in his demeanor.

Josh's eyebrows shot up as he knocked in the seven ball with his first shot. "I've got stripes." He chuckled and walked to the other side to take his next shot.

The bowling alley manager stepped in. "Hey, young man, put out that cigarette. This is California and there's no smoking in public places." The man stood there until Josh snuffed out the butt with the bottom of his shoe and placed it over his ear like an accountant would a pencil.

Josh missed his next shot. As Charles focused in on the two ball, he wondered if Josh's parents knew what was going on with this boy. *Such anger, self-destruction, defiance.*

Charles purposely missed his shot and stood back as Josh tried again to pocket the nine ball. He exchanged small talk with Josh, giving the boy a chance to get comfortable. This would be a tricky interview. Charles had to play to the young man's ego and slowly get to his purpose—a question here, a question there, but always focusing the attention on Josh, his feelings, his activities, his needs.

Charles had his notepad in his jacket pocket, and his jacket was hanging over a chair. He left it there, figuring that "bonding" was more important for now. Maybe when he took Josh to lunch, he could make some notes—to ensure accuracy.

"Do your parents know that we're meeting?" Charles asked.

"Uh-uh," Josh replied, shaking his head. "And I doubt that they care."

"I see," Charles said as he "accidentally" hit the eight ball into the side pocket. "Hey, you win! Wanna go again?"

Charles had to work this carefully. He couldn't release anything to KROX without the parents' consent. But perhaps he could use Josh as his entrée and then get the parents involved—earn their trust too. He could even turn this into an exclusive with Kate's whole family. If not that, at least he should be able to get the parents to agree to let him have a live interview with Josh.

By the end of the third game, Charles had seen to it that Josh had won two. The kid wasn't a very good player, but he was the one with the ego problem, and Charles knew that the real score was Chuck three, Josh zero.

"Let's go have some lunch. You got a good hamburger joint nearby?" Charles asked as they both picked up their jackets and headed for the door.

"Yeah, there's this place called Val's. It's not far. I'll show you," Josh said. "Supposedly it has the best hamburgers in the Bay Area."

Charles pointed out his convertible Mustang and motioned to Josh to get in. Josh was all smiles as he opened the door to the passenger seat.

"Nice wheels," Josh said.

"Yeah, not bad," Charles said. "Get some music on the radio—your choice, my friend."

Booze, burgers, rock 'n roll—I've got him pegged. Now to get him to take me home to Mom and Pop.

chapter eight

Monday, October 1, 3:00 PM

Jamison squinted his eyes and rolled his chair closer to his monitor to avoid the glare from the overhead lights. He reviewed the online charts prepared by the specialists who were working with Kate Craig. He was pleased that the physical therapist wanted longer sessions. This recommendation fit well into his plans. Between tests, psychiatric sessions, physical therapy, and daily check-ups, he should be able to keep Kate at Stanford for a long, long time. She would benefit . . . and so would he. He had convinced Kate's parents that her survival depended almost entirely upon continuous oversight.

Scanning through the charts, he carefully read the notations Kate's psychiatrist had made. Manning's notes stated that Kate was a "poor responder." She was either frightened, reluctant to speak, or very shy.

Jamison sat back in his chair and thought about his interactions with Kate. He had noted similar behavior when he was with her. But he didn't expect much from an eleven-year-old.

Jamison scanned the rest of Manning's notes. He read, "In my professional opinion, the most important factors contributing to the emotional and mental well-being of children are feelings of safety and love, demonstrated through touch and acceptance. The mother is the most important person in Kate's eyes."

Jamison entered the following note to the chart: For months subsequent to the surgery, the only safe place for Kate will be in the hospital. She needs constant observation and therapy until such time as she is deemed functional.

He figured that Kate's mother spent sufficient time with her every day and was very demonstrative with her affection. There could be no question of Kate being loved and accepted—at least by her mother.

Jamison picked up the phone and asked to be put through to Dr. Manning's office.

"Psychiatry. How may I direct your call?" a receptionist asked.

"This is Dr. Jamison. Please put me through to Dr. Manning."

"Sorry, Dr. Jamison, she's with a patient at the moment. But I'll be happy to have her call you when she's through. Oh, wait a minute. She just walked out. Can you hold a minute?"

It was only a few seconds before he heard a click. "Dr. Jamison. This is Dr. Manning. What can I do for you?"

"I'm calling about Kate Craig. I wanted to talk with you about her progress—also to get your opinion on conducting some tests to gauge her mental capacity and assess her education level."

"Intelligence exams?" Manning asked.

"Yes, and tests that provide us with some idea of her education level. I know you're dealing with her emotional needs. But there's so much more I want to know. For instance, although I know the brain was a healthy one and that it came from a young woman, I have no idea of the donor's IQ or whether the donor's level of intelligence was sustainable after the surgery. So I'd like to find out whether we're dealing with a patient who has the IQ of a five-year-old, a ten-year-old, a twenty-year-old . . . or something in between. I think the parents will want to know too." He cleared his throat. "Can you do this?"

"Yes. I have a series of other tests I need to conduct this week, but I'll try to make the IQ and education tests priorities for next week. Is that soon enough for you?"

"When next week?" he asked.

"Um, Let me see. I think sometime early in the week." Jamison could hear Manning's fingernails tapping on the keyboard, and after a short pause she said, "How about Tuesday, a week from tomorrow?"

"Good. Please let me know the results as soon as you have them," he said.

Jamison was about to disconnect the call when Manning added, "Oh, wait. I have a question. This test—um—do you think there's hope that sometime in the near future Kate might be enrolled in school?"

Shaking his head, Jamison said, "No. I think she'll be here a long time—maybe a year or longer—hard to say, but her parents might want to arrange for a tutor. It's important that both her body and her new brain get all the exercise possible."

"That's for sure," Manning said. "I'll get right on it."

3:15 PM

A taste of bitterness filled Liz's mouth. She had been working her body to its breaking point. She picked up the ceramic pitcher that had contained flowers from her parents and filled it partway with water from the hospital decanter. She used this as a weight and lifted it over and over again—first one arm, until the muscles burned, and then the other. Next she worked her leg muscles by trying to undo the tightly tucked in sheets and blanket. When she would succeed, she would call a nurse to repair her bed and then start all over again. She didn't want to hurt herself, but she needed to double her strength in less than a week.

As she did this, she thought about Marcy. Her therapy sessions on Sunday and Monday were with Chet, so she still hadn't seen Marcy since the confrontation. But tomorrow would be another story. Liz had no idea how that would go, but she knew it would be tough.

As she continued her workout, she thought about the challenges that lay ahead. She had already worked out most of the plan, but she needed to discuss some of the finer points with Marcy tomorrow so that there would be time for the therapist to set things up and get the supplies needed for travel and disguise.

Mom. What will I do about her? Somehow she needed to convince her mom to visit earlier than usual on Saturday. She would need to make up something about being in therapy or a series of all-day tests from about eleven in the morning until late afternoon. That shouldn't be too difficult, considering the barrage she'd been going through.

But the tests and exams were an issue. Marcy would need to convince everyone that she was working with Kate in a four-hour session. The other tests and examinations would need to be conducted very early or very late—and on time. This was a big problem. Except for Jamison's early morning visits, her other scheduled tests and exams were often off by as much as an hour due to emergencies and staff illnesses. She'd have to leave those issues up to Marcy.

At that moment, she realized that she was in more pain than she could ever remember—not just physical and not just mental. This was an emotional pain. *Do I hate myself? Or do I love myself? Who is "myself"?*

She rang for the nurse.

Twelve minutes later, the afternoon nurse entered. "Hi, Kate. What can I do for you?"

Although angry at the time lapse, she asked sheepishly, "Would you mind putting down the bedrail? It's bothering me. I feel claustrophobic."

The nurse checked the chart, walked to Kate's bedside, and lowered the railing. "Okay, but it goes back up at night—hospital regulations. You need anything else?"

"No. But thank you so much. I feel better already," Kate said.

As soon as the nurse left the room, she pushed the tray-on-wheels a couple feet away from her, sat up, and slid slowly off the bed. Since the swelling had gone down, the shunt had been removed that morning, and her new pink helmet sat invitingly on the side table. She placed it on her head. Then, holding onto the visitor's chair, she lowered herself to the seat and sat for a moment. Sweat dripped from her brow. Her legs quivered.

Using only her leg muscles, she rose unsteadily to her feet. A rush of dizziness followed but passed as quickly as it came. She gauged the distance between the chair, around the foot of the bed, and over to the window—about fourteen to sixteen feet. This would be her path. She figured that the foot of the bed would provide a halfway point, in case she needed to catch herself or rest.

Unassisted and alone, she placed her right hand and then just her fingertips on the bed. She picked up one foot, placing it in front of the other. Until now, either Mom or Marcy had been at her side to help balance and support her when she attempted to walk. And the distances she had covered during those sessions had been short. Her goal between now and Saturday would be to walk the path for at least twenty round trips without touching anything—and all on her own power.

Her legs wobbled. She set her jaw and willed her legs to be still. She envisioned herself walking with ease. Her first mother had once told her, "If things aren't going right for you, it's because you're not thinking right. Change your thinking." She was changing her thinking.

I can do this. With renewed confidence, she picked up one foot and then another. She reached the foot of the bed and stalled for only a moment before proceeding to the window. From her room, she looked down at the parking lot and then up. As she scanned the horizon, she noted the small, billowy clouds that looked as though they had been flicked off the end of a paintbrush onto a pale blue canvas. She discovered a tear trickling down her cheek. It had nothing to do with the pain. No, this was a tear of gratitude. "Thank you, God," she murmured out loud.

She smiled and began her journey back. As she reached the foot of the bed, the door swung open.

"Sorry I'm so late, honey," Donna said as she walked through the doorway. She stopped and held her breath. "Oh, my word! Look at you," Donna said as she rushed to Kate's side. "Are you sure you should be walking around without anyone in the room to assist you?"

"I'm okay, Mom. By this time next year I'll be dancing. Just wait and see." She leaned forward, grinned, and gave her mom a tender kiss.

Donna cupped Kate's face in her hands. "Oh, I am so proud of you. I can hardly believe how fast you're recovering."

Kate realized that since the accident, the times she'd felt most at ease were when this woman was at her side. A warm feeling of calm and acceptance came over her. She knew that just as she was possessed by an incessant urge to nurture and be with Megan and Mark, this precious woman needed to nurture and be near her.

"I wanted to surprise you," Kate said. "I've been waiting for you.

I'm so glad you're here. I want to keep walking for a while—build up bigger muscles. Will you walk with me?" she asked.

"Of course. What do you think about walking in the hallway?" her mom asked. "The security guard is right outside. So if you want, I'll ask him to make sure the coast is clear before we go."

"Let's do it. But first, what do you think of my new hat?" Kate asked.

"Right out of a fashion magazine," Donna said, eyebrows raised in jest.

"Who knows? Next year it might be the new trend," Kate said, posing like a calendar girl.

Donna shook her head and offered a ready smile. Then arm in arm they took off down the hall.

"How's Dad doing?" Kate asked.

"He's been busy these last few weeks—big project in Portland—a new highway interchange he designed. He'll be home tomorrow and will visit."

"And Josh? How's he doing? I haven't seen him since the press conference."

"I wish I knew. During the week, he leaves for school at about seven-thirty and gets home a little after three. Since your tests and therapies are usually scheduled in the mornings and early afternoons, I leave to see you at about two each day."

"What about weekends?"

"Teenagers are very social," Donna said with a wistful smile. "He's always off with his friends." She patted Kate's hand and continued. "In a couple of years, you'll understand. When I was a girl, I always had plans on the weekends." She gave Kate time to rest before continuing down the hallway. "I'm just happy when Josh shows up for dinner." Donna sighed. "It'd be nice if he'd bring his friends home, but he seems to always want to go to their homes instead."

Kate nodded as though she understood.

Donna squeezed Kate's arm and said, "Now, tell me about your day. What did you learn today?"

chapter nine

Tuesday, October 2, 5:00 PM

Charles sat at his desk and drew Xs on the paper as he thought about trying to locate the donor. Too much time had lapsed since the brain-transplant interview with Jamison. No longer the toast of KROX, Charles grew ever more agitated. It was all so unfair—one day a celebrity, the next, just another reporter. He'd spent a lifetime taking care of everyone else: he'd been trying to support his mother since his father had died, and now he needed to earn enough to put his sister through college. He set the pencil aside and rubbed his face with his hands. The two women he loved most were both so fragile, so vulnerable. He felt a deep, abiding responsibility toward them.

He had to come through for them. But he wasn't going to if he couldn't win the attention of one of the larger markets. The pay at KROX was puny. A chance at a bigger market, a national station, was what he needed.

He held his head in his hands. So far, he hadn't had a single hit with the calls to possible donor families, and he wondered at the number of surviving relatives who just didn't care. He found it hard to believe that some preferred not to know who might have received organs from their donor-relatives—whose precious lives they might have saved.

Some actually seemed to think the inquiries were macabre.

One more day—that's all he had left with the temporary workers and the chance for discovering the donor.

Even Dr. Jamison had become less and less receptive as time passed. Now when Charles called, Jamison's secretary always had a ready excuse: "He's not available right now, sir." "I'm sorry, he's with a patient. Can I take a message?" Jamison hadn't returned his calls in more than three days.

But there was one glimmer of hope—Josh Craig. Charles leaned back as he pondered the troubled young man. Josh had promised him that he'd talk with his parents tonight and try to set up an interview. If the boy succeeded, Charles would win over the parents. If he could get into their good graces, maybe he could eventually talk with Kate. That was what he wanted. She was his ticket out.

6:15 PM

Bruce watched as Megan set the table—paper plates, forks, and napkins supplied by KFC. She folded the napkins and placed them to the right of each plate, the way she'd seen her mother do it so many times. Then she laid a fork onto each napkin. She seemed to do it as a ritual. "You're doin' a great job," he said as he walked over to her.

She slowly raised her head and nodded. "Yeah, I know how to do it. Mom showed me."

Bruce took the lid off the tub of chicken and placed it on the center of the table. He got three serving spoons from the kitchen drawer and placed one in each container as he removed the lids from the mashed potatoes, gravy, and coleslaw. This was the third time in two weeks that he had brought home this same meal.

"I wish Mom had shown me how to cook," Megan said. "We used to have some really good dinners—like spaghetti and meatballs."

"I remember the way Momma would set up all that stuff on the counter so we could make our own tacos," Mark said as he opened the refrigerator door. He took out two Cokes, placed them on the table, and returned to retrieve a third.

"I'll tell you what," Bruce said. "I'll learn how to make the taco stations, if you guys help me. And we'll see if we can find your mom's recipe for spaghetti sauce. I'll bet we can make that too."

"All right!" Mark said.

"Mark, go wash your hands. Dinner's ready," Megan commanded. Mark ran to the sink and Megan rolled her eyes. "Walk. Don't run!"

"Boy, that sure looks good," Bruce said, trying to lighten Megan's spirits. "You two certainly know how to make an old man happy. I'll bet this took you hours to prepare."

Mark ran into the table with hands still wet. "We just bought it at KFC. Remember?"

"Oh, yeah." Bruce pulled the chair back from the table, sat down, and scooted the chair in. "Sit down, kids. You know the routine."

Before eating they always held hands and took turns recounting something for which they were grateful. The smell of the fried chicken made Bruce's stomach growl. He looked over at Mark to go first and hoped the boy would be brief.

"I'm glad it was really windy today 'cause Pop helped me fly my kite over at the park after school," said Mark.

"Pop? Who's Pop?" asked Bruce.

"That's Mr. Thayer," said Megan. "That's what we decided to call him. And we call Mrs. Thayer 'Nana.' " She glanced at him and added, "I'm thankful for Algae. He's always happy to see me."

"And I'm thankful for you two," Bruce said.

They squeezed each other's hands, let go, and passed the cardboard and styrofoam containers to each other.

Bruce tried to look cheerful for his kids, but inside he was hurting. Nothing was the same. The house seemed cold and dark. Liz used to light rose-scented candles and put on soft music. And sometimes in the evening, she would call Megan over and share a dab of hand lotion—a special mother-to-daughter bonding ritual. All of that was gone.

Bruce fidgeted with the hem of his shirt. Even his clothes smelled different. Liz used something in the laundry that gave them a lemony fragrance. The softness was gone too. Everything was different: the food, the smells, the textures, the sounds, and the sights. A feeling of emptiness and sadness swept over him, but he refused to let it show.

Just as he swallowed the last of his dinner, the phone rang.

"I'll get it," Megan said as she wiped her mouth with her napkin and ran over to pick up the receiver. "Hello."

Megan's bottom lip quivered as she whispered, "My mommy isn't here. She's dead."

Bruce jumped from the table and took the phone from her. "It's okay, honey. Sit down. I'll take it." Then in his sternest voice, he asked, "Who is this? What do you want?"

"This is Malcolm Cannon at station KROX calling. Is this the home of the late Elizabeth Lindsay?"

"Why do you want to know?" Bruce felt his face flush with anger.

"We're doing a special on organ transplants, trying to trace donors and recipients . . ."

He saw that Megan's eyes were riveted on his face. It took all his self-control to suppress his rage. He turned his face away from Megan and Mark and then held the phone tighter.

"I don't want to talk about this. Don't call me again," he growled. Then he hung up the phone. For a moment he stood there, motionless. When he finally turned toward Megan again, he noted that her face was white and her hands were shaking. His were too.

"Are you all right, Dad?" she asked. "What did that man want?"

He walked over to Megan, squatted down to her eye level, and drew her to him. He held her tight. "It was nothing, honey. Nothing."

Mark ran over to them. "Is it bad? Is something wrong?" he asked with a tremor in his voice.

"No, Mark. Everything is okay. Sometimes we get calls from people we don't want to talk to and so we hang up. That's all." He patted both his kids on their backs and said in his bravest tone, "Come on, kids. Let's clean up." He picked up the paper plates and napkins and tossed them into the trash. Mark picked up the empty cans and put them in the recycling bin.

Bruce could see the tears mounting in Megan's eyes. She grabbed the forks and took them to the sink, where she began washing them, scrubbing them over and over again as hard as she could—as though trying to wear off the finish.

"That's enough," Bruce said, gently turning her. She dropped the forks on the counter, looked up at him through teary eyes, and put her arms around his waist. She muffled a sob. He drew her close and held her, patting her back and soothing her with soft words.

"It's gonna be hard, Megan. But we're going to be okay." Then he pushed her gently away and raised her chin to look at him. "Megan, honey, I'm sorry if I scared you a minute ago. The person on the phone . . . he just wanted to know some stuff about your mom—stuff I didn't think was any of his business.

Megan acted as though she understood, but he doubted it.

"I'm okay, Dad. I just didn't know what to say after he said Mom's name. But I'm all right now. Really."

Bruce nodded and turned to finish clearing the table. "I have an idea. Let's go put on an old DVD—something really funny. Whadda ya say?"

Out of the corner of his eye, he saw Megan brush some loose hairs from her face. "Hey, Mark. Where are you? Come on down. We're going to watch a movie," Megan said as she walked into the family room. She picked out the DVD and said, "Can we light two of the candles?"

8:00 PM

"Mom, are you there? Anybody home?" Adriana said.

Marcy snapped her head up to her meet her nine-year-old daughter's gaze and smiled. "Oh, I'm sorry. My mind was somewhere else."

Adriana tilted her head. "Did you hear anything I said about the field trip next week?"

"Uh . . . yes . . . next Wednesday, right?" Marcy's mind was racing. She really had been somewhere else—back in the physical therapy room that morning with Kate.

Through gritted teeth, Adriana said, "Would you pa-lease sign the permission slip?"

Marcy looked at Adriana. "Don't get sassy with me, young lady. Here, give it to me."

Adriana held out the crumpled slip. Marcy took it, read it twice, signed it, and handed the form back. "There . . . Now, go put it away. And it's time for your bath. Go draw the water and call me when you're ready to have your back washed."

Her daughter turned, put the slip in her backpack, and walked to the bathroom.

As soon as Marcy heard the water running, she sat back in the overstuffed chair and raised her feet onto the ottoman. Relieved that day was over, she sighed and thought about a glass of Merlot. But she was too tired to get out of the chair.

She kept replaying the events of the day. She hadn't been sure how she could face this day with Kate—Liz—that child. That woman.

Kate had cried, pleaded for forgiveness, said she needed a friend. She had asked repeatedly about what she, Marcy, would do if the situation were reversed.

Could she just walk away? Could she? What was it that the old Marvel comics used to say when two superheroes opposed each other? Something like, "When an irresistible force meets an immovable object . . . " That was how she'd felt earlier that day.

She was still in awe at how this young, fragile woman-child willed herself to walk such a distance. It was obvious that Kate had been in excruciating pain. Marcy could see it in those strained eyes. But the girl kept putting one foot in front of the other, covering a distance totaling over one hundred feet without assistance. She said the next day she would double it, and by Saturday, she would be able to walk from one end of a football field to the other.

"Did you write the poem?" Kate had asked when Marcy had first entered the hospital room.

Startled, Marcy replied, "Are you kidding? How can you even ask me that after blackmailing me and my family?"

"You told me you'd write a poem." Kate hesitated a moment and then turned away, but not before Marcy had seen the tears in her eyes. "I hope you won't disappoint Bruce and the kids," she added.

Marcy glared and said, "I won't."

Kate, with eyes red-rimmed, choked back a moan as she murmured, "I'm truly sorry. I know you don't trust me now. But I need your help—desperately." She had lowered her head as her shoulders sunk inward, then cleared her throat and said, "Please don't hate me. I love my kids and husband. I miss them. What if you lost everything?" she said, hands upturned. "Your home, your family, your identity? I don't know if I can bear another loss. Please, please forgive me, but I have to see them. I must."

At that moment, Marcy had felt herself crumble. She, too, had lost loved ones. What would she do if she lost Adriana? Or her identity as an adult, a mother, a physical therapist? She'd released the pent-up tension she'd been holding, then nodded slowly. "I hate to admit it, but I do understand, Kate. And I forgive you."

Although her career was still on the line, the act of forgiveness was healing. She had issues to resolve, but the destructive power of anger and its awful burden were gone.

She thought about the work ahead. It amazed her that Kate had worked out such finite details for Saturday. Many of those details included several tasks that Marcy had to perform: buy a blonde wig and select some of Adriana's longer clothes that would fit Kate. Marcy knew that their weights were about the same, but Kate was a good four inches taller. Then she had to set up an extended therapy session and ensure that Kate's other tests would be scheduled early or late or rescheduled for another day.

Tomorrow she could begin wheeling Kate around public areas of the hospital, getting the staff used to seeing the two of them together in different areas: cafeteria, atrium, lobby, main hallway, and multiple gardens. That way, if staff or family looked in on Saturday, they'd believe she was somewhere else on the grounds.

Maybe it will work.

"Mom, I'm ready for you to wash my back," Adriana hollered.

"Okay. I'll be right there."

9:00 PM

Josh quietly placed his backpack on the entryway table and walked to the living room. His parents were watching the news. "Hi, Mom. Hey, Dad—glad to see you're back from Portland. How're you two doing?" he asked.

His mother looked taken aback for a moment. "We're fine, honey. And how are you?"

"I'm okay. Uh . . . I was wondering, did you see Kate today? How is she?"

"Oh, Josh, you wouldn't believe it," said John. "I flew in to San Francisco. Your mother picked me up, and we went straight over to Stanford. She's walking and talking."

"She asked about you, dear," his mom said. "I don't think she has many memories, so she asks all about you."

"Really? So she's doing good?" Josh asked.

"Would you like to go see her on Sunday? I know she'd like to see you."

"Yeah. Sure. Can I talk with you about something?" Josh asked.

"Of course. What is it?" his father said.

Josh shuffled his feet and smiled. "Well, uh, you remember that guy who did the interview with Kate's doctor on KROX?"

"You mean, Charles something? The guy who followed us up the elevator?" A suspicious frown crept across his dad's face.

"Oh yeah. I forgot about the elevator," Josh said. "Anyway, I ran into that guy the other day at the bowling alley and he asked me some questions. He seemed pretty nice."

His mom looked tense. Josh knew that she hadn't liked Chuck. "What did he want?"

"Well, he said he was trying to promote organ donation. You know, so that more people who need hearts and lungs—and I guess brains now—can have them. He said he thought Kate's story was inspirational—that was his word. Anyway, it sounded like a good thing to me." Josh looked at his mother for approval.

His mother smiled but hesitated. "Organ donation is very important. I'm glad he's taking that on." Still smiling, she furled her brow and asked, "What does he want from you?"

Josh shifted uncomfortably. "Not just me, but us. He'd like to interview us so we can explain how important it is to donate your organs."

Before his mom could speak, Josh added, "He showed me his license, and he has the stamp. He really means what he says. I think we should do it. We could help save a lot of lives."

His mom took a deep breath, looked over at his dad, and shrugged her shoulders. "What could it hurt?"

chapter ten

Friday, October 5, 6:45 AM

The familiar beeping of the hospital monitors and the buzzing of the florescent lights were now embedded in Kate like a pulse. Other sounds were all that saved her from the constant nightmares. The scene had repeated each night for the last week: ten-foot tall hedges around her, an unending maze. She was running, looking for a way out. But there wasn't one. As she turned in a new direction, the scene grew darker, more foreboding. From a distance, she could hear Megan and Mark calling, "Mom, where are you?"

Her rescuers this morning were the propellers of a small aircraft circling overhead and a cart clattering down the hallway. She sat up with a start—too quickly. A wave of nausea spread over her and then passed. Sweat poured down her stubbled hair, down her brow, and behind her ears. She gasped and tried to open her eyes but couldn't. She started to scream and then rubbed at them. Finally, she was able to pry them open. The blurring and double vision were still there.

During the past three days, her sight had deteriorated. But this current eye problem was new. It was probably just an infection—maybe pink eye. Although she knew the blurring could be the sign of a serious problem, she discounted it. She didn't dare say anything to anyone or all her hopes would evaporate like morning dew.

After the memorial—yes, after tomorrow, I'll tell them.

Tomorrow loomed large. In her mind's eye she could see the word "tomorrow" printed in shocking pink against a black void. It danced across her psyche. Everything rested on tomorrow.

Like a child ready for her first day of school, she was filled with joy and anxiety. But terror shared an equal part of her mind. It gnawed at her. How would she react when she saw Bruce and her children?

Hand trembling, she reached for a tissue, dipped it in the plastic drinking pitcher, and attempted to clean her eyes. With a second tissue, she patted the sweat from her brow and face.

She practiced a meditation exercise to calm her anxiety. But her attempts were in vain. There was no quieting her thoughts, no small semblance of peace. Fantasy scenes from tomorrow's memorial service kept popping into her consciousness.

She could walk the distance. Or could she? There was no place for doubt—not now. And she could sit for hours on end if necessary. Yes, she could. Except for her troubled vision, there were few challenges she couldn't cope with. What she feared most were her yo-yo emotions. So much of her energy had gone into her preparations for tomorrow. It was all that mattered to her.

But suddenly a thought struck her and her eyes grew wide, her mouth dropped. What about after October sixth? What then? Would tomorrow be the beginning . . . or the end?

Dear God, help me. I can't think that far ahead.

"Good morning, Kate," said Carrie, a heavyset nurse's aide. "Something special this morning: eggs and toast and fruit." She smiled widely, placed the tray on the roller table, and lowered the metal side-rail. "I'll fill your hospital container with fresh water. Do you want me to refill that glass pitcher of yours again?" she asked as she motioned to the ceramic pitcher.

"You know me. Can't get enough water. Thanks, Carrie," Kate said as she surreptitiously wiped the last of the gunk from her right eye. But she didn't move fast enough.

"What's wrong with your eyes?" Carrie asked as she moved closer to Kate and peered intently. "They're red and puffy. I'll let the nurse on duty know."

Kate leaned forward in a panic. "Oh, no. I've been crying. I just miss my family. There's nothing wrong with my eyes. In a couple of minutes the swelling will go down."

The aide frowned and stared at her with doubt. Then she shook her head. "I don't know about that, but I'll tell you what; I'll get you a cool washcloth and you can apply it. I'll be back in an hour to help you bathe and we can take another look at them then."

Trying not to show her dread, Kate said, "That'll be fine. See you in a bit." Then, as though it were an afterthought, she added, "Oh, Carrie, could I have some ice chips?"

The aide nodded, disappeared for a moment, and returned with a wet cloth and a tumbler full of ice chips.

As soon as the aide left the room, Kate shoveled the eggs into her mouth—protein for muscle. Then she poured some of the ice chips onto the cloth, wrapped it carefully, and pressed it to her eyes. Five minutes on, five minutes off.

Forty minutes into this routine, she placed the breakfast tray on the bed next to her and opened the lid of the portable table. She glanced into the mirror and could feel the bile rise in her throat. She swallowed it back and closed her eyes as though the image wouldn't exist if she didn't look. Since her awakening, she had seen her reflection in windows and glass doors as she passed, but she had always averted her eyes as quickly as possible.

Kate forced herself to look again. This time, despite her revulsion, she studied her face. She pushed her tongue through the now familiar gap between her teeth and ran her hand over the dark stubble on her head—seventeen days' growth. She looked like an unfit army recruit.

Through blurry vision, she squinted and moved the mirror closer to see her eyes. Her double vision resulted in four eyes staring back. But they were clean, and the swelling wasn't too bad. She didn't have pink eye—the whites were clear. Maybe she could fool them.

Them. There were so many of them: Jamison, the technicians, the pharmacists, the nurses, Marcy, the aides . . . her family, especially Mom.

She gritted her teeth, closed the lid of the portable table, and steeled herself. She could get through this. She would—she was betting everything on tomorrow.

8:00 AM

Jamison was bubbling with pleasure. As he passed the nurses' station, he offered a friendly "hello." The nurses nodded back with smiles and returned his greeting.

As he rounded the corner, Dr. Johnson, one of his assistant surgeons, almost collided with him. "Oh, sorry," she said as she stepped back. Then, as recognition set in, she stammered, "Oh, Doctor Jamison, we're all so proud of you. I heard that you'll be keynoting the next World Congress of Neurology. You deserve it."

Jamison flashed a winning smile at her. "Thanks, Deborah, but credit goes to you and Felix as well." They spoke for a few minutes more. Then he turned and continued his trek toward Kate's room.

He felt magnanimous, even generous. It had been a long time since he'd experienced such joy.

He'd call Charles after the exam to give him another exclusive—Jamison didn't want to ignore him.

Smiling to himself, he recounted his successes: first, Kate was alive with a functioning new brain; second, physically she was doing better than expected; and third, even though like other medical facilities, Stanford preferred to move patients out as soon as they could, the hospital board had just approved his and the psychiatrist's recommendations to extend Kate's stay for at least another thirty days. This was precious time to complete a series of tests and experiments. And when the thirty days were nearing an end, he'd find cause to ask for another extension.

As he approached the open door to Kate's room, he saw her sitting up in the bed. With head lifted, she stared at him. There was something mature, unsettling, in both her stance and expression. His throat tightened. Anxiety replaced his euphoria. "Good morning, Kate."

"Good morning, Dr. Jamison," she replied. But something was wrong. He couldn't put his finger on it. A chill ran through him.

Then the girl curled her lips in a smile, revealed a dimple. "You're right on time, as usual. Do you want me in the bed or in the chair?"

"The bed's fine," he said. "You know, I hear you've been up and about, but I want you to be very careful. You mustn't bump your head or fall. And it's dangerous for you to walk around unassisted."

"Oh, don't worry, Doctor." She pushed back the blanket, sat, and waited. "I'll be very careful." She lifted one eyebrow. "I know my life depends on it."

Jamison walked to the foot of the bed and reviewed the chart. Appetite good, vital signs excellent, meds balanced.

He moved to Kate's side. "Can you sit away from your pillow and bend forward for me?" he asked. She nodded, and he gently assisted her in the movement. He listened to her heart and respirations with his stethoscope and then lightly thumped her back.

"On Wednesday, Dr. Manning, your psychiatrist, will give you an educational evaluation test, and if you're up to it, a short IQ test. Do you know what that is?" he asked.

"I think so. Won't it tell me how smart I am?" she asked.

Jamison relaxed. It was a child's answer. The initial discomfort he'd felt dissipated.

Everything seemed to be in order. Or was it?

11:45 AM

Inhaling deeply, Josh took in as much of the smoke as he could draw. He held his breath until he thought his lungs would explode and then slowly exhaled. He grinned and laid his head on the headrest of the passenger bucket seat. "Let's go, Ron."

"Okay, buddy," Ron replied. "Hey, that freaky sister of yours ever coming home?" he asked as he shifted gears.

"What do I care?"

Ron cranked up the radio. The bass notes vibrated the whole car . . . and the neighborhood. He shouted, "Hey, Josh, your parents know there was no school today?"

"No. But what they don't know won't hurt them."

Ron shouted over the blasting radio. "Today's trip is on me—free of cost. That's what friends are for."

"Man. You're the best," Josh crooned. Then it struck him and he sat up straight. "Oh, I almost forgot. I need to be home by seven tonight; my parents and I are going to be interviewed by KROX. Isn't that sweet? Of course it's about Kate. But the interviewer is really cool—nice car. Almost as nice as yours."

"No worries, buddy. I'll have you home in plenty of time."

1:00 PM

Charles sat across from his manager, trying to hide a grin that extended from ear to ear. He felt as though he could float.

"Yes, that's right, two back-to-back interviews today: first one's at three o'clock this afternoon with Dr. Jamison; then another at seven tonight with the patient's family." He sat up straighter and added, "The camera crews will have to hustle. It's about an hour's drive between the two. And that's without traffic. Plus there's always the setup time."

Penny looked at him with what he could only hope was admiration. "Well, Charles, maybe you didn't locate the donor's family. But these two specials will get nationwide coverage. Good job," she said, giving him a thumbs up gesture.

Finally after years of struggle, he was getting his break. This was his shot to earn a decent living. This pair of interviews would take him over the top. All he had to do was ask the right questions—no mistakes.

chapter eleven

Saturday, October 6, 1:15 PM

Kate walked into the church, accepted a program from the aging Mr. Dodds, and walked to the last row, center aisle. She sat and slouched, barely able to breathe. The walk from the corner where Marcy had let her out, coupled with the heavy clothing she was wearing, the shoes that were too small, and the blonde wig made her feel double her weight. Or perhaps the sights and sounds were what made her chest feel heavy.

She looked at the program. The top lines read:

In Memoriam

Elizabeth Ann Lindsay

followed by her birthday and date of death. Inside, on the left, was a Unitarian hymn and on the right, the speakers and music.

She placed the program on her lap, took a needed breath, and scanned the room through blurred vision, searching for her family. It took all her strength to focus on the separate images and determine the identities of those in attendance.

It wasn't as much by sight as by sound that she found her targets.

Though she couldn't hear their exchanges, she recognized the deep resonating voice of her husband and the fast, high-pitched responses of Maxine, his sister. From the same direction, she heard Megan shushing Mark. She had to press her breastbone to keep her heart inside her chest. She wanted to stand up and yell, "I'm here! It's me, Mom!"

Though she felt torn apart, she held back her tears. It was as though her heart, mind, and soul had teamed up to demolish her like a condemned building. She thought she'd pass out or implode. Finally, she gasped in a breath. The sound drew only brief attention. It didn't take long to realize she was invisible—as good as dead.

Everyone she loved was here—friends, neighbors, and family members. She didn't know so many people had cared about her. Despite the blurring and emotional pain, she began to pick out family and friends and whisper their names.

She yearned to hug her children, kiss her father and brother, and hold Bruce close. Instead, she sat still. Closing her eyes and shutting her ears, she tried to steady the pain. It came to her suddenly that she was grieving her own demise.

Slowly she opened her eyes and tried to disassociate herself emotionally from the scene. She noted Megan at one end of the room, holding Bruce's hand and looking up at him. And Mark, her sweet Mark, stood next to his sister, swinging his arms and turning his head from side to side—his way of releasing pent-up energy.

Her emotions bubbled up again. She ached to hold Mark. He was so vulnerable, so different from Megan. Megan was self-confident, smart, talented, and bossy. Mark, although bright, had an energy level that often got him into trouble. He needed a great deal more than just discipline—he needed unconditional love and forgiveness. He was spontaneous, exuberant, and always in motion. She wondered if Mark would ever again get the level of attention and physical affection he needed. She knew that her young man needed a hug right now.

Her best friend, Maria, and Maria's husband, Scott, were walking hand-in-hand, looking at the displays. They apparently hadn't brought their children—probably thinking the memorial would be too traumatic for them.

She watched as her friends and family members shook hands,

kissed each other, and reminisced around the storyboards that were stationed on the easels or propped on the tables. With her poor vision, she barely recognized some of the snapshots that captured moments of her life.

She stood and walked nonchalantly over to the storyboard closest to her. She squinted and could make out the "It's a Girl" announcement card with her newborn photo. The storyboard also held some of her early school pictures and another in which she was standing with her mom, dad, and brother at Disneyland. Next came a photo of her and Paul, her first boyfriend, in formal attire on prom night.

She shuffled to the other areas where more pictures were displayed: wedding shots; a photo of her holding a day-old Megan; one of Mark's first Halloween, with him dressed as a bumblebee and Megan and herself as sunflowers; and pictures of her with Bruce when they had first started dating. There were also storyboards of holiday gatherings: opening presents on Christmas morning, Easter egg hunts, Fourth of July parades, and Thanksgiving feasts. Her fifteen swim trophies were neatly displayed on one table with an enlarged picture of her and the Hayward High Swim Team.

She was up there on the storyboards in snapshots and trophies. But she was also here in person—and no one, except Marcy, knew that.

She returned to her seat and disappeared again into the background. This was the day she had been waiting for. She had no thoughts about the trip back. That wasn't her concern. She was in the here and now. It was this moment that counted.

She saw Marcy exit the women's room and walk to one of the storyboards. Things were okay now between her and Marcy. The rift was nearly healed. There was still some residual pain, but the forgiveness had been real. Marcy had worked out all the details so well—the timing had been perfect. Marcy had even borrowed clothes from her daughter, Adriana. Although the pants were short, everything else fit well enough. The shoes were new and not yet broken in, and she knew as soon as she put them on that she had guessed wrong at the size—fives were at least half a size too small, so they pinched—but she didn't let that get in her way.

On the other hand, the blonde wig was like nothing Liz had ever seen. Marcy had inserted a small leather helmet inside to protect her soft head tissue. The hair of the wig had medium length, tight blonde curls. It made her look like Shirley Temple's worst nightmare. But no one would ever recognize her, that was for sure.

Liz thought back to the ruse they'd set up so she, or rather Kate, could get out undetected. Not only had Marcy scheduled her for an extended therapy session, but Jamison had told Marcy that it was, in his words, "extremely important that Kate have all possible tests and treatments that might help ensure her recovery." Little did Jamison know that he was aiding and abetting a getaway.

After lunchtime, Marcy wheeled Liz into a therapy room. There she put on the disguise and then simply walked to a sheltered place in the parking area by herself—as though she had been visiting a relative at the hospital. Marcy left soon afterward, drove her car to the designated spot, and picked up Kate.

Liz/Kate pulled herself back to the present and watched as Marcy walked from storyboard to storyboard, studying the pictures and chatting occasionally with others about her "opera buddy." They really could have been buddies—in another life, another time.

She gripped the arms of her chair when she saw Mark suddenly run over to Marcy and tap her on the elbow. When Marcy looked down, Mark held his arms out to her. Liz felt tears well up in her eyes when Marcy stooped down and hugged Mark. They held each other for several seconds. Then Mark took Marcy's hand and pulled her over to where Megan and Bruce stood.

"Oh, there you are. I'm so glad you came," Bruce said in a tone that was a little too friendly. Liz's mouth went dry as she watched Marcy almost trip while approaching him and Megan. It felt as if a weight fell across Liz's chest when Megan positioned her body between her dad and Marcy. But Bruce gently pulled her back a step, whispered something to her, and moved forward.

Disbelief filled her as Bruce kissed Marcy on the cheek and took her hand, holding it longer than necessary. For a moment Liz thought she might have an asthma attack. Even from this distance, and with her poor vision, Liz could see Marcy's face turn pink.

Why am I jealous? They're just being sociable.

But something deep inside told her there was more there—an attraction—whether they knew it or not. Despite the Indian summer heat, goose bumps covered her arms. Bruce was looking at Marcy the way he'd looked at Liz when they'd first met. A pain that had nothing to do with the surgery made her head feel suddenly heavy.

People took their seats as the music started. Bruce, Mark, Megan, and Liz's brother sat in the front row with her dad and his second wife, Vivian. When the music stopped, her minister stood at the podium, draped in a sash that was emblazoned with several religious symbols, including the Unitarian's eternal flame.

The reverend looked solemnly at the congregation and nodded at Bruce and the kids. "Today, we are gathered to celebrate Elizabeth Ann Lindsay's life. Although we miss her and are saddened that she passed too quickly from this earth, we have each been blessed and enriched by having known her. So today we'll share some of the highlights and happy memories we have of Liz, as most of us knew her."

The reverend recounted moments of her life and exaggerated her church volunteer work. Then her brother and dad told stories about their times together. She almost laughed out loud when her brother recounted how, during summer vacation, they would play Monopoly, sometimes all night. And, when she thought he wasn't looking, she would pilfer play money from the bank.

Her dad talked about the swim meets and her championship medals and about how proud he was of her. Funny, she didn't even know that he'd paid attention. He'd always been so busy—gone much of the time.

Maria talked about how their families had shared good times together and how embarrassed Liz was four years ago when Mark and her son, Victor, both then age three, went trick or treating in the middle of July and came home with a bag full of goodies from neighbors.

Liz was doing okay with these stories until the reverend called on Megan to say something about her mom. Liz muffled a gasp.

Lip trembling and speaking just above a whisper, Megan said, "My mommy was pretty and smart. She loved me a lot."

"Me, too! She loved me too," sobbed Mark.

Megan sniffed. "Yes. She loved you too. My dad says she's an angel and she's watching over us. I miss my mom. That's all I have to say." Megan hiccupped and ran over to her dad. He held her and put his arm around Mark.

Liz felt weak. She opened her mouth in a silent scream and felt her world spin out of control.

No more. I can't take any more.

Just as she was about to shout her name and claim her identity, Marcy was called up. As Marcy walked to the podium, she gave Kate a steadying look. Liz took short breaths and closed her eyes.

"You don't know me, but Liz and I were friends. We first met in a computer class and later ran into each other at the Opera in the Park in Stern Grove."

Marcy told the stories they'd made up so carefully, expounding on the opera. Then she added, "I've written a poem in her memory. I call it, 'Dancing on a Star.' " When Marcy looked out to the audience Liz felt she was looking directly at her when she recited the first line.

"Don't weep for me, my sweet ones, for my essence is set free.

"No longer held by gravity, I'm as light as I can be.

"It's relative, so Einstein said, that energy and mass

"And speed of light together form the essence of our class.

"And so I am abiding here, just in a different way:

"A tree, a bird, a fragrant rose, a bright and shining day.

"Take heart, my darling loved ones; I'll never be too far.

"I'm smiling down on you today while dancing on a star."

Marcy cleared her throat and added, "Liz was a good friend. She loved her family more than anything. And, Megan, I'm sure your mother is watching over you."

Liz was overcome by Marcy's sensitive and tender remarks. The stories Marcy had told were so vivid that Liz almost believed them herself—wished they'd been true.

As the service was drawing to an end, the reverend announced, "Before attending the reception, it is Bruce's wish for each person to take a balloon outside and release it in memory of Elizabeth Ann Lindsay. Bruce wants to see all one hundred balloons rise in tandem to represent the beauty of her spirit."

On unsteady legs, Liz accepted a balloon from Mr. Dobbs, walked outside, and looked around at the familiar grounds. As she walked past Bruce, she brushed his arm and felt a warm rush. She closed her eyes for a moment to concentrate on the faint but musky odor of Bruce's aftershave lotion. She wanted to slip her arm through his and tell him how much she loved and missed him.

Someone counted to three, and the balloons drifted like a flock of joyful sparrows, dancing in a ribbon of color. She was late in releasing hers, and it drifted alone, caught by a different current. She watched as it floated past a grove of trees and disappeared.

With a lump in her throat, she looked around for her children, but they weren't in sight. However, Bruce was close by, talking with Marcy. She could overhear them and, although their conversation was casual enough, for a moment they exchanged what seemed to be a special glance. Liz couldn't take it anymore. Bruce was hers—hers! She swung around and grabbed Bruce's hand. "Don't you know who I am?" she said as she looked longingly into his eyes. "Don't you recognize me? Look at me. Can't you tell? I'm . . . I'm Liz-z-a . . ."

She saw Marcy's eyes widen and her mouth drop open. Marcy mouthed a silent "no" as she raised her hand in protest.

In an instant, Liz realized that Bruce and her children would never accept her like this. She knew what she had to do. In her first truly selfless act, she took a step back and forced her fingers open, letting go of her husband's hand.

Bruce looked down at her with concern. His voice was soft, like a father speaking to a child. "No, Lisa, I don't recall knowing you. Are you in Megan's Sunday school class?"

"No. No, I'm n-not . . ." She drew her hand to her face and turned around. She saw through a blur of tears that her friends and family members were all staring at her. "Not in her Sunday school class . . ."

She stumbled backward, away from the crowd. She caught herself before falling, turned, and ran erratically through the paved area, up the grade and onto the road. Like the balloon she had released, she drifted away—all alone. Brokenhearted, broken-spirited, she staggered back to the drop-off point, sank to her knees, and released a torrent of tears.

She knew now that Liz was dead.

chapter twelve

Sunday, October 7, 3:30 PM

Kate was numb—empty. Nothing mattered. Her vision wasn't the only thing blurring; she couldn't remember any part of yesterday's return trip to the hospital. Mystically, magically, her mind had taken her to some unknown place—a quiet, barren place—and left her there. She didn't know, and didn't care, how she'd made it back to the hospital.

She had no more tears. She just wanted to lie in the bed and disappear quietly into nothingness. She prayed for sleep or death, but neither came.

She was half-awake, drifting in and out of consciousness. Somehow she knew that doctors and nurses had been hovering over her. But now the room was quiet. As reality descended on her, she moved her hand over one of her small thighs. She felt sensation. Pain. Her leg throbbed. *I hurt. Therefore, I am. But how? How can I still be here?*

She ran her hands up her torso and felt her small, developing breasts. She slowly shook her head. Then, just as darkness and despair began to fill her again, she heard the rustle of cloth and drew in the fragrance of jasmine. A smooth hand touched her cheek.

"Hi, sweetie," a familiar voice murmured. "How's my angel today?"

Kate opened her eyes. Through a smoky haze, she saw her mom's beautiful porcelain face. With trembling hands, Kate reached up and touched the woman's face, making sure it was real. When her hand touched warm flesh, she pulled the mother figure to her and held her tight. "Momma, oh, Momma. Thank goodness you're here. Oh please, don't leave me. I'm so scared."

"It's okay, honey. I'm here," her mom said as she stroked Kate's stubbly hair. "Did you have another nightmare?"

"Oh, yes . . . a terrible nightmare."

5:30 PM

After finishing with Chet's few Sunday physical therapy patients, Marcy drove directly home. She didn't need to think about the route. She had memorized it years ago.

She parked in her townhouse's garage and sat motionless for several minutes. When she finally exited the car, she stood for a moment, as though unsure why she was there. Finally, she pushed the button to close her garage door and entered her upscale townhouse.

Washed out, without an ounce of energy left, she ambled into the living room, kicked off her shoes, and reached up under her blouse to unhook her bra. With a sigh, she collapsed onto the couch and laid her head on its cushy armrest. She closed her eyes and tried to block out the horrors of yesterday. But every terrifying moment of that outing was imprinted indelibly on her mind, and the experience kept replaying like a slide show in a constant loop. First Kate's quick departure from the church and Marcy's lie to Bruce (she'd told him she had to go home right away because her ex-husband would be dropping her daughter off within the hour). How many lies had she told? Then Marcy had driven her car to the pick-up spot. She gasped as she saw Kate in the fetal position, wig lying in a patch of flowers. Kate had appeared comatose.

Marcy had parked the car, run over, and knelt down to take Kate's pulse. It was barely there and the girl was limp.

Marcy looked around for neighbors but saw no one. She'd fumbled about in her purse and finally located her cell phone. Just as she was about to call 911, Kate, with uncommon strength, reached up and grabbed her wrist. Marcy let out a short yelp.

"No," Kate said as she opened her red-rimmed eyes. "Get me out of here." There was a look of wild determination in those unhappy eyes.

"I can't do that. You need help—now. It's my duty." Marcy's reaction was automatic. She pushed 9-1-

"No. No. You can't call." As Kate spoke, she swung around and batted at Marcy's cell phone, causing it to snap shut and turn off. The girl rose up to her knees and shoved Marcy backward. As she tried to stand, Kate pleaded, "I'm begging you—don't. I can make it."

Marcy took hold of Kate's upper arm to steady her. "You're not all right and you're my responsibility."

"Just get me to the car. I'll be okay. You'll see."

In all Marcy's years of physical therapy she had never witnessed a patient with such drive. Kate was moving on sheer willpower.

Reluctantly, Marcy helped Kate into the car and clicked the seat belt.

"W—water. I need water," Kate mumbled.

Marcy retrieved a bottle of water from the cooler on the backseat, opened it, and started to raise it to Kate's lips.

"I can do that," Kate said as she took it from her. "Drive. Let's get out of here." Kate swished the water in her mouth, swallowed loudly, and then laid her distorted head against the headrest. The next time she drank, it was in large noisy gulps.

"Take it easy," Marcy snapped. "Too much too soon could be harmful."

"What? You think I'm trying to drown myself?" Kate looked up at Marcy. "Wish I could. That would be the easy way out."

Kate turned her face away from Marcy and lowered her head to her chest.

Marcy observed Kate's condition. One tear after another fell silently from Kate's face like the steady drip of water from a stalactite. A wet spot spread across her crumpled blouse.

The sight was tearing Marcy apart. She had to pull herself together. It was still another twenty plus miles back to the hospital.

To Marcy's relief, Kate was soon making muted, raspy sleeping sounds. But her relief was short-lived. The gentle breathing stopped, and a dreaded silence filled the Volvo. Jerking her head toward Kate,

Marcy stared at the girl's chest. Was it rising? Was she alive?

Marcy pulled the car to the curb and placed one hand on Kate's wrist and the other on her chest. Yes, there was a pulse, and although her breathing was shallow, Kate was breathing.

"Kate, look at me. Open your eyes. You need to stay awake. Do you hear me?"

Kate inhaled deeply. Her eyes fluttered open, and she sent Marcy a haunting look.

"Listen to me, Kate," Marcy urged. "You can sleep when we get back to the hospital. But I want you to stay awake until we get there. Do you understand?"

Kate shook her head "no," but Marcy was just thankful there was a response.

"I'm going to keep talking. You must listen. If you don't, I'll turn the music up full blast and squeeze your arm until it hurts." Panic filled Marcy.

Thank goodness she'd been able to keep Kate awake. Every few minutes she reached over and felt for Kate's pulse. She counted the child's breaths per minute.

Now what should she do—drive to the emergency entrance and rush Kate into ER? Tell them what she had done? Or was it possible to get Kate back into the hospital and to the attention she needed without anyone knowing about the outing?

"Oh, no," Marcy muttered. She suddenly remembered the wig. She had forgotten it—and its leather insert helmet. There was no way to disguise Kate and get her back into the hospital, at least not the way they had left. Besides, Kate wasn't able to walk, even a short distance. What should she do?

She was about to give up hope when an idea struck her. She looked at her watch—almost three-thirty.

Marcy drove a few blocks past her regular turnoff and proceeded to Oak Creek Dr. She pulled over in a quiet area near some apartments. After assuring herself that no one was in the vicinity, she turned toward her ward. "Kate, we need to get you out of those clothes and back in your nightgown, slippers, and regular helmet," she said. "Do you understand me?"

"Hmm," Kate responded.

Marcy got out of the car and retrieved the canvas bag that held

Kate's items from the trunk. She looked around again and tried to hide her mounting fear.

"Stay with me, Kate. Do you hear me?" she shouted.

"Yes, but don't blast out my eardrums," Kate murmured.

Marcy struggled to remove Kate's damp blouse, the tight shoes and Adriana's other clothing. Kate barely moved. She was dead weight. Marcy felt her own heart beat furiously. Sweat dripped from her brow, the musty odor from her body mingling with Kate's unwashed odor. After what seemed like hours, Kate was helmeted and back in hospital garb.

Marcy drove to the right of the main hospital entrance. The fountains and well-trimmed hedges conveniently hid them from view. Through the hospital windows, Marcy studied the volunteer at the information center, who was in an animated conversation with an elderly woman. Visitors walking nearby seemed deep in their own thoughts and paid no attention to them. Doctors and visitors walked up and down the main hallway, past the massive plate-glass windows, but, again, none glanced their way.

When Marcy turned the car off, Kate sat up, alert. "Where are we?"

"We're at the hospital. Listen. I need to get you a wheelchair. Will you be okay by yourself for a minute?"

Kate nodded and then lowered her chin to her chest again, like a wind-up toy that had run its course. Marcy bit her lip. She had to get Kate help soon.

Walking briskly into the hospital, Marcy went to the admitting area and took one of the many wheelchairs lining the wall. She smiled at those waiting and nonchalantly wheeled one away. As she walked down the hallway, she saw Brandi, the chatty student volunteer, walking toward her. Brandi smiled. "Hi, Marcy. I heard you're working with Kate today. I'm so glad she's doing well." She looked around. "Where is she?"

Marcy blinked and stalled. "I—I left her in the garden with one of the new volunteers. One of the wheels on her chair was out of kilter, so she's waiting for me to bring another." Marcy forced a grin, turned away, and kept walking. She was relieved when she heard the sound of Brandi's footfalls going in the opposite direction.

"I can't even lie well to a volunteer. What will I do if a doctor or an RN stops me?

Marcy walked out the door and rolled the chair over to her car, relieved when no one called to her. She licked her lips and tasted the salt from her still perspiring upper lip. For the first time since leaving the church, she felt she just might get away with returning her charge unnoticed. When she reached the car, she checked Kate's vital signs. Thank heavens—she was almost stable.

She had only one more obstacle—getting Kate into the chair and wheeling her from the car into the hospital. *I can do this.* Making sure no one was approaching, she quickly lifted Kate into the chair and wheeled her toward the entrance. She pretended she was showing Kate the features of the fountain. Then they entered the hospital. So far, so good. She walked with an air of confidence down the long hallway, past the cafeteria, and toward the children's wing. She nodded at the security guard as she passed his station and smiled cordially. Joe was used to seeing her wheel Kate around. "How's Kate doing today?" he asked in his usual friendly tone.

"Oh, she's over-extended herself again. I think she's ready for a nap," Marcy replied. She was sure that her face was turning red—so many lies.

As she passed the information center in the children's wing, she waved at Vanessa, the desk volunteer. She could tell Vanessa wanted to speak to her, but she smiled, turned her head toward Kate as though she had something special to say to her, and hustled by. She took Kate directly toward her room. As she approached the nurses' station, she motioned to Sonja Manheim, the RN on duty. "I think Kate's overdone it again. Come and have a look at her."

"What did she do?" the nurse asked as she walked over.

"We were in the Atrium Garden, and I turned my back just for a moment. Next thing I knew, she was out of her chair, running through the garden, into the atrium, and then she headed for the elevator. I think she wanted to go to the cafeteria."

Nurse Manheim walked over to Kate's side, lifted the girl's limp wrist, and wrinkled her nose. "Her skin feels clammy." Manheim stood in silence and stared at her watch as she took Kate's pulse. "She'll be okay, Ms. Ames. You go on now. I'll call for the doctor on duty to come and check her over."

"Come and help me, Laura," the nurse said to an assistant. "Help me get Kate back to her bed." She turned and looked sympathetically at Marcy. "It's not your fault. We've had troubles with her before. It's just not possible to keep this eleven-year-old down. Don't blame yourself. We'll take care of her."

Kate looked up at Marcy. Her eyes were vacant, like an old abandoned house. Marcy winced as the nurse focused in on Kate's tear-stained eyes. "Oh, my goodness. Her eyes are red and swollen. What happened?" the nurse asked as she looked over at Marcy.

"You know Marcy—always joking," Kate croaked. "Laughed till I cried." Then she turned, no doubt to hide the quaver in her voice.

Marcy felt waves of gut-wrenching guilt. None of this would have happened if she hadn't taken Kate out of the hospital. "I'm so sorry," she repeated hoarsely.

"I told you, it's not your fault," the nurse said as she glanced over at Marcy.

Hearing the muted echo of footsteps, Marcy turned and saw Dr. Schmidt, the oldest doctor on staff, walking briskly toward Kate's room. He glanced her way with what appeared to be a scowl. For a moment Marcy thought he knew what she had done. The game was over. No, it was just her imagination playing tricks on her. No one knew. But *she* knew, and the guilt was still gnawing at her.

"Mom, I'm home!" Adriana hollered.

Marcy was pulled away from yesterday's recollections as her daughter bounded through the front door.

"I had a great time with Dad," Adriana said.

Marcy sat up and focused on her daughter.

Can't change the past. What's done is done.

"Did ya miss me?" Adriana asked as she threw her arms around Marcy.

Marcy smiled. "I always miss you when you're gone," she said as she folded her arms securely around the body of her treasure—her Adriana.

Lie. Steal. Cheat. Yes, even kill. She would do anything to protect her daughter. She understood all too well what it was that propelled Liz into attending the ceremony. Somehow, she'd find a way to get over her awful guilt and move on.

chapter thirteen

Monday, October 8, 2:35 AM

Jamison swore at the jangling phone. "Who could be calling at 2:30 in the morning?" He turned over and reached for the object of his anger. "I hope the Craig girl's not in trouble," he said to his barely awake wife.

Shaking his head to clear it, he turned on the bedside lamp and picked up the receiver. "This is Dr. Jamison."

"Dr. Jamison, this is Charles Rubenstein—from KROX. Congratulations, sir, it was just announced that you're the next recipient of the Nobel Prize for Medicine."

Jamison sat in stunned silence, unable to comprehend what he'd just heard.

"What is it, Donald?" Inna asked as she sat up. She squinted at the light, frowned, and looked at him with concern.

Still not believing what he'd heard, he said, "Is this some kind of a joke?"

"No sir. It's true. The announcement was just made in Stockholm. It's 11:30 AM in Central Europe. All the major stations monitor the announcement. And it just came in. Congratulations."

Jamison was stunned. He had believed he could win next year, but thought this year was out of the question. Nominations were submitted in February, and the committee submitted their recommendations to the board in September. Someone apparently had nominated him based on his animal experiments and new surgical procedures. The successful brain transplant must have jettisoned his nomination to the top.

"It's true, then?" he said as he ran his fingers over the smooth satin edge of the blanket to calm himself. "I've won?"

"You bet. Expect camera crews around your house and at the hospital today. I just wanted to prepare you for the onslaught."

"Wow . . ." He paused. He hadn't said "wow" since he was a kid. He looked at Inna and gave her a smile. "Thanks, Charles. I'm overwhelmed. I appreciate your call."

"How about another exclusive this evening? We can do a one-hour special."

Jamison looked over at Inna. "Let me talk to my wife, Charles. I'll call you back later this morning. I need a minute to let this sink in."

He hung up and looked at his wife. "My dear, you are looking at this year's winner of the Nobel Prize for Medicine."

He laughed as Inna squealed in delight and wrapped her arms around his neck.

Monday, October 1, 10:00 AM

Because of her mother, Kate thought she might be able to face another tomorrow. Donna stayed by her side all night and slept in the chair. Kate understood her mother's behavior; it was in the nature of a loving parent. For countless hours Donna held her hand, tenderly stroked her face, and made the gentle sounds a parent makes to a hurt or unhappy child. Kate recognized this ritual from dual realms—childhood and motherhood.

Still half awake, one hand clinging to Donna's, Kate flinched when the phone rang. "I'll get it," her mother said, offering Kate a quick "good morning" smile.

Kate tried to observe Donna's facial expressions and study her body language. It didn't take much to note the dark circles under her mother's eyes and her slump-shouldered posture. Her mom needed a real bed to lie down in, a shower, and a good meal.

"Hello," Donna said. "Yes, dear, it's me." She turned toward Kate and mouthed silently, "It's your father."

Donna's expression transformed from a pretense of cheerfulness to unmistakable anguish. "Oh, no, John. How could that be?" She turned her back to Kate and spoke into the receiver in a hushed voice. Although the movement was small, Kate could tell that her mother's shoulders were shaking. She was crying.

Kate felt a pang of apprehension. "What's wrong, Mom?"

She tried to rise, to go over to her mother, but couldn't. The side rail was up, and the IV was back in her hand—had been since Saturday afternoon. She felt helpless.

"Mom, please talk to me," she begged.

Her mom turned toward her and forced a smile. "It's okay, honey. No one's hurt," she said, her hand cupped over the phone.

"Then what is it?" Kate demanded.

Donna frowned and lifted her finger to her mouth signaling Kate to hush. "Yes, I'll be home as soon as I can. It's good that you're home this week. I don't know what I would do if you weren't."

Kate started to ask again, but her mother shook her head and held up a hand. Donna listened for a moment more and then nodded. After a long pause Donna whispered, "Yes, dear, good-bye."

When Donna turned, her eyes were downcast, and all semblance of calmness was gone.

Her anxiety building, Kate said, "Please, Mom, tell me what's going on."

Her mother furled her brow in a manner that spelled confusion. "It's your brother. He's in trouble. He's been expelled for truancy." A look of failure marred her normally smooth features. "They found drugs on him. Cocaine!" She blinked several times as though trying to remember something. "I never would have guessed. I thought he was doing so well. I didn't know—didn't know." A look of bewilderment was imprinted on her features.

Kate felt a sharp twinge of pain. She knew firsthand how a parent suffered and blamed themselves for the failures of their offspring. Her mom was hurting, but what could she do to help?

"Why would he get involved in drugs?" her mom asked.

Kate didn't know what to say. She hurt for Josh but wasn't surprised. She grasped the situation and felt that perhaps she shouldered some of the blame. It was so obvious to her that Josh felt abandoned. She'd sensed Josh's jealousy when they first met—the resentment in his eyes, the undisguised mocking tone of his voice.

"I don't know why he's done this, Mom," she lied. "But you need to go home. Josh needs you." She hesitated for a moment and then added, "I'll be all right." Although she yearned to have Donna at her side, she knew that her brother needed their mom more.

Kate hoped it wasn't too late—that her parents could help Josh straighten out. Her mind was young enough to remember the social pressures that teenagers experience and the temptation of drugs. Yet she was old enough to know that only a big dose of tough love from both her parents would help. And that wouldn't happen if her parents continued to spend all their energy on her.

"It's all right, Mom. I'm not scared anymore. It was just a dream. Don't worry about me. I promise to take it easy—slow down and build up gradually." She faked a confident smile. "I've learned my lesson. You don't have to worry about me."

"I feel so torn," her mother said. "I know he needs me, but you do too."

"I'll be fine. Just give Dad and my big brother a hug from me." With that, she pulled the covers up to her chest and pretended she was tired.

Her mom looked dazed but finally sighed and kissed Kate gently on the cheek. "Okay, honey," she said, worry lines apparent around her pink lips. Then she picked up the phone and placed it on the bed. "But I'll call you later this afternoon—let you know how things are going. Your dad and I, we'll work things out. Don't worry. You already have enough on your plate."

As Kate watched her mother head for the doorway, a surge of guilt washed over her. She could taste bitterness in the back of her throat. It wasn't just her life that had fallen apart; it was everyone she cared for. People were suffering because of her. She closed her eyes tightly and prayed.

Help me, Lord. Someday I'll make it up to them.

11:30 AM

Josh sat at the table and tried to look calm, but he could hardly stay still. He'd been sitting here for hours. He jiggled his feet and tapped his fingers. The questions that the police asked were so screwed up.

"Where'd you get the cocaine, Josh?" the officer asked.

He slouched down in the chair, leaned his head back, and looked up at the ceiling, watching the lights dance.

"I said, where'd you get the cocaine?"

Josh tried to come up with a really humorous answer. Maybe he could get the old fart to laugh—get him off his back.

"Um, let me see—from a poppy field in Afghanistan. It's their number one crop," he said with a smirk.

The cop shook his head. "You don't know anything, sonny boy. Cocaine isn't made from poppies, it's made from the coca leaf—doesn't grow in Afghanistan."

Josh swallowed hard.

"But here's something you need to know. That friend of yours—Ron Andrade—he's been here before. We have a track record on him. Did you buy the stuff from him? Or, on second thought, maybe you're his dealer and just don't know crap about your merchandise."

"Dealer? Well, let's see . . . I deal Black Jack, Seven Card Stud, and Texas Hold 'Em. Give me a deck of cards and I'll deal ya in." Josh laughed—a stupid answer to a stupid question. Besides, he wasn't a snitch. He'd never implicate Ron. Ron was his best friend.

"Well, Josh, we have enough on you to lock you away in juvy unless you come clean with us. I suggest you sober up and get smart."

"Straight A's never got me anywhere, sarge," he said, bitterness lacing his words.

"Well, young man, your parents are here. They've paid your bail. You know, Josh, they're pretty upset. I think they're real disappointed in you." The cop raised an eyebrow as he stood and picked up the file.

"They don't give a crap about me," Josh snarled.

The overweight cop shook his head, let out a long sigh, and walked out of the room.

Somewhere in the back of Josh's mind, he knew that what he had said about his parents' lack of interest wasn't true. Suddenly nothing was funny anymore. He leaned forward and buried his head in his hands.

12:00 Noon

"Yes, thank you. I'm very honored. Yes, I'll see you on the fourth." Jamison hung up the phone and looked at the notes he had jotted down:

December 8—Present lecture at Karolinski Institute

December 10—Receive Nobel award—presented by Dr. Ingmar Holtz.

December tenth. That would be the day when he would receive the medal, and one and a half million dollars. Inna always had a full calendar for December, but this year she would just have to cancel her obligations. He visualized himself being called to the stage, his beautiful wife sitting in the front row at the concert hall. The applause would be deafening. He smiled, wishing his father were alive to see it.

Rubenstein had been right; when Jamison left for the hospital, camera crews were already stationed outside his home, Rubenstein among them.

The hospital's press conference would be held later that day at 3:00 PM. It would be on national news. KROX would be front and center. But he owed Rubenstein something more, so he agreed to give Rubenstein another exclusive interview—from his home tonight. Besides, the young man was now receiving offers of prime-time reporting spots from CNN, FOX, and MSNBC. It might be valuable to keep up a relationship with him. It was possible that they could still help each other.

He pressed a button on his cell phone and said, "Home." After three rings, Inna answered, "Jamison residence. This is Mrs. Jamison."

"Well, Mrs. Jamison, this is Dr. Jamison." He smiled as he spoke.

"And what can I do for you, Mr. Nobel Prize Winner?" she asked.

"I've agreed to do an interview tonight at the house. So ask Margaret to make sure everything is tidy. The place will be full of cameras. And could you make reservations for dinner tomorrow night? Eight o'clock at the Top of the Mark. We're going to celebrate—do it in style."

After Jamison hung up, he brought up the hospital website and viewed the feature story, "Jamison to Receive Nobel Prize."

Life was wonderful. He was floating—he almost felt lightheaded. What he desired most right now was a Seven Up and a sandwich—not that he was hungry or thirsty, but he wanted to get up and move, do something with his hands. Drinking a cold soda and sinking his teeth into a sandwich stacked high with meats and cheeses would fit the bill. Maybe Felix and Deborah would be at the cafeteria too. He wanted to hear their reaction.

As he pushed himself back from his chair, he thought of his father. He wished he were alive today—to help celebrate. Jamison walked from his office, hands in pockets. This time he whistled as he walked down the stairwell. This time he let the excitement spill over for everyone to see.

This one's for you, Dad.

1:00 PM

Charles Rubenstein smiled. Another exclusive—this time with the year's newly announced Nobel Laureate in Medicine.

He wanted a cigarette to celebrate, but this was a non-smoking building. He opened his desk drawer, pulled out a stick of Juicy Fruit gum, and unwrapped it. He pushed the gum in his mouth, rolled the foil and wrapper into a tight ball, and swiveled his chair around as he looked for an appropriate target. Finally, he took aim and pitched the tiny ball nine feet into a trash basket next to Marvin's desk. It made a pinging noise as it hit the rim and bounced in. "Three points," he quipped. Marvin looked up from his computer and frowned.

Charles simply smiled at Marvin. He wasn't going to burn any bridges behind him. He knew better than that. The media was fickle, and unless you were very careful, your reputation could be trashed—especially if you didn't watch your back. So even though he'd soon be leaving KROX, he knew it had served him nicely as a stepping-stone to the next level in his career. He wasn't about to make any enemies now.

He swung the old oak chair around, stood, and headed for Penny's office to talk with her about the exclusive interview this evening.

So far, his only failure had been in locating the donor. But he'd more than made up for it with the Jamison interviews and the Craig family interview. Charles closed his eyes and sighed. For the second time in his life, he was responsible for something meaningful. The first, of course, was his unwavering support of his mother and sister.

But the Craig family interview was having universal consequences. Donor programs all over the country were reporting a significant upswing in registrations since the segment aired. Major stations all over the country had played it.

Charles let his imagination run. He could almost see Kate as this year's poster child for the organ donor program, her story spurring people to place that all-important donor sticker on the backs of their licenses. Because of him, lives could be saved.

When he reached Penny's office, he snapped back to the present. He rapped on his manager's door and heard a quick, "Come in."

Charles flashed one of his winning smiles. Penny looked up from her computer, lifted an eyebrow, and said, "You've done well, Chuck. Are you prepared for this evening's interview?"

Despite his nerves, he tried to appear nonchalant as he walked to the front of her desk and placed a stack of papers in front of her. "I've talked with Jamison's wife, and we're all set. The interview will be at seven o'clock. But we'll start setting up at five and I'll have an hour with them before the interview to go over some of the information we'll be covering. Take a look at my questions and see if there's anything you want to add or edit."

Penny cocked her head. "Give me a quick verbal overview."

His eyes lit up. "I thought we should explore his background. Here's a man who grew up in Arkansas—poor family—his father, a carpenter. I think it's a good 'American Dream' story."

"If I have any edits, I'll call you within half an hour." He could see the wheels turning as she glanced over the papers. "Looks good to me! I'll call down and get the camera crew and lighting arranged. Give me the doctor's home phone number, and I'll see if I can get things set up so you can go straight there after the Stanford thing is over."

Charles handed her the phone number, having already anticipated her request.

"What about the Craig family? Any chance of getting comments from them?" she asked.

He turned and said over his shoulder, "I'll give them a call and see what I can arrange."

"By the way, Charles, nice suit and tie," Penny called back.

He smiled at her and a rush of pride ran through him. He'd purchased the suit today, an off-the-rack gray Macy's suit: it fit him perfectly, no alterations necessary. And the tie was a ruby red silk—the most expensive he'd ever purchased. The crisp white shirt, a never-needs-ironing Van Heusen. He was in a different class now, and he needed to dress the part.

He walked quickly to his desk. By the time he reached it, Michael, one of the camera crew, was there with his gear. Yet as he was leaving, he wondered who he was doing this for—that little girl in the hospital and others like her, or a shot at the big-time?

He didn't want to look too deep, for fear of the answer.

chapter fourteen

Tuesday, October 9, 4:00 PM

Kate kept hearing the words over and over again in her head. "Everything's okay . . . He's home now . . . we're handling it." But when her mom had called last night, Kate could tell that it was serious. As she listened to her mother's carefully chosen words, it became clear that she was downplaying the situation, trying to spare Kate the bad news. Kate cringed as she listened.

When her mother paused, Kate said, "Don't worry about me. I feel fine. And, please, Mom, don't come tomorrow. I'm just going to sleep anyway."

She empathized with Donna—knew that Josh was in trouble, and her mother was in despair. Now, more than anything, Kate wanted to go home—to be with her parents, and help heal the wounds that she had inadvertently caused.

Kate tried to smother her own needs and look for ways that she could help. She hadn't forgotten her prior life and never would, but she had accepted the obscene realities of her situation. She shut her eyes tight and admitted to herself, "I'll never be Elizabeth Ann Lindsay again—never."

She turned abruptly to the bedside table, placed the earphones in her ears, and for the fourth time that day pushed the button on the CD player. The soft, sweet voice of Charlotte Church singing "Pie Jesu" floated over her and calmed her. She sang along, thinking that maybe someday, with training, she, too, might have such a voice. The music helped her shift moods and moved her thoughts to a healthier place.

She wished she could have an iPhone or at least an iPod or some other hi-tech device. But she knew better than to ask her parents. They were dealing with enough right now.

Days ago, when Kate had asked for a CD player and two of Charlotte Church's decade-old CDs, her mom had given her an incredulous look and asked, "Charlotte Church? Who is she? And what kind of music does she sing?"

At which point Kate had simply lied and told her she "believed" most of the numbers were classical and that her therapist, Marcy, had recommended them. Kate told her mother that she could use the CDs with certain therapy exercises.

Her mom had smiled and shrugged. The next day she came in with a bundle under her arms—a small player and the two CDs. They'd had one heck of a time opening the shrink-wrapped CDs. Teeth and nails were of no help. Only a pair of sharp scissors from one of the nurses had done the trick. The incident caused them both to laugh. It was probably the first time in six years, since Kate's near-fatal illness, that this mother and daughter team had laughed together.

Maybe there would be more laughter in her future. But only if she could get well and get out of here. She was certain she could be an exceptional daughter, student, and maybe even a loving sister.

Could this be a second chance? A chance to do more—be more? She thought back to her youth in her previous life. She realized that she had never been very close to her brother. Throughout their childhood they'd fought and competed. Both left home soon after high school and had barely kept in touch. It was as if they'd walked away from their first family. She realized that she was as much to blame as anyone. She'd been self-centered—too busy to be thoughtful, except to her mother. But then her mother had died, and her father remarried just four months later.

She didn't like watching that obnoxious woman, her stepmother, sitting in her mother's chair, eating from her mother's dishes, sleeping with her father. She found Vivian to be nothing more than an ostentatious bore, bragging about her latest cruises or the paintings they bought at auctions.

She pushed thoughts of her dad and Vivian from her mind and tried again to relax into the music. A vision of Bruce with another woman entered her mind. Would he do the same? Marry some bimbo before her ashes were even settled? No, she didn't think so. He would remarry, of course. He was too good a catch to remain single. But he would do it in good time. She was convinced that he was a dedicated father and wouldn't settle for just any warm body.

Charlotte's soprano voice interrupted her contemplation. As she listened, her thoughts ricocheted backward to Puccini's "Un Bel Di" from the opera *Madam Butterfly*. She almost cried out. *Un Bel Di*—One Fine Day—that described what she needed most. Perhaps tomorrow, but certainly not today. Today she was Kate, and would be, she figured, for the rest of her days . . . so she'd better get on with it.

And if she could get out of here, maybe there would be an opportunity someday to watch over Megan and Mark from a distance. And keep an eye on them.

Keep an eye—that was another problem. Earlier that day, during physical therapy, Marcy had noticed Kate's failing eyesight, and now Marcy was worried that it was a sign of a serious problem. Marcy had been standing right in front of her when she asked, "You're not following my finger. What's wrong?"

A flash of light, followed shortly by a clap of thunder, and the sound of rain pelting down on the window startled them both. Rain was common in the Bay Area, but not thunder and lightning. Kate felt it was an omen.

She trembled. "I'm sorry. I should have said something days ago. But I was afraid . . . afraid of . . . oh, never mind. That doesn't matter anymore . . ." Her words trailed off as she blew out a fast breath. "Yes. Things are way out of focus." She tried to sound matter-of-fact. "Sometimes it's not too bad, but other times it's like I'm looking through a heavy fog. Until now, I just wanted to ignore it."

Marcy took Kate's head in her hands and lifted it toward her face. "Open your eyes and look at me." Kate complied. "Oh, you should have told someone sooner. Don't move." She walked to the doorway and called to one of the nurses. Another flash of lightning filled the sky, followed by successive crashes.

A big fuss ensued. Dr. Jamison and Dr. Johnson both came in and looked at her eyes. They asked questions and ordered tests. It frightened Kate. For one terrifying moment, she thought her body was rejecting her brain. She'd overheard the doctors talking about some "thirty-two pathways from the brain to the eyes." Maybe the connectors were failing.

"Am I going blind?" she asked Jamison. She listened to the pounding ricochet of raindrops—waiting for his answer.

Jamison spoke in a hushed tone that calmed her own personal mounting storm. "Don't worry, Kate. You're going to be just fine."

"But I can barely see."

He looked her squarely in the face. "We have an ophthalmologist, Dr. Ahmed, coming over to see you in a few minutes. Do you know what an ophthalmologist is?" He cocked his head to one side.

"A doctor for eyes?" she answered too quickly. She inserted a note of uncertainty to the end of her response. "I'm just guessing."

"You're a very smart girl—very smart. Yes, he's a specialist. You and I will work with him to fix the problem. Okay?"

She was touched by his responses.

Jamison turned to the nurse. "Cancel Dr. Manning's interview with Kate today. I want to reschedule it to another day." Then, almost as an afterthought, he added, "Oh, and get her parents on the phone. They need to know what's happening."

"Please, don't," Kate said. "My mom's not well. Besides, you said we wouldn't know anything for a while anyway. So why bother them?"

Studying her for a minute, Jamison moved closer. "You're very considerate. But I'm sorry. They are your parents and we're required to call them whenever there's a problem that needs treatment." Then he added in a tone that seemed to indicate that he understood her concern, "I promise not to panic them. And you can talk to them first—let them know that I'll be calling."

"Okay. I don't want them driving over here in this storm. It's not safe."

The rain was still heavy, but less fierce. Sounds of thunderclaps trailed off in the distance, muted by the wind.

Jamison motioned to the nurse to hand her the phone. "Do you know the number?"

"Yeah. Thanks," she said, offering him a small smile as she lifted the receiver and began punching the numbers.

Her conversation was short and to the point. She told her mom that she was seeing some blurriness and that the hospital was running tests—but that it wasn't a big thing. "Besides, I feel great! Just a little sleepy. No one needs to bother with me today."

"How bad is it—your vision?" her mom asked.

"It's nothing. So stay home. I'm really tired. Oh, and Mom, I love the CDs. Thanks." Then she faked a loud yawn.

Twice her mom objected and said she was coming down and twice Kate repeated her mantra not to come. Somehow, she managed to convince her parents, and apparently Jamison's call didn't prompt more concern.

Dr. Ahmed arrived at her room a little after two o'clock, and his examination took up the rest of her afternoon.

Kate held her eyes wide as he put drops in them to dilate them. He muttered to no one in particular as he conducted various tests, something about needing more equipment to "conduct all the tests necessary for a thorough exam."

Kate cooperated and said little—just responded to directions. Ahmed made it obvious that Kate's eyes, rather than Kate herself, were the patients. Even though his bedside manner was somewhat cool, it worked well for Kate. She had plenty to think about.

7:15 PM

Bruce sat heavily in his easy chair and pulled the handle to raise his feet. He was pooped. Morning starts were earlier now that he had to feed the kids and get them off to school. For some reason, even his eight-hour shift seemed longer. And then coming home to snail mail, voice mail, email, kids' homework, dinner, dishes, baths, laundry, and what seemed like a hundred other nagging chores cordoned off his days. It felt like time had become compressed—minutes and hours became days and weeks—or was it the other way around?

Now, with dinner over, dishes done, and the kids reading, he had fifteen precious minutes to rest and scan the newspaper. Just then

Algae plopped down clumsily at Bruce's feet. The dog thumped his tail, demanding a scratch or pat. Bruce complied with one hand and turned on the lamp with the other. He was beginning to feel like an automaton. He'd once felt great pride in his career, but now even that seemed rote. It was as though a giant hand had pushed a flush lever, and his happiness was swirling down a deep, dark drain, the flapper closing tight so none could ever return again.

A rotten smell assaulted him. *Garbage. I'll take it out later.*

Perhaps the rainy weather and dark skies were adding to his depression. He listened to it pound—a steady beat with no rhythm. He wondered about other single parents and how they coped.

He banished the thoughts from his head and opened the paper. "Car Crash, Three Teenagers Killed," the headline read. He stared for a moment and then quickly opened to the sports section.

His 49ers had been in a slump. They'd only won two games this season. But they were his team. He knew the names of every player and followed their careers. He celebrated every win and suffered every loss—lots of suffering this year.

He, Liz, Megan, and Mark all had caps, sweatshirts, T-shirts, mugs, and even a large umbrella in red and gold with the 49er insignia. They would get together with friends and watch the games and cheer. Megan had red and gold pom-poms and knew the cheer-chants. Mark was an armchair coach, mimicking his father's actions and words. Bruce would have liked to have tickets, but at a starting price of fifty-nine dollars, he had resigned himself to watching games on the tube.

Bruce suddenly put down the paper and walked in long, quick strides to the calendar on the kitchen wall above the phone. He turned the pages to December. There, circled in red was the date, December 23, with Liz's carefully printed words, "49ers Game!"

Bruce gasped. He'd completely forgotten about the 49er tickets and tailgate party that his employer organized at the end of each season. It was an event they'd always looked forward to. They'd paint their faces, wave their banners, and eat garlic fries. The next one was little more than two months away. Kaiser had set aside four tickets for their family. But now there were only three of them.

Before he could give the game another thought, the smell of the rotting garbage demanded his attention. Bruce gathered the pull strings on the plastic bag and walked outside into the rain.

Algae dutifully followed him. It was as though Algae also suffered whatever sentence had been pronounced upon Bruce.

8:00 PM

Josh had never seen his parents so distraught. His father was pacing, arms crossed, asking the same question over and over again, "Why?" His mother was sitting at the kitchen table, head bowed. She could hardly speak. She would look up, try to say something, and then choke up.

"What were you thinking?" his father asked. "You were doing so well in school. You know, we give you everything. Why would you throw it all away?"

Josh squirmed. He no longer felt buoyant; the drugs had played out. He felt like a dark hole had formed in his chest. Was this what he'd wanted? He had his mom and dad's undivided attention.

He swallowed hard and said between clenched teeth, "I didn't think anyone cared what I did."

His mother's head snapped upright, and her mouth dropped open. She blinked in rapid succession. "Of course we care!" she sputtered. "Josh, whatever gave you such an idea?"

"You don't care about me! All you care about is Kate. Ever since she got sick, you guys stopped loving me. I know that!" he screamed, jumping up from the chair and running from the kitchen to his room. He slammed the door and threw himself onto his bed. "I hate you!" he yelled at the top of his voice, wiping tears from his eyes. "I hate you!"

He clutched his bedspread in his hands and pulled hard, wanting to tear something, to throw something.

Then he heard two gentle knocks on his bedroom door. He sat up and turned with arms raised in anger. But when he saw his father enter with pain written across his brow and his mother follow with tears flowing down her cheeks, he lowered his fists and sank his head to his chest. He felt warm arms wrap around him and heard the words he'd wanted to hear for so long.

"We love you, Josh. We're sorry, so sorry we've neglected you. Please forgive us," his father said as he held him.

"You've always been my hero," his mother said as she took his hand. "You don't know how much I've depended on you. I'm sorry I put such a burden on you. You deserved better. Please don't hate us," she said as she wiped her eyes.

Josh couldn't say anything. He just held his parents tighter and let his own tears flow and cleanse the hate from his heart.

chapter fifteen

Wednesday, October 15, 10:00 AM

"What do you mean by 'wrinkles'?" Kate's mother asked Dr. Ahmed. She was sitting up soldier-straight in the visitor's chair.

"Well, the term, 'retinal wrinkle,' also known as a 'macular pucker' are commonly used to describe Kate's condition," Dr. Ahmed said with a slight accent. He stood near the foot of Kate's bed. "The 'wrinkles' in both her eyes were most likely caused by trauma from the surgery."

Kate felt a degree of relief but stiffened as she thought of other consequences. "Is it possible that my eyesight could get worse?"

The doctor frowned, shook his head, and pursed his lips. "No. I don't think so."

Kate breathed a sigh. Just as she was about to ask about treatment, her mother rose and walked over to the doctor. "Will glasses help? Or can you prescribe something that will improve her vision?"

Dr. Ahmed shook his head. "I'm sorry, but this condition normally doesn't require treatment. And the wrinkles may well disappear in time," he said as though by rote. Dr. Ahmed paused and then added, "Sometimes the scar tissue that causes these wrinkles can separate from the retina. When that happens, then the condition clears up entirely."

"So her vision could become normal?" Donna asked.

Dr. Ahmed nodded slowly. Then he cocked his head to one side and added, "However, if her vision does deteriorate, then there's a minor surgery we may consider at a later date. But at this point it's not necessary. Besides, isn't she—?" He reviewed Kate's chart. "Yes, she's scheduled for the skull replacement surgery in about six weeks."

Kate's eyes widened. She had almost forgotten the scheduled surgery to repair her distorted head. How could she forget? She'd had to put on that stupid Barbie-pink plastic helmet whenever she was up and walking. She equated it with a bedpan. The only difference, she mused, was that it sat on her.

Kate felt a sudden moment of foreboding. "The second surgery—could it cause more damage to my eyes? More wrinkles?" she asked.

Her mother turned and glanced apprehensively at the doctor for his response.

He shuffled his feet. "Anything is possible." Then he added quickly, "But I wouldn't worry. Your upcoming surgery shouldn't be as traumatic as the transplant was—certainly not likely to cause so much stress." He added, "With time, I think you'll adjust to the blurring and the distortion. In any case, I'll come back often and check your vision."

"Thank you, Doctor," Donna said. "We really appreciate all that you've done—you and Stanford."

Dr. Ahmed gave an encouraging smile, turned, and walked from the room.

"Good news," Donna said.

"Yes it is. And I'm so glad you got here as he was coming in with his report. I was a little bit afraid."

"I figured you would be," her mother said as she took her hand and squeezed it. "I told you I'd be here. I'm just sorry I wasn't here yesterday—when you were going through the tests. Did you know that yesterday was the first full day I've missed since we brought you here?"

Kate nodded. "Yes, I know." She hesitated a moment and then added, "Is Josh all right? I mean, tell me, Mom, is he in big trouble?"

Her mother frowned and bit her lower lip. Then she nodded her head. "I think he'll be okay," she said as she patted Kate's hand. "There's no denying that he's in trouble. But I think he'll get through it just fine." She leaned back and shook her head. "We've all learned an important lesson. And I think he's young enough—and your dad and I are old enough—to repair the damage. We'll take care of Josh. Now let's get you well and back home."

"I want to come home," Kate said as a happy thought blossomed. "Do you think I can come home for Thanksgiving? Maybe just for a few days—before I have to come back for the other surgery?" she asked, the pitch of her voice rising with each successive word.

Kate didn't want to beg, but she couldn't hold back her excitement.

Her mother leaned forward and a huge smile lit her face. "That's a great idea. Nothing in this world would make me happier than to have our whole family together—something to really be thankful for. Let me talk with Dr. Jamison and we'll see what we can work out, okay?"

"Yes! Yes! Yes!" Kate said. "I can help make the turkey. And I make . . ." She caught herself just in time. She'd been about to tell Donna about her apple-sausage-pecan dressing recipe. "I . . . I'll help you make whatever you want." She finished the clumsy sentence and quickly recovered her composure.

Then she swiveled and reached her hand toward the CD player. "Listen to this, Mom." Kate pushed the buttons on the player to select track eight. And when Charlotte Church began singing "The Lord's Prayer," Kate joined in.

No one knew that she had been practicing this piece whenever she was alone in her room. As Liz, she had taken voice lessons—knew all the appropriate exercises and warm ups. But Liz's voice just wasn't pure. Kate's voice was something else—crystal clear.

After the first three notes, Kate saw her mother's jaw fall slack and her eyes stare as though transfixed on Kate's mouth.

She hit every note perfectly. She even breathed at the same time Charlotte did. She could feel her lungs expand. She knew she was good. Maybe she didn't look pretty, but she sounded pretty.

As she sang the final phrase, " . . . thine is the king-dom . . ." Marcy and one of the floor nurses opened the door and stood as though spellbound. Kate continued to belt out, " . . . and the pow-er, and the glo-ry for-e-ver—A-men." As Kate finished, she flashed a smile at her mother, her friend, and the nurse.

Applause and soft shouts of "Brava" filled the small hospital room.

11:00 AM

Jamison felt a surge of excitement as he prepared for his next transplant surgery. He was alert, sure of every technique. He was ready. He caught himself gritting his teeth, ever so slightly, and willed himself to relax his jaw.

He hadn't known that today would be the day of his next surgery until early this morning. If he'd had an inkling, he wouldn't have gone out last night. But the dinner and celebration with Inna had been splendid.

He wasn't hung over. He never drank more than one or two glasses with a meal. But he could have used more sleep, and he knew that he shouldn't have eaten so much. An over-indulgence in rich food always caused him to be sluggish the next day. But he was okay today, practically at his peak.

He saw medical students jamming into the viewing room to watch him, the world's only brain transplant surgeon, do his magic. He nodded at one of his prize students and saw the young woman signal him with a "thumbs up." Jamison smiled briefly and then turned to the members of his primary team. "Dr. Yamaguchi, Dr. Johnson, ready?" he asked.

"Ready," they replied.

Jamison glanced at the wall clock. The new donor brain was expected to arrive within the next few minutes. According to the transplant unit, the brain was the right size, the right blood type, and the right age for Brian Jorgensen, his next miracle patient. But he knew timing was everything.

Jamison looked intently at his patient. The young man lay draped and prepped, unaware that he would be the second person in history to have a new chance at life.

Jamison glanced upward, recalling the details about this patient. Twenty-four-year-old—three months in coma—brain dead—bicycle accident—husband and father of a one-year-old.

The young man had languished in this condition because his

wife would not permit life-support systems to be withdrawn. Jamison wondered if she had a religious reason for not pulling the plug or if she had been optimistic about scientific advances. Science—that was his god. Whatever her reasons, this man's wife was a lucky, lucky woman.

Just as Jamison glanced at the clock for a second time, the door swung open and the cooler holding Brian's new brain was brought into the OR.

12:00 Noon

Megan pulled the top of her sweater together as she walked toward the school cafeteria. The top button had come off her blue knit sweater last week, and she had put it in her pocket. She had meant to ask Nana to show her how to sew it on but had forgotten.

It was cold outside. And she felt cold inside. Even her best friend, Amy, wasn't having lunch with her anymore. She and Amy had shared almost everything. Three years ago they'd made a pledge to be best friends forever. But now Amy was walking into the cafeteria with Kari and Jennifer. She was laughing at some stupid joke, and she wouldn't even look at Megan.

Megan wondered what she had done to make them mad—to leave her out. Even her friends in gymnastics seemed to be avoiding her. Why was everybody being so mean?

"Megan, are you all right?" Ms. Andrews, her teacher, asked as she put her hand on Megan's shoulder.

Megan hadn't even noticed that Ms. Andrews had been walking next to her. She looked up at her teacher, faked a smile, and thought fast. "Oh, yes. I'm fine. It's just really cold outside," she said as she wrapped her arms around her shoulders.

"Then is it okay with you if I have lunch with you today?" Ms. Andrews asked. "It won't embarrass you if I eat with you, will it?"

Megan felt her face redden. She didn't know what to say. Teachers never ate with students. "I—I guess it would be okay. I mean, if you want to . . ."

"On second thought," Ms. Andrews interrupted, "why don't we get our lunches and you can come with me to the teachers' lunchroom. That way we can visit without interruptions. What do you say?"

Megan had never been in the teachers' lunchroom. It was forbidden territory for students. What would her friends think when they saw her going into the lunchroom? Still, Megan felt a warm glow in her chest. "Yes, I'd like that."

The fried chicken strips smelled wonderful and made Megan's mouth water. But her interest in eating was nothing compared to her interest in Ms. Andrews. She had never realized how beautiful her teacher was—and Ms. Andrews smelled good too. The reluctant sun seemed to peek its head out above a dark cloud just as they entered the cafeteria.

With a sideways glance, Megan eyed Amy, Kari, and Jennifer as they turned and watched her and Ms. Andrews fill their trays. Megan purposefully became more animated as she talked with the beautiful Ms. Andrews. They were all watching. She would bet they were jealous. She offered Amy and the other girls a quick smile and then turned back to her teacher. "Are you married?" she asked nonchalantly.

"Why do you ask?"

"Oh, no reason. It's just that you're so smart and pretty. I thought you might be married. That's all. Are you?"

"No, Megan. I'm not."

A smidgen of hope thumped in Megan's heart.

8:13 PM

Jamison removed his surgical gloves. Even though he was covered from head to toe in surgical attire, the smell of antiseptic seemed embedded in his skin. He yearned for a shower.

He moved his shoulders in a circular motion. Every muscle hurt. His fingers were almost numb. Despite his exhaustion, he smiled.

"You did it again!" Deborah said as she joined him in the afterglow of a successful surgery.

"Well, he's alive," Jamison replied. "So far, so good." He took in a deep, satisfying breath and let it out slowly. "But, right now, I'm the one who's half dead. I need to go home, take a shower, and get a good night's sleep."

"Me too," chimed in Felix as he removed his mask and booties.

"Just one more thing to do—talk with Brian's family and give them the news. His wife and parents are waiting," Jamison said as a feeling of relief poured through his tired veins.

The thought of telling them the good news gave him another spurt of energy. This was the best part of the job—telling the family when things went well. Brian was the second pioneer to cross the "great divide," and he, Jamison, was the wagon master.

He nodded at his two assistants as they walked together to the waiting family. Jamison knew that their smiles would announce the success of the operation to the family before they spoke.

chapter sixteen

Thursday, October 11, 8:00 AM

Josh sat back in the hardwood chair and looked up at the rotating ceiling fan.

How could I have been so stupid?

He had truly believed that Ron was his friend—his best friend. But according to police records, Ron had lied to the authorities. He'd told them that *Josh* had been the one who'd sold *him* drugs!

Outraged, Josh tried to rise from the chair to speak, but his father, who was standing behind him, gently pressed him back down. "Take it easy, son. Settle down."

Directing his comments to Assistant DA Mulcahey, Josh shouted, "I'll take a lie-detector test. I'll prove to you that it was the other way around."

"Don't worry about Ron Andrade's statement," Mulcahey said. "But you broke the law too, and there are consequences."

"You need to come clean with them, Josh," his father urged. "Tell him what you told your mom and me last night."

"Yes, Josh," his mother said. She reached out and took his hand. "Please do what your father says."

Josh glanced over at his mom, nodded in acknowledgment, and

covertly withdrew his hand.

Mulcahey must have seen the movement because he gave Josh an indulgent smile and cleared his throat. "You're charged with cocaine possession and being under the influence of an illegal drug. If you plead guilty and tell us what you know about Andrade, we can get you before a judge tomorrow and ask for a light sentence—one weekend at the juvenile facility, a six-month probation requiring proof of your weekly attendance at a Narcotics Anonymous meeting, and a $300 fine. When you turn eighteen, if you've kept your nose clean, your record will be expunged."

Mulcahey was waiting for an answer. Confused, Josh frowned and raised his shoulders. "What's expunged?" he asked.

"It means it won't be on any permanent record," his father said. "Isn't that right?" he asked Mulcahey.

"That's right. It will be as though it never happened."

His mother tapped her right foot nervously and sat forward. "But a weekend in the juvenile facility. Why that? This is his first offense. He's never been in any trouble before. Isn't that a bit harsh?"

The DA Assistant looked stone-faced at Donna Craig. "No, we don't think so." He leaned back in his chair, crossed his arms, and stared directly at Josh—a sure signal in Josh's mind that the cop was in charge. "There was a time when we just looked the other way," the DA said as he glanced briefly at Donna and then refixed his eyes on Josh. "But today meth, cocaine, and other illegal drugs are endangering our youth and taking over our school grounds. Zero tolerance—that's our policy. So you can take our offer and serve your sentence. Or you can plead 'not guilty' and we'll go after a harsher sentence—six months in juvy, a $5,000 fine, and three years probation."

Josh squirmed in his chair. He was at a low point—feeling a tug-of-war with his bodily cravings and deep emotional swings. Although he'd only been doing drugs for a week, he had enjoyed the rush the powdery cocaine gave him, and now he yearned for the escape it provided. He wondered if those urges would ever stop.

He had a lot to think about; he needed to make the right decision. At least his parents were here with him now and not at the hospital with his sister. If she hadn't become sick, he wouldn't have to take a back seat all the time; she wouldn't be in the hospital now, and he'd have a life.

Josh leaned forward. "Yeah, I'll tell you what I know . . . and plead guilty." He cocked his head. "But I was just wondering something."

"What's that?" the DA Rep asked.

"The juvy time—can I serve it this coming weekend? Get it finished so it's not hanging over my head?"

"I think we can arrange that. We like swift justice," Mulcahey said.

Josh's father gave him a single pat on the back and walked over to Mulcahey. He nodded and asked, "Then we have a deal?"

"We do."

His mother rose from her chair and Josh followed suit. His hands were sweating, but despite the moisture, he could still feel the oil from the hardwood chair. The oil smelled like lemons—like Kate.

9:15 AM

Charles marveled at the makeshift office that CNN had hastily put together for him. A thirty-six-inch, high-definition, slim-line TV was on the wall opposite a much-used metal desk. He sighed as he watched a rerun of his latest report.

He nibbled a stick of Juicy Fruit gum into his mouth and grinned. He folded the metallic gum wrapper into a small cube and dropped it into the empty metal can next to him. He heard a *ping*—the sound of new beginnings.

No doubt it was his tenacity and smarts, together with some luck, that had elevated him to his current station. The relationship he'd developed with Jamison had given him a leg up. A new donor brain was on its way to Stanford, and a recipient was being prepped. Through Jamison, Charles had accessed the stats on Brian Jorgensen and his family before anyone other than hospital staff knew about the scheduled surgery, giving Charles a jump on all the other stations.

But luck played into it too. The donor family was going public. So even in their greatest moment of sorrow, having lost their eighteen-year-old son, Chris Zigler, in a hunting accident, the parents and two sisters were not only willing but anxious to talk about him.

Even though Charles had given KROX his one-week notice and had made the decision to take CNN's offer to start on October 15, he felt compelled to give CNN the exclusive. And they were more than willing to put him on their payroll immediately. Not only that, but their salary offer went up and their team of experts were on-hand to provide whatever support he needed.

He'd nailed it. Pictures of the dead youth and his short-lived accomplishments were still flashing every hour, on the hour, on every news broadcast. Mrs. Jorgensen's prayers as she stood with her baby on her hip were heart-rending. Plus CNN interspersed earlier clips of Charles's interviews with Dr. Jamison, recapping the events of the last few weeks.

Now, with a new successful transplant and information on the donor, he no longer needed the Craig family. Kate would still go down in history as the first brain transplant recipient. But with donor information, the Brian Jorgensen/Chris Zigler chronicle offered viewers a more complete human-interest story.

For tomorrow's interview, both families had agreed to come together with Charles and his news team to share in the dramatic outcome. Brian would be conscious about forty-eight hours after the completed surgery, if his case was anything like Kate's. This historic moment would be one of the most dramatic in news casting.

Best of all, from Charles's viewpoint, no one except Brian himself, could prevent him from conducting personal interviews with the recipient. Thankfully both donor and recipient were adults this time. Dealing with parents on behalf of a minor wouldn't be a problem. However, the two families' acceptance and trust in him would be crucial to his continued success. So he'd be careful to show them the utmost respect and compassion in his reporting.

He chewed his gum as a segment of yesterday's interview came on.

Mr. Zigler wiped away a tear and choked up as he said, "It-it was only three days ago that-that Chris told us that he'd gone to the DMV to get an organ donor stamp. He did it in response to the broadcast plea from the girl's family through Mr. Rubenstein here."

At this point the camera panned to show Mr. Zigler looking directly at Charles.

Charles shook his head slowly and said, "Your son was obviously a very considerate young man. No wonder you're proud of him."

Mr. Zigler smiled sadly and nodded his head as the picture faded.

As Charles watched the footage come to an end, he swelled

with pride. Not only did he have a brilliant career ahead of him, but because of his actions, Brian, a young father and husband, had a new chance at life.

He grabbed the remote and silenced the TV. It was time to gather his crew and get over to the hospital for another update on yesterday's successful transplant.

1:30 PM

Jamison parked his black BMW in his usual spot in the underground parking lot. He had thoroughly enjoyed his lunch with his financial advisor, Fred.

Jamison seldom ate a hamburger, but Kirk's Steakburgers had the best ones in the Bay Area, and the onion strings were out of this world. He whistled a silly tune from his childhood as he slipped the keys in his coat pocket.

Emerging from the parking area, he heard the roar of a crowd and gasped. He had expected a large media turnout for the two o'clock press conference, but what he hadn't expected were hundreds of protesters circling the complex. Although hospital security and local police seemed to be doing their job, making sure that they didn't block the entrance, the signs stopped Jamison.

The protesters called themselves "The Undeniable Law of God" (TULOG). Their name, acronym, and logo—stone tablets—were emblazoned across the backs of the signs. Cameras were pointed at a young woman who was being interviewed.

Jamison saw Charles in the middle of the media frenzy and quickly shook his head "no" in hopes that Charles wouldn't identify him to the crowd. Charles nodded at him. Then Jamison lowered his head and walked across the driveway between the fountains and the main hospital building. As he listened to the chants and exchanges among protesters, a feeling of dread engulfed him.

"Unethical Heretics" and "Stop Playing God," read the signs. Some even depicted Stanford as the seat of the anti-Christ and Jamison as the devil incarnate.

"Contact your congress members," some were shouting. "Demand that they outlaw the procedure."

Jamison's stomach churned. The onion strings rested uncomfortably in the pit of his belly.

How could these people be so ignorant? Why would anyone

want to deny a young person a second chance at life?

He watched for a few moments in stunned silence, trying to make sense of it all. Then he remembered the initial hubbub over organ transplants, including simple cornea transplants. Decades ago the research was condemned by Bible-thumping evangelists. Even some doctors considered the possibility of a heart transplant unthinkable. It was against the natural laws of God and would lead to the downfall of a sinful nation. The question of ethics in such procedures had always waxed strong. As Jamison recalled, it had taken several years before transplants of any kind were deemed acceptable.

As he turned to enter the hospital, one of the security guards tried to stop him. But then he recognized him and said, "Oh, Dr. Jamison, it's you. Come on in. Hurry."

"It's him!" one of the protesters shouted. "It's Jamison."

The crowd turned in a single wave and moved toward him, shouting accusations and muttering prayers for his deliverance.

He raced through the doorway, and without looking back, walked briskly to the stairwell. He climbed three flights of stairs and scurried down the hall to his office. Even before he opened the door, he could hear his phone ringing.

9:15 PM

The kids were in bed and the house was suddenly transformed from a cacophony of noises to the lonesome creaking of a building settling in its foundation. Bruce tiptoed downstairs, and Algae added the echo of his paw steps as he trailed after Bruce.

For weeks now, Bruce had been putting off the final Liz "chores," but he'd decided he needed to take care of those nagging details tonight. He walked to the family room and sat at the metal folding chair in front of a small desk that held a five-year-old computer. He pushed the startup button and waited for several minutes until the familiar icons appeared. When his browser was ready, he signed in to Liz's email account with her password, "unbeldi."

Bruce sat for a few seconds, trying to determine what to write. He wanted a message he could send to everyone in Liz's address book. Although most would already know about her death, some of her contacts might be friends who had moved away or acquaintances that she only talked to once or twice a year. He didn't want to shock anyone, and he certainly didn't want to receive an avalanche of emails in response. He wanted something simple.

Under subject he entered, "A Message from Liz's Family."

Then he pecked out on the keyboard:

Dear Friends of Elizabeth Ann Lindsay,

Most of you already know Liz was killed in a traffic accident last month. We're sending this message from Liz's email so that you will remove her from your address book but never from your hearts. Thank you all for your kind words and condolences.

Bruce, Megan, and Mark

Bruce clicked on the "To:" box in order to select the first twenty names and addresses in Liz's contacts. It had been his experience that twenty was all he could send at one time. As he scanned the names and started to click on them, the third name on the list stopped Bruce. He stared at the name: Marcy Ames. He didn't want to send the same message to her.

As he clicked on the "Send" icon for the fifth time, he realized he had sent the message to eighty-seven people. Liz had a whole host of friends, just as he'd supposed. And some of them, like Marcy, he hadn't even known.

Before shutting down Liz's email account, he copied Marcy's email address onto a piece of paper. He still had her business card, but he wanted to enter her address into his email address book now, before he lost it.

He typed in Marcy's address and the subject, "Hi." Then he sat at the computer and stared at the screen. Finally he began: "Just a quick note to thank you . . ."

The phone rang, drawing him away from his task.

"Is this Mr. Lindsay?" a woman's voice asked when he picked up the phone.

"Yes," he said.

"This is Ms. Andrews, Megan's teacher. Do you have a moment to talk?"

chapter seventeen

Friday, October 12, 10:00 AM

"You're kidding," Kate said as she swung her legs over the edge of the bed. "I can go home for Thanksgiving?"

Her mom flashed Kate a broad grin as she helped her put on the helmet. Kate thought her mother looked relieved. Even her bright-yellow pantsuit gave testimony of her sunnier frame of mind.

"If you behave yourself, Dr. Jamison says you can come home the week before Thanksgiving and stay until the day before your surgery. Of course I'll have to bring you back weekly for tests and therapy."

Kate's eyes went wide and she squealed. "I was afraid they were going to keep me here forever. What did you say to get them to let me go?"

Her mother wore a thoughtful expression as she touched Kate's elbow in mock support and walked in cadence with her. "Dr. Jamison was easy to convince. He seemed to anticipate the request and was happy to oblige. You probably know he's done another brain transplant."

"Yeah, the nurses are talking about it and it's all over the news. Do you think that had something to do with him agreeing to let me go?" Kate asked as she tried to improvise a dance step. She wobbled and caught herself.

Her mother flashed Kate a proud look despite her clumsiness. "Could be. His attention seems to be diverted to his newest patient."

Kate sucked in her lower lip. She felt a deep sadness for the man housed in the ICU. "I hope Brian will be okay. I saw the story about him—with that same television reporter who interviewed you."

"He needs our prayers," Donna said as she patted Kate on the arm. "You know better than anyone else what he'll go through."

Kate's legs felt weak and her head began to spin. "Mom, I feel funny. I need to sit down."

Her mom scooted a chair over, and Kate sank down with a thud. A trickle of sweat dripped from her forehead. Unsettling thoughts raced through her head. Would the surgeons get it right this time, or would they leave Brian with the memories of that teenage boy? Maybe the demonstrators were right. Maybe Congress should ban the procedure.

"Are you okay?" her mother asked as she placed a warm hand on Kate's shoulder.

"Yeah, I just got up too fast." Kate mopped her forehead with a tissue.

Just then Marcy peeked her head in. "If the diva is accepting audiences, may I come in?"

3:15 PM

Bruce tried to stay focused on the elderly patient in the MRI tube as he looked at the screen, but he was bothered by the conversation he'd had last night with Megan's teacher, Ms. Andrews. He kept slipping back to the words "withdrawn, angry, belligerent."

Bruce had always known Megan was more serious-minded than most nine-year-olds. But on the other hand, she'd always had friends and been outgoing, gregarious, almost bordering on bossy. Now, according to Ms. Andrews, Megan was quiet, sullen, acting out toward those who had once been her closest friends. And they were avoiding her, leaving her out of their conversations and activities.

Bruce fought back his own emotions. Apparently Liz's death was more traumatic for Megan than he'd realized. Perhaps he was dumping too much responsibility on her. Maybe he needed to back off. But he was certain that if he didn't keep her engaged in activity, she would sit and brood, letting herself wallow in self-pity. What could he do?

He snapped his attention back to the job, realizing he had completed the procedure on auto pilot. He needed a break.

"Okay, Mrs. Johansen, we're through now," he said as he turned off the machine and the table returned to its position outside the MRI tube. "Stay there and I'll be right over to help you sit up."

He offered Mrs. Johansen an outstretched hand and walked her back to the dressing room. Then he glanced at his watch. He had fifteen minutes before his next appointment. Slipping his hands in his pockets, he walked through the double doors and down the hallway to the cafeteria. The aroma from the grill caused his stomach to contract. He purchased a Diet Coke and a peanut butter cookie and then walked to an empty table in the far corner so he could have a moment of solitude and gather his thoughts.

The carbonation soothed his parched throat and refreshed his spirits. He unwrapped the giant cookie and broke it in half. He leaned back, downed one half in three bites, and wiped the crumbs from the corner of his mouth with his thumb. He wished he could cure Megan's sadness with a cookie. What could he offer to bring her out of her doldrums? Was there anything special coming up? Ah, yes, Halloween.

He shook his head—bad idea. For most kids, Halloween was a time of diversion—for trick or treating, dressing up, and pretending to be someone else. But for his family, the date loomed as an added burden, since that was the date when they'd always celebrated Liz's birthday, even though she was born shortly after midnight on November first.

If Liz hadn't died, she would be turning thirty, the big three-oh. In two weeks she would have been entering her prime.

Bruce mused at Liz's obsession with Halloween. She'd once told him that until she was five years old, she had believed that the candy and costumes were in honor of her birthday. She was crushed when she learned otherwise but made up for her disappointment by melding the two events into one.

On second thought, maybe avoiding the holiday was a mistake. Perhaps he needed to make a big to-do over it, let the kids celebrate. It might help them deal with their pain and move on.

Intrigued by the prospect, he removed a pen and a small notepad from his pocket and began writing ideas for decorations. Then he started a list of people he'd invite: the Slagle family; the Thayers; his sister; Manny, a fellow worker, and his family; some of their friends from church . . . maybe even Marcy Ames and her daughter. Yes, he'd invite Marcy. He wanted to learn more about her connection to Liz.

He'd ask Megan to help him plan the event—a party to end all parties. Megan and Mark could invite their friends too.

His next X-ray appointment was due in less than a minute, so he rewrapped the leftover cookie and slipped it into his jacket pocket. He walked back to his station with more energy in his step. He smiled to himself and looked at his watch again. In two hours he had an appointment to meet with Megan's teacher. He'd run the idea of a party by Ms. Andrews and get her opinion.

8:14 PM

Jamison was still upset about the demonstrations taking place outside the hospital. But he was certain that this newest triumph would send the naysayers home apologetic and ashamed of their behavior. How could they—how could anyone—deny life?

Jamison inhaled a long, satisfied breath as he studied his patient's vital signs. Brian's pulse felt strong, his respirations somewhat shallow but still within the normal range. There was no fever, no sign of organ rejection. His skin was clammy and a shade jaundiced, but his overall signs were much better than Kate's had been shortly after surgery.

Now that Jamison had an estimated timetable, based on Kate's recovery, he was intent on being present when Brian woke up. He was sorry he had missed Kate's awakening. This time he would taste the pleasure of the miracle.

Sitting next to her husband, hands clasped in prayer, Brian's wife looked at Jamison and smiled, hope in her eyes.

Jamison swallowed, feeling emotional, something he couldn't allow—not that he wasn't human, he just needed to stay alert.

"How's he doing?" Felix asked in his soft tenor as he entered the ICU and closed the door behind him.

Jamison looked at his colleague, grateful for the diversion and a chance to bask in his achievement. "He should be coming around soon. Everything looks positive."

chapter eighteen

Sunday, October 28, 10:00 AM

Staring out the window and taking in the Indian summer day, Kate tried to pull herself out of her depression, but it was useless. She frowned. How could Bruce host a party just six weeks after her accident?

Last week, when Marcy told Kate that Bruce had invited her and her daughter to a Halloween party, Kate couldn't believe her ears.

Marcy's face had reddened, and she'd sputtered when she tried to explain. "Bruce thinks that Megan needs a diversion to prod her out of her melancholy," Marcy said.

Kate almost bought that explanation until she learned that the party would be held today, the Sunday before Halloween. She and Bruce had never held a party on a Sunday. The birthday/Halloween celebrations were always on Saturdays so kids and friends could stay late. It didn't take long before the truth set in—Marcy worked on Saturdays and was off on Sundays. It was painfully obvious to Kate that Bruce had planned the party around Marcy's schedule. He wanted to see her.

"Bruce is doing this for Megan," Marcy said meekly. "He's just trying to do the right thing."

Kate chewed on the inside of her cheek. "And did you accept?" she asked as she jutted out her chin.

"I told him I'd call him back and let him know. I thought I should talk with you first. I won't go if you don't want me to."

Kate was trapped. How could she refuse? Maybe Bruce was out of line, but Marcy was her only contact with her former family. She didn't dare break this critical connection.

"Bruce wants us to wear something funny—nothing scary. What do you think, Kate?" Marcy asked.

Kate could tell that Marcy was trying to act like it didn't matter to her whether she attended or not. But Kate knew better. She remembered all too well the way Marcy had looked at Bruce—and the way Bruce had looked back at her at the memorial service.

Kate's mouth twitched. "I hope you do," she said and then added, "but I don't want to wait until you're back to work on Tuesday to be filled in. Promise me you'll call me on Monday." She turned away so Marcy wouldn't see the pain in her eyes. She tried to keep the anguish from her tone. "I want to know if Mark is still taking karate classes and if Megan is in gymnastics.

"Oh, and don't go as a fairy queen," she said with a rasp. "That's what I was going to be this year—if I hadn't died." She turned back and glanced briefly at Marcy, who looked stunned.

That conversation reminded Kate of how different things were now. Just two weeks ago, when the second brain transplant patient died, she had panicked—sure she would soon follow Brian to a cold, dank grave. In addition, the failed surgery had almost cost her the free pass to go home for Thanksgiving. Dr. Jamison had started spending more time with her and was unduly obsessed with her progress, ordering more frequent tests. But her parents held Dr. Jamison to his word. He couldn't deny that she was growing stronger every day or that her vital signs were normal. So, in about two and a half weeks, her parents would take her home. To their home.

She kept trying to associate that word with a place somewhere in Castro Valley. But whenever she heard or spoke the word, a small two-story abode in Hayward came to mind. She muffled back a sob.

Her mind jumped to other issues. Just the day before learning about the party, Kate had taken her postponed IQ test. For a so-called eleven-year-old she rated "genius" with an IQ of 163. She knew that because of the differences in the adult and children's measuring scales, her actual adult IQ was more like 128—still well above average but certainly not genius. She'd given the test her full attention because she didn't want to redo middle school and high school. She figured that scoring well on the test would provide her with an opportunity to skip grades and move quickly back into college. Now she wondered why she cared.

The only thing that gave her any pleasure was her voice. And thanks to the singing lessons her mother had arranged, she was learning to increase her volume. Singing added a new dimension to her life—a welcome diversion. When she sang, calmness and joy filled her.

Walking back to her bedside, Kate whistled through the gap in her teeth. Then she pushed the play button on the CD player. She had listened to the two Charlotte Church CDs at least three dozen times, so she knew every song, every word, every note. She returned to the window, leaned against the sill, and tried to sing in harmony.

I'm almost thirty. A single tear trickled down her cheek. She mumbled to no one in particular, "Who will sing 'Happy Birthday' to me?"

10:45 AM

As the organ music filled the sanctuary, Josh glanced at his mom. Her soft two-toned green pantsuit looked freshly pressed. She smelled of gardenias. Even seated, she was a good six inches shorter than Josh.

He lowered his head, pretending to read through the program provided by the United Methodist Church of Castro Valley. His family had been attending this church for as long as he could remember.

A small flicker of hope grew inside him as he saw his friends. Maybe after the service he'd have a chance to talk with some of his buddies. So far, the entire weekend had been spent under the watchful eyes of his parents.

He glanced to the left at his father, whose steely blue eyes were fixed on Josh, his thin-lipped smile forced. They still didn't trust him. Couldn't they see that he was following their rules?

As the preacher spoke about love and forgiveness, Josh fidgeted with his small white shirt buttons. One of his parents was always by his side, and if he spent more than ten minutes in the shower, they were knocking on the door to "check on him." He felt smothered by their constant attention. Then he realized something and almost laughed out loud. *Isn't this what I wanted?*

His mom was still spending a lot of time with Kate. But his dad had cut back on his work commitments and was spending "quality time" with him. His parents even monitored his computer time. He was only permitted to be online for school research—no chat rooms, no blogs, or email. How lame was that!

He'd thought juvy was bad. But now he was as much a prisoner as he'd been in that dump. The only difference was the food at home was better. But juvy was only for a weekend! He closed his eyes as the pastor called for prayer.

In just eighteen days, his sister would be coming home. She would be sharing the same house, eating at the same table, and he'd take a backseat all over again. The prayer ended and they all said, "Amen." Then the pastor said, "Open your songbook to page 110."

"Stand up, son," his father said, nudging Josh's arm.

Josh stood and helped hold the hymnbook. He pushed away thoughts of Kate and added his tenor voice to the congregation's: "When the trumpet of the Lord shall sound . . ."

2:15 PM

Jamison sat, head in hand, for several minutes, his mind numb. Perhaps it was the lack of sleep that was catching up with him. How could he sleep? There were so many unanswered questions.

The bags under his eyes were so noticeable that this morning his wife had threatened to use something called "concealer" on him. He'd pushed her away—even shouted at her.

He clicked open the autopsy report on his computer. How many times had he reread the report? He'd lost count. He reviewed every step of the surgery. The only difference between Kate and Brian was that Brian was in much better physical shape than Kate. He slapped his hand onto the desk. *So what went wrong? Why did Kate pull through and this strapping young man die?* It didn't make sense.

The brain of that boy was a perfect match: no damage, right size, same blood type. The personal memory was erased and all functional skill areas protected. The organ had been properly removed and maintained during transport. But it wasn't the brain that had failed. It was the heart. Yet the autopsy showed no signs of pre-existing disease. For some reason, the heart had just stopped beating.

It had been years since he'd ached for a shot of whiskey. But in the last few days, when answers eluded him, he'd indulged heavily. It helped to drown out the images of Brian's young wife; her screams of despair were embedded in his memory.

He opened his desk drawer and drew out a packet of aspirin, washing three down with a cup of lukewarm tea. Although the Nobel Prize would soon be presented to him, this failure had caused widespread hostility. His colleagues and the entire medical profession were focused on this disaster. And he couldn't tell them what went wrong.

He stood and walked over to the window. The media pundits were having a field day at his expense. When interviewed, all he could say was, "There are risks in all surgeries and this is still experimental." Unfortunately, his carefully parsed statements seemed to only stoke the flames of unrest. Even Charles Rubenstein sounded skeptical, acting as though Brian's death was a personal loss to him. Both the donor's family and Brian's family were featured on one newscast after another.

It wasn't so much the loss of a patient; Jamison had seen death many times. It was the death of this, his second brain transplant patient. If he'd had two successive triumphant surgeries, his procedures would have become standard in a few short years.

He turned away from the window. The tragedy had been further punctuated by the news that TULOG, the protesting group, had passed a resolution condemning the surgery and had found Congressional sponsors for a bill to halt future brain transplants. Jamison was certain that such a bill would never pass. No one would support something that would set back medical research and development to the Dark Ages—making all experimental surgeries subject to political whim. Still, he balled his fists. What was it that made Kate so robust? Why was she still alive and young Brian dead?

Jamison moaned and then moved the mouse to close the autopsy report. He turned off his computer and pushed back his chair.

5:30 PM

Marcy hadn't felt like this since high school. Her insides were a jumble as she drove to the party. Adriana was listening to some teenage singer on the radio. Marcy told herself that she was being ridiculous as she tapped on the steering wheel to the beat of the music. After all, Bruce had only been widowed for one month and ten days. But who was counting?

She breathed deeply as she remembered how he'd looked at her. Just the memory created a spark that warmed her to the core, despite the cool air rushing through the partly rolled-down window. How could she even think about the possibility of such a friendship?

Kate/Liz stood like a steel door between them. Memories of Liz were a barrier for Bruce and his children, and Kate's existence was a barbed wire fence between Marcy and Bruce. It was impossible. She needed to refrain from these silly fantasies.

As she rounded the final corner, she realized that she shouldn't have accepted Bruce's invitation and shouldn't have told Kate about it. Instead, she should have politely declined. But it was as though an outside force was dragging her to some preordained juncture.

As she pulled up in front of the Lindsay residence, Marcy flashed a nervous smile at her daughter. Adriana was excited about attending the party and had chosen their costumes after much deliberation. Adriana was a perfect Kermit the Frog and Marcy was dressed as Pig-o-Patra—Miss Piggy dressed up as Cleopatra—complete with pig's ears and nose, a long wig with a hundred black braids, a gold-fringed white gown, and elbow-length purple gloves.

Marcy was amused by their attire and hoped that Bruce and his kids would be too. However, as she parallel parked, her mind shifted to Bruce. Here she was, in her mid-thirties, thinking about his eyes, his deep smile lines, and his wavy dark hair. And there was something needy in his expressions, something that said, "I wasn't meant to live without the love of a woman." Or was that just her imagination?

She wondered why Bruce had invited her. She hoped it was because, somewhere deep in his subconscious, he wanted her too. If this was true, what would Kate do when, and if, she found out? Then again, how could Marcy even think of being with a man whose wife was still alive, albeit in an entirely different form? The thought of it made her head ache. She would think about the logistics later.

Right now Adriana needed help getting to the entrance. Her flippers made walking a challenge, and the outfit was warm because of the unseasonably hot day. But Marcy figured that the sun would soon set and Adriana would welcome the added insulation.

"Mom, tell me again, how do you know these people?" Adriana asked.

I know . . . uh, *knew* . . . the children's mother. She was a friend of mine. She died last month," Marcy said as they approached the front door.

"How come we were never invited before?" Adriana asked as she struggled with her costume.

"Probably because we live on the other side of the bay."

Just as Marcy was about to knock on the door, it swung open. Bruce, dressed as Captain Jack Sparrow, smiled and stood mutely for a moment studying their faces. Then a large smile erupted on his face and his kohl-lined eyes lit up. "Oh, Marcy, I'm so glad you could make it." Then he looked at Kermit the Frog, lifted one eyebrow, and said, "And this must be Adriana."

There was a rustle by his side and Megan, dressed as a pixie, grabbed her father's hand. Megan looked up at Bruce and smiled sweetly. Then she threw a sharp glance at Marcy. "Daddy, why don't you come and dance with Miss Andrews? She's a really good dancer," she said, eyes blinking innocently.

Bruce looked down at Megan, winked at her, and said, "Why don't you take Adriana outside and introduce her to some of your friends?"

Marcy could see the disappointment on Megan's face, and then a small version of Spiderman came running down the hallway. "Hi, Marcy. Yeah! You came." The comic book figure jumped up and down. "Daddy said you were coming."

Marcy recognized Mark's voice and couldn't help grinning at his obvious enthusiasm over seeing her.

Mark cocked his head to one side. "Gosh, you look funny," he said to Marcy. Then he shrugged his shoulders and took her by the hand. When he finally spied Adriana, he laughed. "Ha, and you came as Kermie. Hey, you wanna go out in the backyard and jump around in the bounce house? It looks like a giant dragon," he said.

Adriana took off at a fast pace, trying to keep up with Mark as he ran to the backyard.

Megan's expression turned sour. Then she tugged at her father's arm again and repeated her suggestion. "Come and dance with Miss Andrews," she said, giving Marcy a warning glance.

Bruce patted Megan's shoulder. "Yes, Megan, I will. But first, let's introduce our new guest and make her feel welcome. Okay?" He took Megan's hand and offered Marcy his other arm.

"Sure," she said, eyes narrowing. "But you know, Miss Andrews can't stay late. She has school tomorrow."

9:30 PM

Bruce sighed deeply as he sat and rested for a moment. As he took in a slow draft from a bottle of Corona, Algae sank to the floor at his feet and almost instantly fell asleep. The party had ended at eight-thirty sharp, and although there was still garbage to take out, streamers to take down, and general cleanup to attend to, at least the kids were bathed and tucked in. For a while it had been tough going with Megan. But as the evening progressed, she became more and more animated. She laughed, danced, and bounced along with her friends.

Bruce was no fool. He could tell Megan was smitten by Miss Andrews and felt animosity toward Marcy. But after he danced twice with the matronly, very unattractive Miss Andrews—who was probably a good twenty years his senior—Megan finally relaxed and enjoyed the remainder of the party.

He couldn't help but be amused by Megan's attempt at matchmaking. He understood how children often saw beauty differently from adults. Perhaps they had better vision. Indeed, Miss Andrews was a kind, gentle woman who showed deep concern for Megan. Bruce wanted to encourage that relationship, hoping that someday Miss Andrews would be a close family friend. However, the relationship Megan so obviously wanted was out of the question.

Bruce took a sip of his beer. When Megan prodded Bruce to invite Miss Andrews over for dinner next week, he'd capitulated. Miss Andrews respectfully declined—said she already had dates planned for "almost every night for the next several months." She told them that the only reason she had been able to attend the party was because her "boyfriend" had a cold and had to postpone their date. The woman was wise beyond her fifty-some years.

As the evening wore on, Bruce managed to be attentive toward Marcy, despite Megan's interruptions. Twice he'd danced with

Marcy—one fast, one slow dance. Her hair smelled like honey. And her skin was smooth like iridescent satin.

Marcy had brought up the subject of Liz. Unfortunately, he flinched and stammered as he tried to respond. After that, Marcy didn't mention Liz's name again except when Maria made the toast. Then everyone raised a cup "To Liz."

After folks had helped themselves to the taco buffet, it was time for cake and ice cream. The frosting on the Costco-decorated carrot cake said, "Happy Halloween," and Charlie Brown's image was pictured with a giant pumpkin. It was the first time the Halloween cake he ordered didn't also say, "Happy Birthday."

Five more minutes. He'd sit for five more minutes before finishing the cleanup duty. He couldn't get the image of Marcy out of his head. Even as a pig, she looked beautiful. Toward the end of the evening, he'd gotten up the courage to mention the December football game.

"Do you like football?" he asked.

"Only when the 49ers are playing," she responded. "As far as I'm concerned, they *are* football."

"Don't answer me now, but I have tickets to the final home game in December. I have an extra ticket and I'm sure I can get another. I would love it if you and Adriana would join us."

Marcy's eyes had grown wide. "I need to think about it."

"Of course." He swallowed. "I'll call you next month . . . if that's okay with you. Just before Christmas."

chapter nineteen

Thursday, November 15, 10:00 AM

Kate let out the air she'd been holding with a quick puff and tried to calm the butterflies in her stomach. She glanced again at the clock as she placed her CDs in their cases and packed them, along with her pajamas, robe, and slippers, in the small blue suitcase her mother had brought her when she visited yesterday.

Her new jeans and orange sweater contrasted with the pink helmet. But she liked wearing street clothes and was especially fond of the sneakers.

Her parents were due any minute now, and she'd be on her way to Castro Valley. Kate sat on the edge of the bed, trying to recall the details of the conversation she'd had with Marcy. After the Halloween party, Marcy had spent almost an hour on the phone giving Kate a rundown on all she had learned about Megan, Mark, and Bruce. According to Marcy, they were coping "as well as could be expected." Marcy had learned from Mrs. Thayer that Megan had finally mastered the back flip. The next thing she would be attempting was an aerial—a cartwheel-like flip, except without touching the floor with her hands. Liz had always been Megan's spotter, catching her when she fell or providing support for a spin or lift. Now Mrs. Thayer and

Maria Slagle took turns spotting for Megan. Even as Kate packed for her new life, she ached to be with her former family.

Luckily for Bruce, the Thayer and Slagle families had become surrogate grandmother, grandfather, aunt, uncle, and cousins. The relationships with those families had been developed and nurtured for many years, not by Bruce, but by her—when she was Liz. Bruce had always been too busy with his career to give much time to "idle chitchat." Although he'd been outgoing and kind to her many friends, he'd left all social planning and arrangements to her.

Now he was reaping the benefits of her years of outreach. But she thanked God for these wonderful people, knowing that they offered the type of community her spouse and kids needed.

Kate stared out the window but saw little. At the moment, Megan was her greatest concern. Images of Megan replayed over and over again like a rewound tape. Marcy reported that during the party Megan had tried to play matchmaker with Bruce and her teacher, Miss Andrews. Although Liz hadn't met Miss Andrews, she knew the woman was single. Upon hearing that her daughter was already trying to replace her, she'd developed a rash and tears welled in her eyes now. According to Marcy, Megan had even tried to cajole Bruce into inviting the woman to dinner. What's more, he *had* invited her. She balled her fists, but then the itching returned, and she once again started rubbing the red bumps.

Kate withdrew a tissue and applied a small torn edge to the spot she'd irritated. The whole interchange had been deeply troubling. Kate was sure that unless she could think up some diversion, Megan would try to talk him into inviting Miss Andrews again—and next time she might say "yes."

All packed now, Kate pulled the hospital tray over and poured herself a glass of water. She downed the water in large gulps. As she placed the cup down, a crazy thought shot through her. The notion bordered on the ridiculous. If Megan tried to get Marcy together with Bruce, then Kate could get periodic reports—keep abreast of her children and her husband. At least she would have a friend positioned in a strategic place. But if Megan's teacher or some other woman came into the picture, Kate would lose all contact.

Kate stood and paced the room. Up until now she'd been trying to impede a relationship between Marcy and her family. She'd been wrong—so wrong. Now she could see that such an alliance could work to her benefit. The therapy sessions would provide private opportunities to talk with Marcy. And if Marcy had regular contact with Bruce and the kids, then maybe, at some future time, Marcy could help set up visits—from a distance.

She rubbed her upper arms to comfort herself and tried to speculate on how she could pull this off. As she closed her eyes, a pleasant smell caught Kate's attention. She opened her eyes and spied the piece of chocolate-covered toffee she'd left lying on its wrapper near the window. Even though it was raining outside, the glass window had magnified the surface temperature, and the milk chocolate was melting. *That's what I need: chocolate.* She hurried over, picked up the morsel, and bit down on the crunchy, buttery toffee. The bitterness she'd tasted moments ago disappeared.

The idea of promoting a relationship between Marcy and her family and the instant sugar high from the candy prompted her to swift action. She picked up the phone and punched the familiar sequence of Marcy's cell phone number. She tapped her foot, impatient to hear Marcy's voice. One ring, two, three, four. She cringed when she heard the too-familiar recording, "Hello. This is Marcy Ames. I'm sorry but I'm unavailable to answer the phone now. Please leave your name, number, and a short message, and I'll return your call as soon as possible."

She waited for the beep and then said, in her most pleading voice, "Marcy, I need to talk to you. Something important has come up."

"What's that, dear?" her mother asked as she and Kate's father entered the room.

"Oh, nothing," Kate said as she clumsily replaced the receiver. "I was just trying to reach Mrs. Ames, my physical therapist—to say good-bye."

"She's such a sweet woman. But you'll see her every week," her mom said as she reached over to give Kate a quick embrace and a peck on the cheek.

"Wasn't it Mrs. Ames who got you to perform in the hospital concert series?" her father asked as he picked up her suitcase.

Kate nodded.

"Gee, I wish you would have let us know sooner. We would have loved to have heard you," her mom said. "Everyone's talking about it. They say you have the voice of an opera star."

Kate grimaced. "I'm glad you guys weren't here. I would've been so nervous."

Her mom started to object, but before she could speak, a volunteer entered the room. The plump young woman pushing a wheelchair introduced herself as Amber. "Looks like you're all set to go home." She motioned to the wheelchair that she'd brought in with her. "Hospital rules. We're going to run you around back to avoid the media."

"Yes, we know," her father said. "I've made arrangements to pull the car up to the south wing. I'll sneak out to get the car."

Media—that was the last thing Kate wanted. Too much attention would ruin her chances of getting close to her children.

11:00 AM

Sneaking out of the hospital was a challenge. Two reporters were waiting at the side door with microphones and cameras. But Kate played dumb and kept her head down as Amber wheeled her to the car and her mother kept moving.

"Mrs. Craig, how do you feel about the death of the second transplant patient?" asked a brash, pushy woman with a microphone.

Donna simply opened the passenger door and slid in. Then Amber and John, Kate's dad, took over. John held the back door open and, with his other hand, shielded Kate's face from the cameras while Amber helped her into the back seat and shut the door. He walked to the driver's side, hopped in the car, and drove off without a single word to the reporters.

"How are you doing back there, Kate?" her father asked as he pulled onto the freeway.

"I'm okay." She sighed. "Thanks for your help with those reporters," she said, impressed at both her parents' poise and assertiveness.

"There will probably be a mob of them when we get to the house. We hired a security guard to keep them off our property," her mom said.

"So don't worry about the crowd," her dad echoed. "We'll take care of it. And we changed our home phone to an unlisted number to put an end to the nonstop phone calls. Your mom's cell phone and mine have caller ID so we can stay connected to our work and only answer the callers we know."

"Enough about security. We're going to get you enrolled in school," her mom said as she turned and smiled warmly at Kate.

"School?" Kate asked.

Her dad turned his head ten degrees but kept both eyes on the road. "We have a terrific teacher for you—a good friend of ours. Her name's Connie Wong. She'll come to the house two hours a day, Monday through Friday, starting tomorrow."

"And your voice instructor will come to the house twice a week—Mondays and Thursdays."

Sitting back, Kate pondered how drastically her life had changed. It had only been two months to the day—September 15—since everything had turned upside down. Back then she was Liz. Today she was Kate. Two months ago she was taking care of everyone. Today, people were taking care of her.

A little while later she glanced out the window and caught her breath. *We're less than a mile away from my old home.* She clutched her forearms, bent forward, and let out a long moan.

Her mother turned her head, her eyes narrowed in concern. "What's wrong, honey?"

"It's nothing—just a little pain—but it's passed now," she said in a low voice.

But the truth was that she yearned to grab the wheel and spin the car around, run up to her house, burst through the front door, and embrace her children. Then she would kiss her husband and . . .

She bit down hard on her bottom lip to keep from crying. The further they drove away from her former life, the easier it was to breathe.

They drove up Center Street, then Redwood Road, and up the hill. Two more turns and she saw the reporters. The block was lined with upscale homes, classy cars, and perfectly landscaped yards, but she could hardly see them through the crush of people and cameras. As they pulled into a long driveway, cameramen followed their every move and reporters shouted questions.

Kate caught a glimpse of her new house. It was large—three or four times the size of her old home. It was brick with a columned portico, double front doors with stained-glass side panels, and an attached three-car garage. The grounds were better than manicured—they were pedicured. But she could scarcely take it all in for the noise and crush of bodies.

The garage door opened, and her dad drove the Mercedes in. He pressed a button on the interior roof panel with his left hand as he turned off the motor with the other. The garage door descended and a light came on automatically. The garage was lined with custom shelving and cupboards. It was oversized—probably as large as the lower level of her Hayward home.

She gazed in awe. This was the type of house she had once lusted over.

Be careful what you wish for.

3:30 PM

Josh had successfully avoided the reporters outside his home by slipping behind his neighbor's trees and shrubbery until he was within sprinting distance of his front door. The security guard held back the reporters and opened the door for Josh.

He hurried inside and slammed the front door to make sure that everyone inside knew he was home. He was aware that today was the day his sister would be here. Now he'd be back to playing second base to the star pitcher.

"Hi! I'm home," he said as he swung his backpack off his shoulder and onto the floor in the entryway. He sauntered into the living room and glanced around. No one was there.

"How was school today, dear?" His mother's voice came from her in-home office.

He opened the door and peeked in. She was seated at her computer, working on some bookkeeping project for one of the few accounts she had kept over the years.

He pushed the door all the way open and entered. "Good. I aced the Spanish test and, well, everything's . . . fine."

His mom turned from her work and looked up at him. "There are fresh cookies in the kitchen. I'll be through with this in less than two hours, but I need to give this my undivided attention right now. I have to transmit the payroll to Acme Janitorial Services before five today." With that she smiled and turned back to her work.

Josh's mom had once owned a large CPA firm, A-Plus Accounting, with twelve employees. But that was before Kate's illness. After that, she sold her firm with the agreement that she could keep ten of the smaller business accounts. That way she stayed up on tax laws. Josh didn't understand all the ins and outs of her business, but he knew that most of the money she made went to Kate's care.

"Where's Dad?" Josh asked as he walked into the hallway.

"He's out back. There's something wrong with the awning. He's trying to repair it."

Josh nodded, walked from the room, and gently closed the door behind him. He went directly to the kitchen, opened the refrigerator, and took out the milk. He poured himself a large glass, selected the three fattest chocolate chip cookies from the plate, and bit into one. It was still warm.

He studied every inch of the kitchen—no sign of Kate. Maybe she hadn't come home. But if that was the case, why weren't his mom and dad upset? Why was everything so normal?

As he shoved the last half of the third cookie into his mouth and washed it down with milk, he heard a rustling sound behind him and jerked around.

"Did you like the cookies?" Kate asked.

There she was with a bicycle helmet on her head and no shoes, just socks. She wasn't quite as scary looking as the last time he'd seen her. Still, she wouldn't be winning any beauty contests.

"What's it to you?" he asked.

The gap between her front teeth seemed larger than he'd remembered. "I made them especially for you," she said, eyes smiling.

He stared at her and then at the plate of cookies. "You? No way!"

"Mom said she had a recipe for your favorite chocolate chip cookies. She said you liked them with walnuts, so I mixed up the batter and put them in the oven."

He turned his eyes from her and stared out the back window.

Confused, he muttered, "I'm going to help Dad." Then he turned and didn't look back.

4:30 PM

Kate spent the better part of an hour going through the clothes in her closet and trying them on. She had pushed the scene with her brother from her mind, knowing that she'd find a way to deal with him later. There had to be a way to break down that concrete wall of resentment. For now, she had other concerns.

She flopped on her bed, rolled over, and picked up the figurine of Sneezy from her nightstand. Apparently her bedroom was much as it had been six years ago before her near-fatal disease. It was obviously meant for a five-year-old, not an eleven-year-old: pink and white walls, framed posters of Tinkerbell, and a collection of Disney figurines. Even her daughter, Megan, had outgrown this décor.

Megan was her number one challenge.

Kate tiptoed out of her room and down the hall to the kitchen. No one was there, so she walked over to the built-in desk and removed the walk-around phone. She stepped into the walk-in pantry, turned on the light, and closed the door. For the second time today, she punched in Marcy's phone number.

One ring, two, three. Finally, Marcy picked up.

"Marcy, it's Kate," she whispered into the receiver, cupping the mouthpiece close to her face.

"Kate. You're home. How do you like it?" Marcy asked.

"Oh, it's beautiful. But that's not why I called."

"What's up?" Marcy asked.

"I've been considering what you said about Miss Andrews. I . . . I'm worried about Megan trying to push her on Bruce."

"Oh? So what do you want me to do?" Marcy asked, her words clipped.

Kate tried to think of the right words. "I need your help. I was wondering if you would mind calling Bruce and inviting him and the kids—along with your daughter, of course—to go someplace you might all enjoy." Kate spoke quickly, taking small breaths.

"Why do you want me to do that?" Marcy asked.

"I thought maybe Megan would become less enchanted with Miss Andrews and perhaps refocus her attention on . . . you." There, she'd said it.

"Why me?" Marcy asked.

Kate heard the tightness in Marcy's voice. "You could keep me apprised of what's going on. Please do this for me."

Marcy hesitated. "Really?"

"And I can help you win them over."

A long pause followed. "Please," she said holding the word longer than she meant to. Another long pause ensued.

"All right," Marcy finally conceded. Then she added, "But I'll have to ask them out for either this coming Sunday or the first Sunday in December. A week from Sunday is part of the Thanksgiving weekend, and Adriana and I already have plans."

Kate breathed a sigh of relief. "Try for this coming Sunday."

"Okay. But won't he think I'm being forward? And what will your friends think?"

"It'll just be a platonic relationship. Right?" Kate asked.

"Of course."

"Oh, and I won't be able to call you often, but we can talk when I'm at the hospital for my weekly appointments. Okay?"

"Sure," Marcy said.

"Great, I have to go now. I'll see you on Tuesday. Bye." Kate smiled hesitantly as she hung up the phone, but as soon as she placed the receiver back in its nest, she massaged her stomach to quiet the mounting nausea.

Then she turned off the light, opened the pantry door, and peeked around—all clear. She returned the phone to its base and silently made her way back to her bedroom.

At least she had a plan in place to keep in touch with her family. And she would start her tutoring tomorrow—Friday.

Yes, tomorrow will be better.

4:35 PM

Josh finished half of his algebra homework and put down his pencil. His parents had confiscated his cell phone and removed his laptop, but he still had the landline. Angie had given him her cell phone number at school, and he wanted to call her. He picked up the receiver and started to press the number she'd written on the scrap of paper but then he heard a noise.

He put his hand over the mouthpiece and listened. Kate. "Try for this coming Sunday."

Then another female voice said, "Okay. But won't he think I'm being forward? And what's more, what will your friends think?"

"It'll just be a platonic relationship. Right?"

He listened to the rest of the conversation and frowned. *Friends? What friends? Platonic relationships?* Where had Kate learned a word like that?

Josh grabbed his dictionary and rifled through the pages, *M . . . N . . . O . . . P.* "Platonic." He read the definition and shook his head.

"A relationship without sexual desire."

Sexual desire?

4:40 PM

Marcy amazed herself at the stealth that she'd used to get Kate's approval; no, not just approval, but encouragement, in pursuing Bruce. She had been sneaky, making it appear that Miss Andrews was "a catch." But she hadn't told a single lie. She'd simply left out a few facts.

She swallowed back a thrill of excitement, which was quickly followed by a tremor of guilt. *What am I doing? This is Liz's husband. He's married . . . no, a widower. Liz is dead . . . No, she's an eleven-year-old.*

Marcy warred over what to do next, but the truth was that she liked Bruce, and she liked his children. And she and Adriana needed something more in their lives. Someone who could be there for them—love them.

As much as Marcy wished it otherwise, the hourglass had turned and there was no going back. She closed her eyes and took a deep breath, then slowly opened them. Not only would she accept Bruce's invitation to the 49ers game, she would invite Bruce and his kids out Sunday—all of this with Kate's blessing.

Both she and Adriana loved the Exploratorium. They'd been there countless times and knew the locations of the most fun exhibits. Marcy felt confident that if she played it well, Megan would soon approve of her.

Marcy took a sip of her Earl Grey tea and thought about Mark. He was such a sweet child. She wouldn't have to work at winning him over. Plus, he and Adriana had already become fast friends. But Megan and Adriana were a different matter. They hadn't hit it off well.

Marcy put the cup down, sat back in her chair, and rotated her shoulders. What could she do to break down the wall Megan was building? She had to make this outing a success.

The Exploratorium offered a good setting. For one, it would be in Marcy's territory. Secondly, the exhibits were interactive and several required partners. She'd make sure the two girls were coupled up. Even the Grinch couldn't hold a grudge there.

She wanted to call Bruce now, but she knew he'd be at work. He put the kids to bed at eight-thirty, so by nine, he should be free.

This would be a whole new venture for her. She'd never called a man before to ask for a date. *What will I say?* But then she thought of Liz and buried her face in her hands.

chapter twenty

Sunday, November 18, 11:00 AM

Megan tossed her head and stuck out her bottom lip as she undid her seatbelt and slid across the backseat to exit the car after her brother.

She was suspicious of this outing. Both her dad and brother looked at Marcy like she was a Snickers bar. And she especially didn't like that stuck-up Adriana.

Stupid "esploratum," or whatever it was.

Although it was sunny, the cool air and breeze caused her to pull her sweater tightly around her. She fastened her sweater, and when she came to the button, she remembered how Mrs. Thayer had taught her to sew her missing button back on. She wished she were with Mrs. Thayer now, practicing her gymnastics instead of spending the day at some dumb science place with people she didn't even like.

She took in a deep breath and caught the faint taste of salt, but kept her head down.

"Look at the swans, Megan!" her brother shouted.

Megan looked up to see Mark running toward a small lake. She caught her breath and stared at the fairytale scene. The lake was full of swans, ducks, and other birds. The wind rippled the surface of the lake, and it sparkled like a million diamonds beneath the sun. A water fountain spouted upward from the lake and cascaded down a wall into it. On the far side of the lake stood a tall round structure with long orangish-pink columns and statues of women at the top. They looked as though they were holding up the large domed roof. Behind the round structure was a building that seemed to stretch for a city block.

Megan looked from one end of the grounds to the other. It was beautiful. "Is this it, Daddy?" she asked as she turned toward him and shaded her eyes with her hand.

"Yes, Megan, the jewel of San Francisco. The Palace of Fine Arts—built for a worldwide expo."

Megan screwed up her face. "Palace of Art? I thought it was a science thing."

That's what it is now. But when it was built back in 1915, it held hundreds of paintings, sculptures, and other art, brought here from many countries."

"Megan, hurry up." Mark jumped up and down at the shoreline of the lake and motioned to Megan. "You gotta see this."

Megan took her father's hand and pulled him to the side of the lake where people were feeding popcorn to black and white swans and different colored ducks. As Megan and her dad walked over to Mark, the woman and young girl who were feeding the ducks and swans turned toward them.

"Would you like to feed them?" the woman asked as she held out a microwaved bag of popcorn.

Marcy and Adriana were standing there smiling. Megan hadn't recognized them before Marcy spoke. She'd never seen Adriana in regular clothes, just that silly frog costume at the party. Marcy was wearing jeans and a blue sweater, and her hair was pulled back in a ponytail—different from the other times Megan had seen her.

Mark lost no time. He practically leaped to Marcy's side. "Marcy. Adriana. Yeah, you're here!" he exclaimed. "Can I feed the ducks?"

"Of course, Mark." Marcy held out the bag and Mark reached in and brought out a handful of popcorn. He grinned at her, knelt down, and held out his hand. A duck swam over and waddled up the shore. At first it seemed scared. Then it took two quick steps toward him and seized the morsels. It backed up, jiggled its head, and gobbled the food.

"Want some?" Adriana asked.

Megan cringed. She wanted to say yes, but instead she shook her head.

"Aw, come on," Mark said as he got up and dug his hand deep into Marcy's bag again. "It's fun!"

Megan rolled her eyes, then let out a loud sigh and muttered, "Oh, all right."

Megan stared as Adriana waltzed around her mother and moved over to her side. "You go ahead. Take this," she said as she handed her the half-eaten bag of popcorn. "We've been here for a while. Your turn now."

After a moment's hesitation, Megan let go of her father's hand and snatched the bag. "Okay," she said.

"You ever been here before?" Adriana asked.

Megan hunched her shoulders in reply, stooped, and held out the popcorn to a little brown speckled duck. "We've been to Candlestick Park in San Francisco before, but not here."

Screwing up her face, Adriana said, "Candlestick Park? What's that?"

"You don't know?" Megan asked, eyes wide. "That's where the 49ers play football."

Adriana turned downcast eyes. "Maybe I've never been to Candlestick Park, but I bet you'll like the Exploratorium better. It's our favorite place."

"Better than Disneyland?" Megan asked.

"Of course not. Nothing is better than Disneyland." Adriana put her hands on her hips. "But this is the best place in San Francisco. We'll have so much fun."

Megan blinked to avoid the bright sunlight and dumped the remaining popcorn in the water, bringing all the ducks and swans to the goodies like paper clips to a magnet. Crushing the empty bag, Megan ran to a trash can and deposited the litter. She yelled over her shoulder, "Come on, you guys. What are we waiting for?"

1:00 PM

As they exited Applebees after church, Kate noticed that Josh was sidling her way. Her parents were a good twenty feet ahead of them. For three days now, Kate had felt like she'd been on a balance beam—teetering on the edge. Minutes after she'd ended her phone conversation with Marcy and had returned to her bedroom, Josh knocked on her door. He entered before she could even say, "Come in."

"You just got off the phone, didn't you?" He squinted his eyes and cocked his head. "I heard you talking to some woman. What was that all about?"

Kate recoiled. How much of her conversation with Marcy had Josh actually heard?

"So who's the lady?" he asked. "And why were you talking to her about 'platonic relationships'?"

At first she couldn't respond. Her blurred vision made him look like a phantom as she tried to focus both her vision and her attention.

"Do you always listen in on private conversations?" she asked. "And who said you could come into my room? I don't remember inviting you."

Josh hesitated for only a second. "I wasn't snooping, just trying to call a friend. But you were on the line. What are you up to?"

Shifting tactics, Kate said in as nonchalant a voice as possible, "I . . . I made lots of friends at the hospital. Unlike you, I don't have any friends here in Castro Valley." She sucked her bottom lip and released it with a popping sound. "I was hoping we could be friends," she said, looking up at Josh.

"Don't change the subject, sis. You're hiding something, aren't you?" His voice was so low it was almost a whisper. "How do you even know what 'platonic' means? You're four years younger than me."

Kate flinched. "I . . . I heard it on TV. The meaning seemed self-evident."

"Self-evident—there's another unlikely word."

Kate felt caught in a vice. She was sure that the more she said, the worse it would get. Finally, in a fit of confusion she said, "You don't know anything." Then she pointed to the door. "Just get out."

Josh stormed out and slammed the door.

From that moment on, she had kept running her conversation with Marcy over and over in her mind, trying to create scenarios that she could present to Josh to assuage his suspicions.

For the past three days, Josh had pressed her for answers and threatened to tell their parents about the conversation. Every time he pushed, she tried, without success, to convince him that the phone exchange had been harmless—just a girl talking to an older friend.

Now, walking toward the family's Mercedes, Josh glanced at their parents and held Kate back. He whispered an ultimatum. "This is your last chance, Kate. Either tell me what's going on or I'm going to go tell Mom and Dad."

Kate halted, arms akimbo and said, "Go ahead and tell Mom and Dad. I don't care. Besides, what do you think they'll do to me, spank me?"

He stared back, red-faced as he hastened his steps, abandoning her side and joining their parents. Kate watched him through hazy vision. She could tell that he was whispering something to them, but she couldn't hear. A chill ran through her. Even though she couldn't see clearly, she intuited that Josh was glaring at her.

What would she say to her parents if he told them? She wasn't sure. But she knew with certainty that she'd have to do a great deal more than bake batches of chocolate chip cookies if she ever wanted her brother to like her.

5:00 PM

Driving home from San Francisco, Bruce sneaked a peek at his kids through his rearview mirror, but he couldn't see their heads. He turned and glanced over his shoulder and understood why the car was so quiet. Both Mark and Megan were sound asleep in the backseat and were using each other as pillows.

He placed his right arm on the center armrest and steered the car with his left as he hummed. Without a doubt, this was one of the most enjoyable days he'd spent in weeks. He broke into a wide grin as he thought about his kids. Megan had dropped her guard and by the end of the afternoon, both she and Adriana were giggling and whispering young girl secrets. The effect on Megan was transformational. She'd gone from sullen and withdrawn to her old self: energetic, talkative, or as Liz used to say, "a fart in a skillet." And Mark seemed absolutely smitten by Marcy. He'd walked hand in hand with her and looked at her adoringly with star-struck eyes. *Boy's got good taste—takes after his dad.*

Bruce smiled to himself. It wasn't just his kids who had enjoyed the many exhibits at the Exploratorium. The place was amazing. And Marcy's actions had moved him. She'd been graceful and magnanimous, seeming as interested in the needs and concerns of his children as her own daughter.

Although he'd acted as though he and Marcy were just friends, he had to admit that he felt an undeniable attraction to the woman. He wanted more—so much more. But he knew it was unthinkable, especially so soon after Liz's death. The familiar heaviness returned when he thought of Liz, but he fought back the shadows and forced himself to focus on the present.

He had to admit he was thrilled that Marcy had accepted his invitation to the 49ers' game next month. It had brought him out of the fog he'd been in for the past several weeks. Between now and then, he'd refrain from calling her. Perhaps he would email her once or twice, but he'd hold off on calling her until a week before the game. Then he'd call just to confirm the date and give her details about the tailgate party plans.

"Date." *Well, that's what it is.* The mere thought of it both frightened and excited him.

6:00 PM

Charles Rubenstein couldn't help feeling sorry for Dr. Jamison as he reviewed the recent tapes of the doctor on his computer screen. In Charles's opinion, the doctor was being unfairly vilified. But the public was clamoring for news about the brain transplant and death of Brian Jorgensen. And Brian's young wife and baby son were featured on one talk show after another. More important, Charles knew that he had established himself as the nation's brain transplant reporter, and as such, couldn't ignore the public's cry for more details.

Exhausted by the late nights, he closed his eyes for a moment. He was poised and ready to give the viewing public their due, but the rants and ravings of TULOG and its activists were unnerving. It was damaging enough that they were asking Congress to enact a law to ban future brain transplants, but their demand that Jamison be charged with murder was ridiculous.

Still, he couldn't defend Jamison on camera. He had to objectively report what was happening. His best opportunity to help Jamison would be to provide balanced interviews. Perhaps he should resurrect

Kate Craig's case—feature the miracle of her rebirth. That way he could counter the mob.

Charles cringed as he studied the sudden deterioration of the once-proud Dr. Jamison. He viewed recent pictures from different news programs and could see the strain that the negative media coverage and angry demonstrations had taken on the doctor. The poor man looked beaten. His usual straight posture and self-confidence were gone. He walked stooped, seemed to drag his feet. His complexion was sallow, and the dark circles under his eyes were deepening by the day. He was coming undone before Charles's eyes.

Drumming his fingernails on the arm of his chair, Charles leaned back. He rubbed his temples to relieve the pressure. It didn't take a brain surgeon to interpret the results of recent polls. They indicated that the public felt that the experimental surgery, if performed as a last hope, should not be denied. But the TULOG activists were so vocal and persistent that their minority voices were gaining momentum. They were even threatening to send hundreds of their demonstrators to Norway to block Jamison's acceptance of the Nobel Prize, an event that should have been the highlight of the man's long, illustrious career.

Charles yawned loudly. There wasn't much time left between now and December tenth, the date of the Nobel presentation. If he wanted to help Jamison, it would have to be soon. Perhaps with good research, he could pull together a documentary on past medical procedures that groups had once labeled "sinful" but that were so commonplace today that denying them would be considered "criminal."

He began to sketch out the documentary. Perhaps at the end of the broadcast he could ask viewers to vote on whether the brain transplant procedure should be banned—except he couldn't do that because TULOG would just send a hundred responses per person.

I'll do something, but I won't jeopardize my family or career.

chapter twenty-one

Tuesday, November 20, 10:00 AM

The last two days had been awful for Kate. Josh's conversation with their mom and dad had almost unraveled her plans. Josh revealed, word-for-word, what he'd overheard between her and "the woman on the phone." Her mom and dad were visibly shaken. They had demanded to know who she'd been talking to. She hated to lie to them. But she couldn't lose her relationship with Marcy. She felt a sharp stabbing pain in the small of her back as she made something up. "I was talking with one of the volunteers—a girl named Brandi. She's a teenager, a friend of mine."

"I see. And just what was this conversation about?" her mother asked.

"Nothing, really. Brandi has this guy friend. He invited her to a football game on Sunday. She wasn't sure whether she should go. I said she should and told her not to worry about what other people say. That's all it was. Honest." The last word stuck in her throat.

Her father looked at her with one eyebrow raised.

Since then, Kate had sensed that both her mom and dad were concerned. Or was it distrust? At the same time, Josh seemed pleased with himself. Every chance he got he made some snide remark or uttered the phrase "platonic relationship." Her only response to his taunts was to shrug her shoulders.

Then last Tuesday when she returned to Stanford for therapy and tests, her mom stayed glued to her side. It was impossible for her to talk with Marcy about the outing or to make additional plans. Luckily, Marcy took her cue from Kate and kept all conversation appropriate to the therapy.

"Everything's going as planned," Marcy said as she tested Kate's range of motion and agility. "We're right on schedule."

"I'm glad to hear that. So, did you have a nice weekend?" Kate asked.

"Oh, yes. I took my daughter and three of her friends to the Exploratorium," Marcy replied.

"Really? What's the Exploratorium?" Kate asked, covering up her pleasure at Marcy's response.

Marcy went on to describe the exhibits, but Kate barely listened; she already had the information she came for. Nothing Josh could do or say could take that away. Maybe next Tuesday she would have some time alone with Marcy and be able to find out more.

But tomorrow was Thanksgiving Day, and their destination was her grandparents' home in Ben Lomond.

chapter twenty-two

Thursday, November 22, Thanksgiving Day

It was nearly a two-hour drive from Castro Valley to Ben Lomond. Until two days ago, Kate had never even heard of the small hamlet nestled in the Santa Cruz Mountains. But according to her parents, she'd been going there for family gatherings every year, except last year when she was too ill to travel.

During the ride from Castro Valley, she learned that Grandma and Grandpa Kelly, her maternal grandparents, had selected the site on Love Creek Road some forty years ago. Her grandfather had single-handedly built a bridge across the crawdad-filled creek, and a two-story house as well as an immense deck that spanned the entire front of the building.

As they drove down the tree-lined lane and turned to go over the bridge, Kate held her breath.

Though her eyesight was still problematic, she could discern every shade of green imaginable—the trees, the dark ivy climbing up the evergreens, the ferns, and the house—all silhouetted against a gray-blue fall sky.

As they exited the Mercedes, a blond dog wagged its tail and ran up to Kate, then stopped and bared its teeth. Kate drew back.

"That's Corky's way of greeting you," her mother said. "She's not growling—just smiling."

Kate had to laugh. Indeed, the dog's front lip was lifted in a silly grin, displaying four front teeth. Kate bent down and stroked the ridiculous creature. At that moment an elderly couple came onto the deck and waved hello.

Her grandparents stepped down the few stairs from the deck and walked briskly over to them, with a ready embrace and an offer to help carry the feast that Kate and her mother had prepared.

The elderly woman embraced and kissed Josh. He responded sheepishly, but he hugged and kissed her in return. The woman then turned to Kate, took Kate's face in her hands, and asked, as a tear of joy streaked down her face, "Did you know that your grandpa and I were at the hospital every day from the date of your surgery until you regained consciousness?"

"Mom and Dad told me."

"You were in the ICU and only a limited number of family members were permitted. But we were there, sweetie. We were there."

Acceptance, love—those were the emotions that caused a lump to rise in Kate's throat. Grandma and Grandpa Kelly were family. She knew it—felt it.

Grandma planted a kiss on Kate's cheek and then went to the trunk and lifted out the small lightweight cooler that contained a fresh garden salad. Kate adjusted her helmet as she bent toward the trunk to pick up the basket of cookies that she and her mom had made. Her grandfather came over and took the green bean casserole in one arm while offering Kate his other. With a strong arm, he led her up the stairs. "It's so good to have you here, darlin'. And you're looking so well. It's what we've prayed for, every day." As they reached the top of the stairs, he gently squeezed her arm and then let go and opened the front door. Corky brushed by and ran in first.

As Kate entered the cozy house, the unmistakable smell of roasting turkey and baked bread wafted through the room. She stood at the doorway, her mouth open. The pine-paneled living room was cavernous, and at the far end stood a majestic eight-foot-tall stone fireplace with a blazing fire that warmed the room. Wood-carved words, so delicate they looked like lace, were framed and hanging over the fireplace. It was the Lord's Prayer. "That's beautiful."

"I carved it myself," Grandpa said. "Took me two years."

Josh nudged her and pointed to a cuckoo clock hanging over a piano. "He carved that too."

Kate looked at her grandpa in wonder and then scanned the room. This house was a little piece of heaven tucked in the corner of a very complicated world. If she had her way, she'd stay here forever. It was a place of healing—a house of love and peace.

The window seats under the two corner windows were big enough to serve as extra beds and looked inviting with their large paisley-printed cushions. There were three mismatched sofas, each with a crocheted afghan, plus several chairs, two rockers, shelves of books, and lots of musical instruments. There were so many details that spelled out their lifetimes of caring. But something was missing. At first she couldn't put her finger on it. Then it struck her.

"Gramma, Gramps, don't you have a TV?" she asked.

"It's downstairs in the basement," Grandma replied with a sigh. "We prefer to entertain guests, read, and play music."

Kate frowned at this foreign idea.

"Come, put those cookies on the dining sideboard," her mom said, pointing to the kitchen.

Kate followed her mother. At the far end of the kitchen/dining room was a long table with a dozen chairs. The dining area was lined with windows, and the far end had a glass-paneled door leading outside to a patio. Just then, she heard another car pull up. She looked out the windows and saw a couple with three children get out of their SUV.

"Karen, Allen, and the grandchildren are here," Grandma announced.

From the window Kate saw the front door fly open and the smiling dog leap out to offer her special welcome as the rest of the family followed behind.

I have more family. Family gatherings had been sad affairs for Liz with her mother gone.

More baskets, bowls, and platters of food were brought in. Kate became "reacquainted" with her Aunt Karen, Uncle Allen, and cousins: Rebecca, age ten; Erin, eight; and Nick, five. Although the older cousins stared quietly at Kate and made her feel uncomfortable, little Nick said, "Why ya wearing your bicycle helmet in the house?"

Kate pointed to her head. "I had an operation and I have to wear this until my next surgery."

"When is that?" Nick asked.

"If everything goes well, on Monday."

Nick scrunched his face and narrowed his eyes. "Aren't you scared?"

"A little. But I'm looking forward to getting rid of this helmet."

Nick shrugged and Grandma ruffled Nick's red hair as she walked over to the piano. She sat on the bench and motioned to Gramps, who picked up a guitar from the stand and sat next to her. "How about a little sing-along?" she asked.

Grandma handed Kate a book full of the words to popular oldies. Kate recognized all of them, but pretended she'd never heard them before.

"I play the tambourine," Nick said, then tapped it against his leg.

"I'll play the wooden spoons," Erin chirped.

Rebecca chose a ukulele, and Kate's mom picked up a mandolin. All three began tuning their instruments as Grandma struck notes on the piano. Josh picked up a set of bongo drums and started pounding out a rhythm. Uncle Allen, her mother's brother, opened up a set of harmonicas while Kate grabbed a maraca from the top of the piano.

When they began singing, she heard Josh add his strong tenor voice to the family choir. It was Kate's first ray of hope for a possible bond with her brother.

5:45 PM

As Charles helped his mother and sister place the last of the leftovers from the prime rib dinner in the fridge and clean up, he felt a pang of anxiety. He was his own worst critic. Still, he hoped his family would find tonight's special primetime production, "A Millennium of Miracles" worthy of him and that he could watch it with them without becoming ill. He'd worked eighteen hours a day for the last two days and used every resource and expert available to develop a ninety-minute documentary that tracked the history of medical science: the horrors, the successes, the obstacles, and the failures. It was objective. It was honest. And it was his creation.

He closed his eyes and tried to remember all the famous physicians and scientists who had contributed to present-day knowledge and capabilities. He depicted the years of sacrifice that were spent to cure the suffering of others. He'd had no idea of the plight of early physicians—how many difficulties they'd had to overcome: grave robbing to study anatomy; Maria Montessori, the first female physician in Italy, conducting her university lab work on cadavers at night, because it was inappropriate for a woman to work on naked bodies in the same laboratory as men; Jonas Salk, who spent eight long years developing the polio vaccine and tenaciously worked into his seventies searching for a cure for AIDS; Norman E. Shumway, pioneer cardiac surgeon and the first doctor to successfully perform an open-heart transplant operation in the US and who persevered even though few patients survived for long in the early days and other surgeons abandoned the procedure altogether.

"Charles, what are you doing?" his mother asked, tapping him on the back.

His head snapped up. Here he was standing in front of the refrigerator with the door open and the appliance's motor groaning. He closed the door. "I guess I was on Mars."

"I've never seen you so nervous," his sister said as she poured gel in the dishwasher's cup, closed the door, and hit the start button.

"You're right." He walked to the wine rack and withdrew a bottle of Seven Deadly Zins and studied the label. "How about a glass of vino?"

"I'm so stuffed I couldn't eat or drink another thing." His mother patted her stomach.

"Sis?"

"You go ahead. You're the one who needs it."

Charles stared at the bottle intently and then put it back. Instead, he walked to the cupboard and surveyed his options.

"You've put so much of yourself into this project," his mother said, taking off her apron and hanging it on a hook inside the pantry door. "We're both so proud of you."

"Little bit prejudiced, aren't you?" He smiled and then turned to study his mother. She looked better than she had in years. He credited her improved health to his current career success. They were finally meeting all their expenses. He hoped tonight's performance would be another step in a long and prosperous career, one that would profit his mother and sister as well as himself.

"Let's go into the living room and get ready for your big show," his mother said.

With a nod, he followed his sister and mother into the room and sat at the far end of the sofa. He removed his shoes, and placed the Pettit point ottoman that his paternal grandparents had made in front of him. His father had been so proud of it, often pointing at it and bragging about how his father had built the base and carved the mahogany legs and his mother had sewn the beautiful rose design. Besides his sister and himself, that ottoman was all that remained of his father's family. And as Charles placed his feet on the precious relic, he hoped that he'd inherited just a smidgen of their creativity and that someday, years from now, someone would look at what he had done and feel inspired.

7:28 PM

Jamison sat squeezing Inna's hand as the last credits for the cable special flashed across the screen.

"I don't understand. Why did that reporter pretend to be your friend and then ignore you in this special?" Inna asked with an inquisitive look that quickly turned to hurt.

He pressed the power button on the remote to turn off the TV. "No, my dear, don't you see? He showed how every great researcher and scientist has been challenged—some even tortured and killed for their discoveries." He felt a heavy burden lift off his shoulders. He knew now that he couldn't stop, couldn't let the naysayers win.

"You think he did this to help you?" Inna asked.

"I do. I've been such a fool. There was nothing new in it, nothing I didn't know, but now millions of others know too. It was a masterpiece and I owe him a note of thanks."

"Oh, that reminds me," Inna said as she handed him a small cream-colored envelope. "This came for you yesterday."

Jamison looked at the handwritten return address, "Mr. And Mrs. John Craig." He paused for a moment and then carefully lifted the sealed flap and withdrew the small card. He read it out loud to his wife.

Dear Dr. Jamison,

There are no words to express our heartfelt thanks for all that you have done to restore our daughter to us. At this time last year we held little hope that Kate would be alive for another Thanksgiving. There is no greater gift to parents than to restore a lost child to them. Thank you for her life.

Yours truly,

John and Donna Craig

PS: Congratulations on the Nobel Prize. No one deserves it more!

Jamison looked up at his wife and saw that her brown eyes shimmered with moisture and her bottom lip trembled. "That is so sweet," she said in a choked voice. "And they're right. She wouldn't be alive today if it weren't for you."

"Thank you for standing with me," he said as he wrapped his arms around her and tenderly kissed the tip of her nose.

He knew now what he had to do. Kate was the answer. There was something different about her—something special that had made her survive when Brian, who was physically stronger, died. What was it? He would not, could not, rest until he had the answer.

Yes, the Craigs were right. He was responsible for Kate's new life. But he needed more than gratitude from them: he needed unfettered access to Kate.

chapter twenty-three

Tuesday, December 2, 2:30 PM

Muted sounds pulled Kate out of a dark abyss. Her head throbbed. She blinked and squinted at the glaring rays of the sun—no, not the sun, just a bright light fixture. Several days had passed since Thanksgiving, and she was back in the hospital after her surgery. She'd been dreaming about Josh. He had been shaking her, telling her he knew the truth about her. *The truth.* No one could ever know the truth.

Still groggy, she tilted her head toward her mother's familiar fragrance and heard her soft voice. It seemed to come from slightly above Kate.

She craned her head and looked at her mother. "Am I still alive?"

"Very much alive. And you'll be happy to know that yesterday's surgery went well."

"Yesterday? You mean I've been asleep for a day?"

"You've been in and out of consciousness now for the last twenty-four hours. Don't you remember? Dr. Jamison said it would be like this."

"Oh, yeah. It's just strange losing a whole day," she said feeling a strain in her throat.

Her mother rubbed her hand. "You're doing great. By tomorrow they'll move you out of the ICU and into the Surgery Care Unit. Then, in a couple of days, you'll be ready for home."

Kate could feel her mother's warm breath on her ear, and her smile was heartwarming. Donna bent over and planted a soft kiss on her cheek. Kate choked out a combination of a laugh and whimper in the same breath. She couldn't stop shaking. She lifted her hand to her head. It felt sore but solid. And the two months' worth of hair growth was still intact. *Thank you, God.*

She remembered how excited she'd been when Dr. Jamison had told her that the prep routine for her skull replacement surgery wouldn't include shaving her head. It had been bad enough to have a distorted head, but adding baldness to the equation had multiplied the hideous effects. Now she had a solid crown topped with short dark curls.

A nurse walked over to Kate's bedside and touched Donna on the shoulder. "Sorry, Mrs. Craig," she said. "I'll have to ask you to leave now. She's scheduled for some tests."

Donna nodded in acknowledgment.

"You can come back in an hour," the nurse said as she adjusted the flow of Kate's IV. "By then she should be sitting up, ready to carry on a more coherent conversation with you and your husband."

Kate was still sleepy, but her energies were fully focused on the people around her.

"I understand." Her mother sighed as she squeezed Kate's shoulder. Then she rose from the chair. "We'll see you in an hour, hon. Do whatever the doctors say."

"I will," Kate murmured with a weak smile. She looked at the nurse and added, "You guys do your best. I'm expected home in a few days."

The last words came out in a rasp. Her throat was sore—probably from the tube they'd put down her throat during surgery to keep her from swallowing her tongue or closing off her breathing passage. In any case, the sore throat was a small price to pay for a hard head. She couldn't wait to dispose of the pink Barbie helmet. Maybe she'd hold a special service and bury it.

"Any plans to honor us with a song or two at the next concert?" the familiar-looking nurse asked.

Kate shook her head. "My throat is sore. I feel like I swallowed a porcupine."

"Porcupine, huh?" Dr. Jamison had entered the room so quietly that Kate hadn't seen him until she heard his voice a few feet from her side.

Kate felt a warm, welcoming sensation. Her opinion about the doctor had changed. Were it not for him, both Kate and Liz would be dead. Now, part of both of them lived.

"It's nothing. Besides," she said, touching her scalp, "my head feels like a real one." The words came out in a whisper. To make up for it, she flashed the biggest smile she could manage under the circumstance.

He patted her hand.

"I'm sorry . . . about Brian," she whispered. "I know you did your best. Those stupid protesters . . . from the Dark Ages."

Dr. Jamison looked at her quizzically. "And what do you know about the Dark Ages?" he asked, turning his head to one side and studying her face.

The realization of what she'd said acted like a splash of cold water across her face. She forced herself to be more alert, but she was having a tough time thinking. "History class," she lied.

Through narrow slits, she watched intently as Dr. Jamison sucked in his bottom lip and looked at her as though he was dissecting a specimen.

"History class?" he asked, brow furled.

"Mrs. Wong comes to the house a couple of hours every day." Her voice began to fade but, in spite of the pain, she said, "Maybe someday I can go to a regular school." How dumb, trying to cover up one lie with another. She was sure he could see right through her.

"You'd better save your voice—sounds like it's getting worse," he said as he bent over and listened to her heart through his stethoscope. "Now, take in a deep breath and hold it."

She took his advice and kept her mouth shut. When would she learn?

3:15 PM

Jamison sat back in his office chair, the fingers of his hands locked together, and held to his chin as though in prayer. But he wasn't praying. He was thinking. He knew that Kate's new brain retained the life skills of its prior owner, but there was something too mature about the way she talked, the way she behaved. It wasn't just reading, writing, and talking. It was the way she looked at him and the way she phrased her words. Her expressions—even her body language didn't fit that of an eleven-year-old. Her body memory wasn't as influential as he had expected. The only outward sign of body memory was Kate's quick bonding with her mother. He had observed their interactions. They weren't just from mother to daughter. They were from daughter to mother too. And from early animal experiments, he knew that body memory was a strong influence. After studying animal reactions, both he and his surgical team had assumed that if Kate survived the transplant, within two or three weeks she would adapt to her family and her body's age.

Jamison drummed his fingers on his desk. A couple of hours ago, when she first awoke from the skull replacement surgery, her actions were appropriate for any patient in recovery. But within minutes she was saying things and doing things that were years beyond her age.

Jamison clasped his hands behind his head and stretched. He needed to know more before the next surgery to avoid another repeat of Brian. There was something uncanny about her actions—something unnervingly mature.

Scooting his chair closer to his desk, he brought up Kate's computer file and typed in an order for additional psychological testing. Maybe by the time he returned from Stockholm, additional information would be available to him—info that might help him solve the riddle.

3:30 PM

Almost as soon as the MRI was completed and Kate was returned to her room, her mom and dad came walking in. Her dad was casually dressed in a blue plaid Pendleton shirt—sleeves rolled up—and a pair of deeply creased tan trousers. He was carrying a bouquet of multicolored balloons in one hand, and his other arm was linked together with her mom's. They both had broad grins on their faces and a bounce in their steps. Hope surged through Kate. She felt as though life was on her side again.

"Hi, sweetheart," her father said. "How's my gal?"

"Got a splitting headache. Other than that, I'm glad it's over . . .

and I can't wait to go home again." She pressed the remote control to bring the head of the bed upward.

Her father walked to her side, bent over, and kissed her on the forehead. "You look great." He set the weighted balloon bouquet on her side table and then lightly brushed her short curls with a finger. He seemed to glow when he looked at her. It was the first time Kate felt a real parent-child connection with her dad. She knew then that he loved her and that he was an important factor in her life—so different from her other father. "You have no idea how much you look like your mother," he said as he glanced over at his wife. "The most beautiful woman in the world."

Kate's mother blushed.

"I want to see. Help me raise the lid on the tray so I can see myself in the mirror," Kate said, excitement filling her voice.

"Sure, hon. Here, let me lift it," her mother said.

Kate held her breath and faced the open lid, her heart beating so fast she thought she might pass out. A cold chill ran up her legs, through her chest, and then straight through the back of her head.

Suddenly, someone turned off the lights. "What's happening?" Kate asked. "Why is it dark in here?"

"Kate, the lights are on," her mother said.

Gasping, Kate blinked and moved her eyes from side to side—but there was only darkness. "No!" she shouted. "Not my eyes. Oh, please, not that." A freezing bottomless pit seemed to open up and swallow her, pulling her downward.

Someone was shouting. People were moving. Someone was touching her. But all she could do was thrash about. A high-pitched scream escaped her lips and soon morphed into a moan.

Strong hands gripped her and she felt a prick on her upper arm. She struggled, but to no avail. Then a floating sensation took her to another dimension where she no longer cared.

4:00 PM

Josh cursed and threw his jacket onto his bed.

The phone had been ringing when he entered the house and when he'd answered it, his mother was crying. "Kate's blind," she said, her words choked. "They think something went wrong with the surgery."

"Mom, don't cry. Please don't cry."

He heard his father's strained voice in the background and then on the phone. "We may be late getting home. Will you be okay?"

Even before the phone conversation was over, guilt shot through him. He'd been such a jerk and now this. After they hung up, he swallowed back guilty tears and fell on his bed. He beat his clenched fists into his pillow. *Not blind. No, not that.*

He didn't know how long he stayed there, curled up in a ball. But he wished . . . prayed for someone who might understand his feelings. Maybe he didn't like his sister, but he didn't want her to be blind. That was the most terrible of all possible outcomes. Hot tears coursed down his cheeks. He had wished her dead. Now she had lost her eyesight. Maybe it was his fault.

Oh, God, I'm sorry. Please, give her back her sight. Don't let her be blind.

chapter twenty-four

Wednesday, December 5, 10:00 AM

Jamison stood silently over Kate's bed and stared at her pale face. She was breathing heavily—a child's gentle snoring. He touched her forehead and felt the cool clamminess. The enormous trauma she had undergone had taken its toll.

Eyes still closed, Kate moved her head, a small frown on her brow as she scrunched the edge of her sheet with a clenched fist and released it, her dreams obviously unpleasant. Her lips moved but no words escaped, just indecipherable moans.

Suddenly her breathing came in short pants and after several seconds, her eyelids quivered. Bending over her and speaking in his gentlest voice, Jamison said, "Kate. Can you hear me?"

Kate whipped her head from side to side as though trying to deny some terrible accusation. "Kate, it's Doctor Jamison. Listen to me; you're going to be okay."

She snapped her head in his direction, her face distorted in anguish as she covered her eyes with both hands. "Oh, no. I'm back here with you."

"Kate. Listen to me. You're not blind. You're fine. Open your eyes."

Kate dragged the palms of her hands and curled fingers from her eyebrows to her mouth, disfiguring her appearance. Then she opened her eyes and sat up with a jerk, eyes widening. "Oh, I can see! I'm not blind!" Large tears welled up and streaked down her face. Color filled her pale cheeks. Her bottom lip trembling, she reached out and touched the back of his hand, motioning him to come closer. He bent closer to hear her choked words. "How can I ever thank you?"

He froze when Kate squeezed his hand, not used to such displays of emotion from patients. His throat constricted and, for a brief moment, he thought he was going to add his tears to hers. He pulled his hand back, cleared his throat, and gathered himself. Then he clumsily patted her hand and lowered himself into the chair next to her. As he brought his eyes level with hers, he shook his head. "What happened was just temporary. The clinical name of the condition is 'amaurosis fugax,' which is brought on by anxiety."

"It was only temporary? Could it come back?" she asked, a look of dread clouding her face.

He shook his head. "We don't think so. But you need to stay calm." He rose and opened the chart. "We ran tests while you were sleeping. They all came back negative, but we'll keep a close eye on it, okay?"

Kate's grimace turned to a grin as she wiped her nose on the sleeve of her hospital gown. "Is that a pun?"

He shook his head, taken aback by her quick retort, then squelched a chuckle. At that moment he realized he cared deeply about this child, not just as a patient, but as a father might feel about a daughter. The insight frightened him. He had never wished to be a parent, but now he wanted to protect her, keep her alive, not for his glory, but to watch her grow and prosper.

He harrumphed as he rose from the chair and then walked toward the doorway and called back over his shoulder, "Your parents are in the waiting area. They're anxious to see you. I'll let them know you're ready."

As he walked toward the waiting room, he pondered the enigma of Kate—a girl on the brink of womanhood who seemed to have already celebrated the rites of passage. A girl who had come to him as a wide-eyed gargoyle and whom he had transformed into a curly headed cherub whose songs could melt the coldest heart. Little did she know that twice he had stood at the back of the hall, leaning in the shadows, while Kate sang during the Stanford Hospital concerts. He had been entranced by her sweet voice. But he'd also been concerned that she would gain too much notoriety, too much public attention. She was already a celebrity and, in his opinion, her fame was an obstruction to her treatments and development. She didn't need to draw more interest to herself.

He drew in a deep breath as he entered the waiting room. Kate's mother and father stood. "You can go in now. She's awake and is waiting to see you," he said, with an emphasis on the word "see."

"She has her eyesight back?" her mother asked.

"It's as we told you earlier. Her condition was only temporary. Go on in."

Kate's father pumped Jamison's hand in thanks, and her mother gave him a hug and a kiss on the cheek. "Thank you for saving my baby."

He nodded and then said his good-byes and hurried down the hall. At the small sink, he took a paper cup from a holder, filled it with water, and drank it down in two large gulps. He crumpled the cup, tossed it into the trash receptacle, and then held the sides of the sink and leaned toward the mirror.

He would not—could not—get emotionally involved with Kate or any other patient. Such feelings would surely interfere with his goals. Like his father had always told him, "Keep your eye on the prize."

Despite the stress of the protesters, he'd readied his staff for a third transplant. It amazed him that even after Brian's death the hospital had received hundreds of requests for transplants for brain dead patients. The statistics on each perspective patient had been studied in depth, and if a viable brain became available, he would find a match.

On the one side, desperate family members were begging for the procedure, some offering hundreds of thousands of dollars if their loved one was selected. On the other, protesters were condemning the procedure and trying to block his life-saving surgery.

However, he wouldn't perform the third transplant until after he and Inna returned from Norway. He felt confident that the lecture and Nobel Prize ceremony would give him some much-needed media coverage to counter the cries of the protesters. Plus, he badly needed a vacation—time to renew his energy as well as his waning confidence.

His and Inna's early flight tomorrow would take them first to New York and then, after a short layover, to Stockholm. He figured he would have plenty of time to recover from any jetlag and would be fresh for the upcoming events. What's more, he'd promised Inna several days of first-class pampering, and he meant to keep his promises.

He walked to his window and looked out at the small group of protesters. Although their numbers had declined, they still badgered visitors as they entered the premises, trying to get them to sign their petition. These few "faithful" had worked themselves into a frenzy and were driving the hospital staff crazy. It would take a miracle to stop them. A miracle.

Jamison slapped his forehead with his palm. Kate. She was the only one who could bring those dissenters down. If she would speak on behalf of the transplants, the protesters would lose their momentum. She'd do this for him; he was sure. It was brilliant.

He returned to his desk, sat back in his leather chair, and buzzed his secretary.

"Yes, Dr. Jamison?"

"Beatrice, I'd like a hot cup of coffee and one of those muffins from the cafeteria. Would you mind?" he asked.

"No problem. I'm glad to hear your appetite has returned."

12:00 Noon

Josh sat at the far end of the cafeteria, avoiding conversation or eye contact with his peers and stared at the ground beef with suspicion. He had doused his so-called hamburger with mayonnaise, pickles, and ketchup to cover the dry, tasteless meat. It was like sawdust mixed with oatmeal. He licked a gob of mayo oozing from the bun and nibbled at the lettuce.

He had a lot to think about. His mom had called the school with the good news that Kate was okay—she could see. Josh was relieved that she wasn't blind, but for one fleeting moment he actually thought that maybe God had made her blind because of the way he'd behaved. He pushed thoughts of Kate from his mind when someone brushed his shoulder. He turned and looked. A shot of pleasure bubbled through him as Melissa Arnett sat next to him.

"Whatcha been up to?" A dimple danced at the corner of her right cheek as she added, "I haven't seen you much lately."

"Been busy," he said and quickly added, "but not now."

"Busy, huh? Too busy for friends?"

He turned his chair toward her and inched it a little closer. Then he flashed her his most practiced smile. "I've always got time for you."

Melissa giggled. "I hear you've been hounded by reporters. There's something about your sister every week on the news. Don't you find all this attention exciting?"

"Sort of." He took a sip of his soda. "That reporter, Rubenstein—he calls me all the time," he said as he leaned the plastic molded chair onto its back legs.

Her eyes grew wide and she licked her glossy, pink lips. "Really? If someone pointed a microphone at me, I think I'd just freeze. But you . . ." She just stared at him in awe without finishing the sentence.

"No big deal," he said with a shrug. "Hey, are you doin' anything Saturday night?" He tried to look detached as he willed his tone to sound nonchalant. "We could go to Val's for dinner and then see a movie."

"You got a car?" she asked.

"Of course," he lied. "Well, I mean it's my parents' car. I'll get my own later this year—" He hoped. "But I can drive one of the family cars." He took a bite of the cold burger and had to take three long gulps of his cola to wash the food down. "Anyway, I'll take care of the transportation." He knew this was impossible. Since the drug bust, his license had been pulled. But if she accepted his invitation, he would find a way to go out with her.

"Well, I have a car. So if it's a problem, I can always pick you up," she said as she pierced a cherry tomato with her fork.

At first Josh felt deflated by the thought of a girl picking him up. But under the circumstances . . . "Yeah, maybe that would work better." To hide his awkwardness, he turned away, as though interested in a debate going on at the next table.

"Good," she said. "It's a date."

3:00 PM

The terror of blindness had passed. The soothing words of the doctor and her parents gave Kate comfort, especially when her mother told her that Josh had said he hoped her vision would return. She felt relief. Maybe Josh didn't hate her after all. Kate counted this as a breakthrough.

After her parents left the hospital, she sat alone in the room and pulled the mobile hospital tray in front of her. She opened the mirror and stared into it. Finally, she lifted her hand to her face and gently traced the shape of it. It was soft, but firm. She carefully ruffled her short, dark curls, careful not to touch the almost invisible stitches around the edges. For an eleven-year-old, she was almost cute, except for the space between her two front teeth, but maybe she could talk her parents into braces in a year or two. She looked closer and found that she could adjust to the blurring caused by the wrinkled retina—just as Dr. Ahmed had predicted. She let out a short gasp, almost a laugh. In the two and a half months that she'd been Kate, she had never noticed that her eyes were a deep bluish green. They sparkled and were downright beautiful. For the first time since the accident, her chest swelled with the possibility of a near-normal existence.

She reluctantly closed the lid and then stared at the four walls of her hospital room. It wasn't the same one she had been in last time she was here. It was more cheerful, with bright primary colors. A balloon her father had brought her was on the windowsill. There were no words printed on it, just a single red rose—a symbol of love and hope, or so he'd told her, two emotions that now seemed to blossom within her.

5:00 PM

A sudden darkness passed over Kate's room as a cloud temporarily obstructed the late afternoon sun and cast dark shadows across her bed. She felt a tingling in her spine when she heard a rustle at the doorway. Dr. Jamison was staring at her. She knew instantly that something was wrong. The physician looked more like a beaten dog than the world's next Nobel Prize winner.

He hesitated for a moment and then walked to her bedside and clasped his hands together, bobbing them up and down like a beggar. "I have something special to ask of you, Kate," he said.

"What?"

"Those people down there—?"

She listened to the chanting and nodded.

"They want us to end the trials, the research into brain transplants. That will mean people like you, people who have suffered a car accident or a stroke, will have nowhere to turn. I've heard your singing." He paused to clear his throat. "You have amazing talent. That talent would have died with you if you had never been given a second chance at life."

She nodded in agreement.

"I need your help, Kate. I can't do this without you," Jamison said, his vulnerability showing in the set of his mouth.

"What do you want me to do?"

"Tell the public that brain transplants are life-saving procedures. Tell your story and be our champion," he said, his eyes looking deeply into hers.

She blinked and chewed the inside of her mouth as a dozen thoughts rushed through her head. Why hadn't she expected this? To give her time to think, she picked up the hospital-issued plastic water jug, took a quick sip through the straw, and swished the cool water between her teeth. She considered the consequences. If she agreed, would she ever be able to enjoy a modicum of privacy? Could she ever attend a public school and not be the target of hurtful taunts? Could she help him and avoid the fallout?

Jamison bent closer. "Look, Kate, you don't have to decide today. Just think about it. We can talk more tomorrow. And of course talk it over with your parents."

She noticed a slight tremor in his voice, and her heart ached for him. Hadn't she asked him just a few hours ago how she could ever thank him?

She pulled her blanket up higher. "I understand, but I do need time to think about it."

"Of course."

Even though the room was cool, his forehead was shiny with sweat. Kate knew how difficult this was for him.

"Don't worry, Dr. Jamison. Everything will work out okay."

His glassy eyes seemed to hold back a torrent of raw emotion. He stepped back, gave her a brief nod, and then turned and walked out.

chapter twenty-five

Monday, December 10, early

Kate turned over, stretched, and opened her eyes. She fumbled in the darkness and then finally located the lamp on her nightstand and switched it on. For several seconds, she stared at the Mickey Mouse alarm clock and tried to focus on the dial. She rubbed the sleep from the inside corners of her eyes and peered again—5:45 AM, still pitch black outside.

She fluffed her pillow, placed it against the backboard of her bed, and sat partially upright. She smiled at the thoughtfulness of her parents as she picked up the remote to the small television set they had purchased for her as a "welcome home again" gift. And Josh had actually been nice to her since the blindness episode, until he saw the gift their parents had given her. Then, as the day progressed, his sullenness had returned and increased.

Kate sighed. Well, she couldn't do anything about it now. Besides, she needed to find out what was happening with Dr. Jamison. She listened intently for a few seconds to make sure that the rest of the household was still asleep. Then she pushed the on/off button, muted the sound, and changed the channel to CNN. She didn't need to listen. Just watch. She figured that with the time difference, it would be early afternoon in Stockholm and there might be something on about the Nobel Award ceremony.

However, instead of Jamison's tall frame, there was a slender woman pointing at a map of the United States that indicated rain across the plains, snow in the northern and eastern areas, and sunshine in Hawaii and Phoenix. Kate sighed and switched to CNBC—financial news—not good. Then she turned to FOX—sports. She surfed all the channels in her limited cable service but found nothing about the doctor.

Kate tried to picture Dr. Jamison at the podium. Would he make an acceptance speech? Or would he just go up, smile, and shake someone's hand? She tried to remember earlier recipients and how the media had reported their achievements. She recalled black-and-white photos of the awardees and short statements that television commentators or newspapers printed about what they had done. But that was all she could remember.

Perhaps because she was so intimately involved in the doctor's success, she thought more should be made of it. She figured that there would probably be something about the Nobel winners on tonight's news. She could watch it with her parents.

Disappointed for now, Kate turned off the set, pushed her pillow down, and switched off the light. She tried to relax and go back to sleep, but visions of Dr. Jamison and the obvious joy he'd displayed last Thursday when she had agreed to advocate for him and his brain transplant procedure kept flashing through her thoughts.

"You will? You'll do it?" he'd asked, a grin spreading across his usually composed face.

"Well," she'd said with a nod, "I'll ask my parents. But I think they'll let me."

"Thank you, Kate. That means a lot to me."

Oops. She hadn't yet mentioned it to her parents. *I'll do that tomorrow—today.*

She sat up with a start when she heard a gentle rapping on her door and an almost indiscernible squeak of a turning doorknob.

"Who is it?" she said in a loud whisper.

"It's me, Josh," her brother said as he tiptoed into the room. "What are you up to now?"

What do you mean?" Kate replied.

"I saw your light come on from my window. You were supposed to be asleep hours ago not watching TV. What's going on?"

In a low but firm voice she whispered, "Josh, you're being paranoid. What's with you, anyway? You know, you're only hurting yourself with your passive-aggressive behavior. Now go to sleep and leave me alone."

Kate could see the dark outline of Josh's frame as he folded his arms. "There you go again with those big words, 'passive aggressive.' Something's just not right about you, sis. And I'm gonna figure it out." Josh turned on his heel and left as quietly as he'd entered. He pulled the door closed without a sound.

And I thought he was beginning to care.

7:00 PM Stockholm time, 10:00 AM Pacific Time

Jamison felt the muscles in his back tense. Any minute now he'd be accepting the prize from the King of Sweden. His tuxedo fit well enough, but the heavy starch in the shirt chaffed his neck and wrists.

He was surprised at how nervous he felt. The hard work was already behind him. On Monday he'd delivered his lecture at the institute to a full house in the theater-style hall. That had been the real trial—a forty-five minute lecture, complete with thirty-eight slides. It had been a hit. He'd received an ovation that lasted a full three minutes. Cameras rolled and admirers had sidled up to shake his hand afterward and offer him congratulations. He felt vindicated. The protesters were thousands of miles away, while in this country he was considered a genius and a hero.

But here he sat, front and center in the enormous Stockholm Concert Hall. Inna was seated to his right, staring up at him and smiling. She touched his hand as Dr. Ingmar Holtz came to the microphone to make the presentation speech. Jamison inhaled deeply and whispered his mantra, "For you, Dad. This is for you . . ."

He knew every word that Holtz would say because he'd provided the requested information about his background and discoveries. Nonetheless, he sat spellbound as Holtz delivered a twelve-minute recap of his accomplishments. It was as close to an out-of-body experience as he'd ever had. Then, after a short pause, Holtz finally announced, "And now, Dr. Jamison, please step forward to receive the Nobel Prize from the hand of His Majesty the King."

Thunderous applause echoed throughout the hall. He stood, glanced at his wife, and walked to the center of the ceremonial area. The King handed him his medal and Nobel diploma. The air was filled with electricity. Jamison didn't want the evening to end.

6:29 PM

Kate clicked off the TV, disappointed that neither KROX nor CNN had showed any part of the Nobel Prize ceremony. They just made cursory announcements that Jamison had received the highly coveted award. Both stations treated the event like an afterthought.

Kate was glad she hadn't asked her parents to record the coverage. She would have been embarrassed by the outcome, and she was particularly annoyed that after the short announcement, the stations had focused on the protesters from TULOG who were out in force at the hospital that night. She choked back a lump in her throat and decided that now was the time to ask her parents if they would support her endorsement of Jamison and the procedure. But she wanted the words to come out right. She wouldn't use the word "endorsement." That was too adult. Maybe she'd just say she wanted to help Dr. Jamison by talking to the media and telling them how thankful she was for the operation—use simple language.

"Time for dinner," her mother called from the dining room.

Kate's stomach growled and she realized she hadn't eaten much today.

"Coming," she responded as she continued to figure out exactly how she would broach the subject. Things were so complicated now.

6:30 PM

Marcy loved living in the Bay Area; it was almost winter and she could still use her outdoor barbeque. The aroma of barbecued ribs wafted into the kitchen as she brought the platter inside. It was such a pleasure to actually cook a whole meal rather than to heat up a frozen dinner or bring home Chinese take-out.

"Adriana, dinner is ready," she said as she placed three ribs, some French fries, and a large spoonful of coleslaw on each of the two dishes.

"Okay, Mom," Adriana replied as she clomped down the stairs.

"Get some napkins from the pantry." Marcy placed the plates on the kitchen table. With one hand, she took two glasses from a cupboard and then opened the fridge and extracted a plastic half-gallon container of milk. She closed the refrigerator door with her knee, walked to the table, and filled the glasses.

"Is anyone else coming? You only make ribs when we're having company," Adriana said.

"Just you and me. You're my special guest."

That wasn't the entire truth. Marcy hoped that someday she could serve them to Bruce, Megan, and Mark and that they would be as fond of ribs as both she and Adriana.

As she bit into the spicy ribs, her thoughts focused on the Lindsays. After the school bus had picked up Adriana that morning, Marcy had driven to the mall to find Christmas gifts to give to Bruce and his kids at the tailgate party before the football game—small things, not too expensive.

Although she'd been looking forward to this date for weeks, she still felt pangs of guilt for her thoughts about Kate's "husband." For this reason she had already decided that she wouldn't present the gifts herself. She'd leave that up to her daughter. That would be less awkward and might help build the relationship among the children. The gifts would simply be a way of saying "thank you" for the outing.

Although Marcy had been focused on appropriate gifts, the first item she'd bought was a special neck scarf for their dog, Algae. For some reason she'd been drawn into the pet shop. The blue doggie neck scarf, emblazoned with little snowmen and the words "Let It Snow," seemed to beckon to her—an impulse purchase, especially since it seldom, if ever, snowed in Hayward.

"What's so funny, Mom?" Adriana asked.

"Oh, I didn't know I was laughing out loud." She wiped sauce from the corners of her mouth with a napkin. "You remember that big dog at the Lindsays' Halloween party?"

"You mean Algae?" Adriana asked.

Marcy nodded and then told her about the scarf.

"I don't know, Mom. I think he'd rather have a bone."

"You're probably right. When we're finished eating, we'll put some of these rib bones in a plastic bag and put them in the freezer. Then we can find out if he has a taste for fashion and for ribs."

Adriana rolled her eyes.

"Oh, I almost forgot. I have some good news," Marcy said, trying to steer her thoughts away from the guilt she felt at having kept her silence.

"Tell me," Adriana said.

"Starting next week I'll have both Saturdays and Sundays off. We'll have more time to spend together."

"Cool," Adriana said. Then she cocked her head to one side. "What about Dad? When he's in town, will you still let me spend time with him?"

"Of course. We can take turns on alternating weekends. When it's our weekend, we can take short trips. I was thinking we could go to Tahoe for a weekend in January and take skiing lessons together."

Adriana's eyes crinkled and her mouth formed into a wide grin. "I would love to learn to ski."

Marcy pretended to be engrossed in her ketchup-dipped French fries while she recalled the tough negotiations at the hospital in order to work Mondays and take Saturdays off. She felt a tinge of regret as she admitted to herself that the reason she had requested the change wasn't so much to spend more time with her daughter but to pave a way to spend more time with Bruce, should the opportunity arise. After all, Kate now approved of the match as a way to learn more about her children and husband.

Guilt weighed down Marcy's shoulders. The mind of Liz—the soul of Liz—was still alive. Remorse swept over her. *But it isn't my fault. I've been her friend*, a little voice inside her said. *Some friend.*

It had only been three months since Liz died—still too soon to enjoy the type of relationship Marcy wanted—still too unacceptable to friends and family. But how long could she wait? It had been seventeen months since she'd broken up with John. He'd been a nice man, but not the right man. She knew in her heart that the right man was Bruce. How much longer would she have to wait?

"You okay, Mom?" Adriana asked, looking up at her with deep concern.

"Oh, yes, I'm okay—just tired, I guess."

8:00 PM

There couldn't have been more than two seconds between the time the doorbell rang and Josh answered it. He'd been pacing the hall, waiting for Melissa to arrive at his house and meet his parents.

Since their date Saturday night, he'd been unable to get her off his mind. He kept replaying the scenes: them entering the theater and her leading him to the far corner in the back row; him putting his arm around her as she placed her hand on his thigh and gave it a squeeze. Then, as he pulled her closer, she had turned, lifted her head, and let him kiss her. The rest of the evening was a blur of kissing.

As he drew open the door, he felt a surge of heat shoot through his body.

"Hi, Josh," Melissa said, fluttering her long dark lashes at him.

He felt wetness under his armpits. "Uh, come in. My family's waiting to meet you," he said in a louder-than-normal voice. He had to play it cool in front of his parents. Then they could go to her house to do "homework." Saturday, at the end of their date, she had let him know that on Monday evening her parents would be "out for the night."

He led her into the living room and tried to remember the proper way to introduce her. Was he supposed to present her to his parents? Or vice versa? He was so flustered that he couldn't remember, so he just fumbled through it. "Um, Mom, Dad, this is my friend Melissa." He felt his face flush.

His mom put down her pencil and Sudoku book. "Hello, Melissa."

"Josh has told us a lot about you," his father chimed. Then he turned toward Josh. "Don't forget to introduce your sister," he said, motioning to Kate, who was walking down the hallway.

"Yes, sir," he said as he turned and introduced Melissa to his sister.

Melissa threw a surreptitious glance at Kate. "Um, hi, Kate. Josh's told me everything about you." Josh saw Kate's eyes flutter and her face go pale, followed by a look of dislike and distrust. Fortunately, the two girls were facing away from his parents.

"Melissa, tonight's a school night," Josh's father said, "so our boy needs to be home by ten."

Josh felt his face burn, and he gritted his teeth. He knew better than to say anything. After his conviction and two months of them constantly reining him in, his parents were finally letting up. He didn't want to blow it.

"Oh, no problem, Mr. Craig. We're just going to study for our history test. That shouldn't take long," Melissa said with conviction. Josh was surprised at how well she delivered their practiced lines.

"Don't worry, Dad. I'll be home on time," Josh said with a wave, as he grabbed his jacket and opened the door for Melissa, carefully avoiding Kate's forlorn expression.

He put his arm around Melissa and then guided her briskly toward her car.

8:15 PM

A deep depression enveloped Kate. That little display her brother had just orchestrated was too much to bear. How could she survive in such a hostile environment? And how could she ever see her kids again with Josh watching her every move? She fought back tears.

School would be letting out for the holidays on Friday. Then he would be hanging around, watching her all the time.

A cramp caused her to massage her stomach and she felt a sudden wetness between her legs. Oh no! Not puberty . . . again!

chapter twenty-six

Sunday, December 23, 11:45 AM

Adriana peeked out the living room window. "Shouldn't they be here by now?" she asked her mom. "I hope you gave Mr. Lindsay good directions to our place."

Marcy smiled patiently at her daughter. "Yes, dear, I gave him good directions and I'm sure they'll be here any minute now."

Marcy walked to the window, stood beside her daughter, and peered out. She noticed that dark, billowy clouds were racing toward them. The weather channel had promised only a 10 percent chance of showers. But how often was the weather report right? Nonetheless, rain or shine, she and Adriana were committed to a tailgate party and a day at Candlestick Park.

Despite the wintry day, her daughter's eyes danced with excitement. This would be her first professional football game.

"They're here!" Adriana shouted as she waved from the window.

"Okay. Button up and wrap that 49ers scarf around your neck. It's cold outside," Marcy said as she drew her own jacket tight around herself. She grabbed her purse and the bag full of gifts.

As she and Adriana came out the front door Bruce exited the driver's side and ran around the car. He opened both passenger doors and said to Mark, "Move over to the middle and let Adriana in."

Mark scooted over and Marcy swung the bag of Christmas presents onto her daughter's lap. She then slid into the front seat of the car and smiled at Bruce.

As Bruce pulled away from the curb, he looked at Marcy and grinned. His deep smile lines accentuated the shape of his strong, square jaw. Marcy caught her breath. "Sorry I was late," he said with that same vulnerability in his eyes as she'd seen earlier.

Marcy wanted to touch him, kiss him, take away the pain of having just lost his wife. She struggled to compose herself. "No problem."

"Traffic is always bad when we have a home game, but don't worry. We have special stadium parking reserved for Kaiser staff tailgate parties. I gotta warn you though, we make quite a ruckus," he said, a wry smile forming on those irresistible lips.

"Yes. I know," she said without thinking.

"You do?" he asked, confusion written across his brow.

"Er, Liz told me about the annual outings . . ." Her words trailed off as she realized she had just opened a wound.

Silence invaded the car. Even the children quit their jabbering. Within seconds, loud drops began to splatter on the windshield. Why couldn't she keep her big mouth shut? Gloom mounted as the windshield wipers tapped out the warning, "Hush, hush, hush."

After several minutes, Bruce broke the silence. "Hey, kids, what's the first thing you guys want after we get there?" he asked in a tone riddled with false hubris.

The only sound from the backseat was the shuffling of feet that kept time with the windshield wipers.

Finally, Mark said, "I'd like fries. Will they have them?"

"Sure they will—best garlic fries in California. That sounds good to me too," Bruce said, sounding as though it was the best idea since the invention of microchips.

Then Adriana and Megan chimed in and the spell was broken. Bruce surreptitiously reached over, took Marcy's hand in his, and squeezed it. Without turning her head, she glanced at Bruce. He was staring straight ahead, but she could see a small, almost indiscernible smile at the corners of his mouth.

Marcy closed her eyes, inhaled, and ever so gently squeezed back. In that instant, all doubts left her. She knew that he wanted her the way she wanted him. It was as though an electric blanket, set on high, was suddenly thrust on top of her. Heat rose from her body, only intensifying as the rain abated and the sun peeked out from behind a cloud.

She sucked in her lower lip to stifle a moan. When would it happen? When could they have time alone together?

In an instant, Kate's image leapt into Marcy's mind and crushed her fantasy. Marcy pulled her hand away from Bruce and stared straight ahead.

Go away Liz . . . Kate . . . whoever you are.

12:15 PM

Trembling, Kate collapsed into a heap on her bed and curled into a ball. How could God do this to her? Wasn't it enough that she had lost her first mother to cancer?

She had sensed something was wrong last Friday when her mom had received that awful call. Her mother's face had gone white and her small mouth had formed an "O." When she hung up the receiver, she stood there like a sculpture with her hand covering her mouth.

"What's wrong?" Kate asked.

"It's nothing for you to worry about, dear," her mom said. But it was a lie. There was something wrong—terribly wrong.

"Mom, tell me. Maybe I can help," she pleaded. But Donna just shook her head and said that she needed to lie down for a while.

It wasn't until this morning, during the "Cares and Joys" part of the church service, that Kate and her brother learned the terrible truth. As parishioners shared their blessings or concerns, Kate saw her father's hand go up. When called upon, he stood and said, his voice choked, "Please pray for my wife, Donna. Friday she learned she has breast cancer. She starts treatments after Christmas."

Kate felt like she'd been knocked down. Memories flooded her like a tsunami. In precise detail, she relived the interview with her mother's doctor, the weeks and months of chemotherapy, the radiation treatments, her mother's nausea, and the final wasting away of her mother's body. She remembered that last day when her mother had motioned for her to lean over.

She whispered, "Liz" and started to reach up to touch her face. But then a startled expression came over her and Liz heard a final exhalation as her mother's hand dropped.

Again. Again. All over again. She balled her fists. She had no one to talk to about this terrible news. She couldn't tell her mom. And with Josh acting as her shadow, she couldn't call Marcy.

Kate crossed her arms, digging her fingernails into the flesh on her upper arms. What should she do?

Suddenly, Kate recalled the significance of today—The 49ers' game. *Marcy is with my family.* She grabbed her pillow and turned over on her bed, face down. Then she curled the pillow over the back of her head to muffle her sobs. She didn't want anyone in the house to hear. They were all suffering.

Moments later, she realized that someone was pulling her pillow away. "Kate, it's Mom. We need to talk."

Kate shook her head. "I can't," she said between sobs.

"Honey, I'm sorry you learned about my condition this way. I didn't know your dad was going to do this today. I wanted to tell you myself—after I learned more about the treatments. Most of all, I don't want you to worry."

Kate turned over and threw her arms around her mother. She hugged her hard. "This is my fault."

"What are you talking about?" her mother murmured, as she stroked Kate's face and pushed a short curl off her forehead. "You're my joy—my sweet, sweet girl."

Kate looked up at her mother's serene face. "But you have ca-cancer."

"Look, honey, this isn't going to slow me down," she said, wiping a tear from Kate's face. "Right now we need to get a bite of lunch, finish packing, and then we still have two more presents to wrap before we can leave for your grandparents' house."

"We're still going?" It didn't seem possible that this small woman could function with a cancer sentence hanging over her head.

"Of course we are. There are some traditions that must go on, and this is one of them. We have to live every day as fully as we can. So go wash your face and help me with lunch. We're going to have one of the best Christmases ever." Her mother handed her a tissue. "We'll take this one day at a time." Then she added with a look of pride, "In the meantime, you'll be entering public school—seventh grade—and helping Dr. Jamison. You have a lot on your plate, young lady, and you can't accomplish anything by sitting around here crying. Now get moving!"

Her mom smiled at her, rose, and walked to the door. Then she motioned for Kate to follow.

Kate blew her nose and stood. She would follow this woman wherever she led. She was, without a doubt, the strongest, kindest woman she had ever met.

12:30

Josh paced back and forth, one hand jingling the change in his pocket and the other clutching the cell phone to his ear. "Please answer."

After five agonizing rings, Melissa picked up. "I thought you were going to your grandma's house," Melissa said after a brief hello.

"We are. But something happened . . ."

"What is it, Josh? What's going on?"

"It's . . . it's my mom." Josh pulled his hand from his pocket, doubled up his fist, and brought it down hard against the dresser top. "She has . . ." He couldn't say the word. It kept catching in the back of his throat. He coughed and tried again. "She's sick. She has can . . ."

"Cancer? Oh, Josh, that's terrible. What kind is it?"

"It's b-breast cancer."

"Oh no, I'm so sorry." For a moment he thought she'd hung up. Then she asked, "Do you know what stage?"

Josh felt on the verge of tears, but he would not cry in front of Melissa. He swallowed back the lump that was forming in his Adam's apple. "We don't know yet," he blurted, "but I think I know what caused it. I heard that stress causes it. And Kate is the number one cause of stress in my house."

Melissa paused. "I don't know, Josh. I mean, yeah she's got her flaws, but—"

Josh barely heard her as he paced faster. "You're the only person who understands how I feel. What do you think I should do?"

"Don't do anything right now, Josh. When you get back from your grandparents', we'll figure out what to do."

"Okay, but there's something wrong with Kate. I don't know what it is. But I'm going to find out."

"And I'll be right by your side, Josh." Then her strong voice became a whisper. "I love you."

"I love you too," he said. "I'll call you tonight after we get to Ben Lomond."

wrapped by her mom, but nonetheless she experienced a sense of joy at the prospect that someday Josh might want to give her something more than grief.

5:30 PM

"Want more popcorn?" Marcy whispered to Adriana.

Adriana reached over and dug her hand deep into the butter-stained bag. But just as she was about to put her hand to her mouth, Adriana burst out in a belly laugh and popcorn went flying.

A G-rated movie was one of the Christmas traditions Marcy had invented for herself and her daughter after she divorced Earl. A second tradition was for Adriana and her to serve lunch to the homeless at the local Salvation Army kitchen. Marcy believed that both of these activities made them part of a larger community.

Marcy put her arm around Adriana. It haunted her that the two of them had no other family with which to share the holidays—and hadn't for almost six years now.

Marcy closed her eyes and tried to remember her parents' faces. But the images were blurry. In her mind, they had always been old. Both were in their forties when she, their only child, was born. They had doted on her and given her what they could from her father's meager earnings—a solid foundation and a good education. But both passed away within three months of each other the same year that Marcy and Earl divorced. The combination of these events, falling one upon the other, had left her without a village—without a tribe. For too many years now she blamed herself for her parents' passing—as though her divorce had destroyed them and their dreams.

Why did remorse hang over her head like a big black cloud? First her parents and now Kate. Visions of Bruce kept popping into her mind. Unlike the indistinct images of her parents, his hair, eyes, lips, and strong muscular arms were clearly visible to her. Two days ago, during the football game, he had reached over and moved a strand of her hair off her forehead. Then he'd asked her if she and Adriana would like to spend Christmas with them. She had wanted so badly to say yes. But she couldn't. It was too soon—much too soon. But maybe someday she could say yes. Maybe someday the guilt would go away and she would be free.

Everyone in the theater began laughing again. Freddy the Fearless Fly was boldly buzzing the Black Widow as the villain spider frantically weaved a web to capture Freddie. But he darted back and forth so fast that the spider ended up wrapping herself up like a mummy. Freddie finished her off by tying a neat bow on her head. Then he joined his other friends and they filled their cups with spider cider. Marcy wished it were that easy to get rid of the guilt that had been stalking her.

She squeezed Adriana's arm gently to let her know she loved her. More than anything, Marcy wanted her daughter to have a full life. *Maybe next Christmas will be different. Maybe we'll be a family.*

But one terrible thought kept shredding her dream. *What if Bruce finds out? What if he learns that Kate is Liz? Most important, what if he finds out I've known all along?*

9:28 PM Pacific Time

"Hey, soldier, what's your name?" Charles Rubenstein asked as he held the microphone up to the soldier's mouth.

"Lieutenant Andrew Baker, sir."

"How long have you been deployed here in Afghanistan?"

"Seven months, sir."

"And to whom would you like to send a holiday greeting?" Charles asked.

Long white clouds ejected from the young man's lips. "I want to say hello and Merry Christmas to my mom and dad; my little brother, Colton; and my fiancée, Julie. I love you and miss you all. Thanks for the warm socks and cookies."

"Thank you, Lieutenant Baker." Charles turned away from the soldier and spoke into the mic. "That wraps up our live CNN broadcast from Kabul, Afghanistan, and our holiday tribute to the brave men and women of our military who make sacrifices every day to keep you and me safe at home."

As the cameraman turned off the camera, Charles hugged himself to fend off the freezing morning air. Thank goodness they'd conducted the earlier interviews indoors, but the last four were moved outside so the nation could get a glimpse of the rugged terrain and weather conditions. By sending live between 8:30 and 9:00 AM Afghanistan time, the broadcast would be viewed by those on the West Coast between 9:00 and 9:30 PM. Charles hoped that his mom and sister had been watching.

This was his first Hanukkah season away from home, as well

as his first assignment outside the U.S. He had always dreamed of being a CNN reporter. But spending the holidays in Afghanistan, interviewing soldiers so they could send greetings to their folks back home, had never been a part of his fantasy. Sure CNN treated him well, but he was just one of many, and if he wanted to stay on top of his game, he had to be ready and willing to go wherever they said. He told himself over and over again that these men and women had families at home too, and they missed them as much as he missed his family. His career wishes had come true, but the price he was paying was more than he'd ever expected.

He hurried into the barracks. "Can I have a cup of c-coffee?" he asked through chattering teeth. The soldiers laughed and one of them poured him a steaming cupful.

He took off his gloves, stuffed them into his pocket, and wrapped his hands around the warm cup.

9:30 PM

Jamison shook his head as he turned off the television.

"Did you hear the quaver in Rubenstein's voice?" he asked his wife.

Inna nodded her head sleepily. The annual holiday banquet with their good friends, the Morrisons, had left her in a stupor—probably too much wine and turkey. Jamison got up from his chair, walked over to the couch, and then moved Inna's discarded shoes to one side and lifted her legs onto his lap. Lying down, with her head propped on one of the decorator throw pillows, she asked, "Why do you suppose he was so nervous?"

"Think about it, Inna. A Jew in Afghanistan is a target. He started out the broadcast with 'Live from Kabul, Afghanistan—this is Charles Rubenstein with a special CNN holiday edition.' " Jamison let out a deep breath.

Inna raised her head, a frown on her brow. "You're right. I hope he gets home safely. He's a good man and he's been helpful to you."

"True. But it looks like he has more on his plate than just following me around."

Jamison knew the cost of fame; it didn't come cheap. But Rubenstein was gambling with his life. Jamison's face reddened as he acknowledged that, unlike Rubenstein, his gamble was with other people's lives. He'd saved one and lost another. But the trip to

Stockholm had renewed his faith and energy. He was ready for the next surgery. This time he couldn't fail.

10:00 PM

Kate couldn't believe her ears when her mother told Grandma and Gramps, just before bedtime, that the lumpectomy surgery would take place on Thursday at Kaiser Hospital in Hayward. When Kate heard the words she gasped out loud.

"What's wrong, honey? You knew my surgery would be on Thursday," her mother said, head tilted to one side. Everyone was looking at her. They expected her to say something, but she stood there, mute.

Kate pulled the wool blanket to her neck and tried to drive the scene and the words from her mind. It couldn't be. Not at Bruce's hospital. How was it possible that her mother and her husband would be at the same place at the same time while she was relegated to staying with her "Aunt" Karen?

It had never entered Kate's mind that her family's medical coverage could be through Kaiser or that future medical visits might put her within reach of Bruce. Since her treatments had been at Stanford, she'd assumed that the family had a private plan. Was this providence or karma? Whatever it was, sleep would be difficult tonight.

chapter twenty-eight

Thursday, December 27, 11:00 AM

Kate craned her head toward the door to the X-ray area as she, her father, and Josh walked toward the surgery recovery area.

"What are you looking at?" Josh was so close to her that she felt crowded.

"People," she answered.

Kate's lungs felt heavy. She wished she could shout out the truth: "I'm looking for my husband!" Instead she had to stand silently by and wait.

She counted it a miracle that she had been able to convince her mother she should be there when she awoke from the lumpectomy surgery. But when her mother finally gave in, it meant that Josh would come too, and his presence made Kate uncomfortable.

"It's no place for you," her mother had said when Kate first broached the subject.

"How can you say that? I've been in and out of hospitals for months. I'll go stir-crazy if I have to wait at the house," she'd argued. All of this was true, but the fact that Bruce worked at this hospital was the clincher. She was determined to be there.

As they were passing the elevators, the doors swooshed opened and Kate turned. In that moment, her world stood still. Bruce looked directly at her, smiling.

He recognizes me!

Kate turned on her heel and rushed to his side. Just as he was about to walk past her, she reached out, tugged at his sleeve and whispered, "Bruce." The word came out a plea. He said something to her, but his voice sounded as though it came from a deep echo chamber.

The lobby began to spin. The blood drained from her face, and her knees went weak. A curtain of darkness floated down in front of her like a theater drape at the end of an act.

A pungent smell caused Kate's eyes to jerk open. Bruce was holding her hand while waving a small capsule in front of her nose. "Bruce," Kate cried out. Tears flooded her eyes. She reached up and touched his face, pulled him closer, longing to kiss him as she had in the old days . . .

Suddenly she drew back her hand. No. No. No. It wasn't Bruce. She recognized the man: one of Kaiser's male nurses.

"Everything okay?" Malcolm asked her. "You were sure out for a bit."

"Where's Bruce?" She tried to sit up, but her chest felt heavy and she could only prop herself up halfway. But Malcolm wasn't looking at her. He was talking to someone at the head of the gurney. She'd forgotten about her dad and brother, who were standing there, looking down at her. Her father appeared conflicted and in pain, whereas her brother seemed puzzled.

"Who's Bruce?" Josh asked, suspicion written in his eyes.

Malcolm cocked his head and then snapped his fingers. "He was the employee who called emergency for help and stayed with her until we could get a gurney."

Josh frowned and directed his question at Kate. "How do you know everybody's name here?"

Before she could think of an answer, Malcolm pointed to his name badge. "All staff members wear name badges. She must have read it."

A flood of emotions washed over Kate. Could Bruce tell she was Liz, his wife? Surely he must recognize some spark of her former self and see her for who she was, the same Liz who had "died" on the operating table weeks back. She fought back tears. She had lost everything.

"I—I'm sorry. I don't know what happened." She wiped her tears. "Please help me up. Mom's coming out of surgery now."

Malcolm shook his head and pressed her back down. "You need to rest. Your father says you had a very serious surgery a few months ago." Then he directed his conversation to her father. "We'll call her doctor at Stanford and let him know what happened today—see if he wants her transferred there."

"No!" Kate shouted, pushing Malcolm's hand away. "I promised Mom I'd be there when she woke up." She clutched her father's hand. "Please."

Her father turned to Malcolm. "Can't we wheel her up?"

Malcolm lifted his eyebrows. "You need to sign some paperwork first."

"Can't that wait?" her father said. "After the visit, I'll come back and sign the releases. I promise."

"Okay," Malcolm conceded. "I'll get a wheelchair."

12:00 noon

Kate's insides were churning as she sat next to her mother, squeezing her hand. She kept reliving the moment when she had seen and touched Bruce. After her fainting spell, she had recovered her senses long enough to come to her mother's bedside to be with her. Now, it all seemed to be part of another nightmare.

"Hi, Mom. We're here—Dad and Josh and me. How are you feeling?"

Donna's eyes scanned the three of them. "I feel great. I'll bake something delicious when I get home."

Déjà vu—her first mother, Diane, had behaved the same way. All the conversation following her surgery had been about trivial things. It was as if by not talking about tragedy, it didn't exist.

Josh piped up, "You look great."

It was a lie. Donna's face was pale, and the blue surgical cap hid her usually coifed hair.

Then Kate's mom turned her head and her smile fell. "Why are you in a wheelchair?"

"I'm—"

Kate's father interrupted. "She slipped in the lobby—didn't really hurt herself. But I told the staff about her earlier surgery and they insisted we put her in the wheelchair."

"You fell?" her mother asked.

"I wasn't hurt, but you know how hospitals are. Anyway I don't really need the wheelchair. See?" She stood up and pushed the chair back.

With a reluctant nod, her mom finally accepted that she was all right. When they said their good-byes, Kate left the wheelchair behind. As they returned to the emergency room to sign the papers for Kate's release, she looked around for Bruce, but he was nowhere in sight.

The ride home was miserable. Although it was warm in the car, Kate felt like someone had poured ice cubes over her body. Her fingers, toes, and nose were blue. But Josh was the real cause of her chills. He sat next to her dad in the front seat but kept turning around and staring at her.

Once they got home, it only got worse. Josh was her shadow. He seemed to be right behind her at every turn. And whenever their dad was out of earshot, Josh would ask, "Who's Bruce, Kate? What's he to you?"

"I don't know what you're talking about," she answered.

But he repeated the question over and over again, until her only escape was her bedroom.

She didn't know how she was going to do it, but tomorrow she was going to contact Marcy. Marcy was the only person who would understand—the only person who could help.

6:00 PM

"Okay you two. Now I want you to play fair," Bruce said. Megan and Mark nodded in agreement.

Bruce motioned to them to sit on pillows spread out on the floor by the coffee table where he'd set the steering wheels for the Wii. Algae snuggled in between the two kids as though he was part of the contest.

Bruce chuckled. "It'll take me about thirty minutes to get dinner on the table. Algae, if they misbehave, you come and get me."

When Algae heard his name, his ears perked up and he sat straighter.

As the sounds of the speedway filled the room, Bruce turned and walked to the kitchen. He counted himself lucky to have found a Wii for sale just two weeks before Christmas. Despite the poor economy, the contraptions seemed to sell out as fast as retailers could get them.

As he took the frozen fish sticks from the freezer, he thought about the emails he and Marcy had been exchanging:

> Would Megan like to come to Adriana's birthday party in February? Her birthday is on the 14th but we're celebrating the next weekend so she can have some friends over for a slumber party. If so, when you bring her over, maybe you and Mark can stay for the pizza party. I'll bring her back to your place on Sunday.
>
> MA

Bruce had responded:

> What time do you want us there? P.S. Mark has a crush on you. LOL!—BL

Marcy answered:

> Mark has a crush on me? Well, tell him the feeling is mutual. Oh, and bring Algae along. Adriana thinks he's the best thing since garlic fries.
>
> Love, MA

"Love." She had written "Love." He could feel the closeness building between them despite the fact that both of them seemed to choose their words carefully.

It had been little more than three months since Liz died. But by February 16th—the party—it would be five months. Bruce raked his fingers through his hair. He felt like he was betraying Liz's memory, and yet there had been a void since she died that nothing had been able to fill, until Marcy. *Why does this have to happen now? Why couldn't it happen a year from now?* Then he might not feel such guilt. But he did, and there was no getting around it.

He rubbed his hands over his face and moaned. Friends and family were already introducing him to one single woman after another. And there were the single women at work who hovered around and found excuses to be near him. It was flattering, but if he couldn't have Liz, he wanted Marcy.

Bruce popped the fish into the oven along with the tater tots. Then he went to the refrigerator and removed a bag of premixed coleslaw, pulled the tear tab, and poured the contents into a bowl.

As he set the table, images of the young girl at the hospital popped into his head. There was something unnerving about her—about the way she'd called his name—but he couldn't put his finger on it.

He shook his head and sat at the kitchen table. He had twelve minutes before the timer would go off on the stove.

As he sat there his thoughts turned to Marcy. She was so different from Liz. She was tall, svelte, dark haired, and bashful; whereas Liz had been short, buxom, a strawberry blonde, and an extrovert. But he couldn't deny his attraction to Marcy. It was intense, and he was determined to pursue it, even if he would pay the consequences later. He closed his eyes and tried to imagine himself with Marcy, but he couldn't help returning to the thought that he was betraying Liz.

8:00 PM

Even though a thin veil of fog lay over Josh's backyard, it was the only place where he and Melissa could talk. He pulled the chaise lounge into the middle of the brick patio so he could see the house and its exits clearly. He didn't want anyone to overhear their conversation. As they sat, he put his arm around Melissa. "Seriously, Melissa, something's wrong, and it seems like I'm the only one who can see it." Josh licked his lips. "You should've seen my sister at the hospital, reaching out to this stranger. She knew him. I know it."

Melissa frowned. "How could she?"

He shook his head. "I don't know. It was just too weird." Josh licked his lips again and then lowered his voice. "When I asked the guy how she knew his name, the dude pointed at his name badge. But she has something wrong with her eyes. Even if she could've read the nurse's badge, there's no way she could have read that first guy's."

"So what are you saying?" Melissa asked.

Goose bumps rose on Josh's arms as he whispered his theory into Melissa's ear. "I think she's possessed."

Melissa's eyes popped open wide. Then she removed his arm from her shoulder and hugged herself as though she'd experienced a sudden chill. "Oh come on! I know she drives you crazy, but that's not even possible."

Josh reached out. "I know it sounds strange, but what if . . . what if a spirit invaded her body while she was sick and now it's taken over?"

Melissa stared at him as though he had flipped. "You mean like in *The Exorcist?*" She pushed him away. "Josh, you're scaring me."

"Listen to me, if it hadn't been for my mother just coming out of surgery, I would have said something, confronted her."

"She's going to be okay, isn't she? Your mom, I mean," Melissa asked.

Josh felt a burning at the back of his throat. "My mom has cancer."

"So the surgery didn't work?" Melissa asked.

"I doubt it."

"Well, they've come a long way with cancer treatments. My neighbor, Mrs. Betman, had breast cancer seven years ago and she seems just fine."

"Mom says she's supposed to go see a specialist on Monday. I've heard about that chemo stuff—makes them sick, go bald . . ." Josh's voice trailed off as he thought about the awful things his family would have to face. Hadn't they already faced enough?

chapter twenty-nine

Friday, December 28, 8:00 AM

Sleep hadn't come for Kate last night. Yesterday's run-in with Bruce had weakened her. Despite her anguish, she put down her spoon next to her bowl of cereal and watched her brother as he poured milk and sprinkled sugar over his Cheerios. She had hoped that their shared concern over their mother's recovery might create a tie between them.

"Good morning, Josh," she said in her most pleasant voice.

"Don't 'good morning' me." He leaned forward, eyes narrowed. "When did you take over my sister's body?"

It felt as though an electrical current had surged through her. She choked on the toasted oats in her throat. *He knows.* She stared back at Josh, dumbstruck.

"What's your real name?" he asked in a growl.

Kate tried to speak, but her mouth wouldn't cooperate. *Who am I? Kate? Elizabeth? How do I answer his question?*

"It's okay. I already know," Josh bellowed as he shoved his bowl across the table, sloshing his Cheerios and sweetened milk onto the table and splashing it onto Kate's lap.

He rose from his chair and, like a genie loose from its bottle, seemed to grow taller as he spoke. "I'm not afraid of you. When my mom and dad learn what you've done to my sister, they'll call for a priest and we'll have you exorcized."

Kate wasn't sure she'd heard him right. She tried to decipher his meaning. "What are you talking about?"

"You're possessed."

Kate laughed, but upon seeing his serious expression shook her head to clear her thoughts. Then a light went on. *He doesn't know.* In spite of her best efforts to control herself, she burst out laughing again. "Oh, Josh, I thought you were serious," she said between chuckles.

Josh's face turned red, and Kate knew her laughter wasn't helping matters. "I am. As a matter of fact, I'm sure of it. You took over my sister's body during the surgery."

Thankfully, the television in the family room muffled Josh's words so their parents couldn't hear Josh's ravings. Kate wiped the smile off her face. "I'm sorry. I didn't mean to laugh," she said. "But think about it, Josh, if I were possessed, would I choose to enter the body of a physically impaired minor who can't even sneeze without someone holding a tissue to her nose?"

Josh looked puzzled—but only for a moment. Then he grimaced, folded his arms, and stared at her. "People are more likely to trust a child, especially one who seems helpless. But I've got you figured out, and you're not helpless at all. Your words keep giving you away—'physically impaired minor'? That's not something a kid or a teenager would say."

Kate's mind was racing. She needed a moment to think. She took her napkin from her lap and wiped the spilt milk. Then, deciding that the best defense was a strong offense, she said in a calm voice, "You don't have me 'figured out' at all. I'm Kate, your sister. And whether you believe it or not, I'll never do anything to hurt Mom or Dad, or for that matter, you. I'm not an angel, but I'm definitely not the devil."

Josh turned and looked beyond Kate into the family room as their dad walked from the hallway into the kitchen, newspaper tucked under his arm. "What're you two up to?" he asked as he poured himself a cup of coffee.

Neither Kate nor Josh answered. Their dad joined them at the table and, spying the remainders of the spill asked, "What's this?"

"Ask her," Josh said, pointing a finger at Kate. Then he rose, walked out the back door, and slammed it behind him.

Her father turned toward her and lifted his eyebrows.

"He's just worried about Mom," Kate said, believing that it would only make matters worse if she relayed their conversation.

"I suppose," he said as he rose. "We're all concerned."

With a deep sigh, her father walked to the back door, opened it, and stood there looking as if he'd lost something.

Emptiness filled Kate. She'd lost something too—hope. Although someone was always nearby, she felt isolated, cast off, like a lone tumbleweed blowing across an arid desert at the mercy of the shifting winds.

My brother thinks I'm possessed; Jamison wants me back at Stanford for tests; today my mom comes home from Kaiser; and Monday she starts cancer treatments. Kate knew she had to find a way to contact Marcy—the only person in whom she could truly confide.

8:30 AM

"Are you ready, Doctor?" Yamaguchi asked as Jamison inserted his hands into the surgical gloves.

Jamison nodded, but inside he didn't feel ready. A new donor brain had been flown in early that morning, and a thirty-two-year-old female, Consuela Rodriguez, was prepped and ready to receive it.

But yesterday, when Kaiser had called about Kate's fainting spell, he'd wished he had the power to have her brought to his side on command. He wanted one more round of tests before conducting the next transplant surgery. He wanted reassurance that the fainting spell wasn't a sign of organ rejection or some other chronic condition.

But how could he refuse to operate? Everything was in order; the recipient and donor were a perfect match. All the required equipment, the surgery team, and the necessary facilities were ready.

He swallowed his insecurities and walked briskly to the operating table.

One of the nurses reached over and wiped his brow. He hadn't even realized sweat was dripping from his forehead. He glanced at his hands and noted a nervous quiver. He whispered to himself, "Dad, if you're up there and can see me, help."

5:12 PM

Marcy couldn't get into her car and leave the grounds fast enough. She yearned for the comfort of home—to hold her daughter. Like September 11, she would forever remember where she was and what she'd been doing on this day.

Marcy was still dealing with the news that the third brain-transplant patient had died on the operating table when her phone rang. Kate was on the other end, blubbering and telling her about her run-in with Bruce, sobbing and upset about her brother, and worried about her mother's health. Kate rambled on in one run-on sentence after another.

Marcy listened and responded to each of Kate's concerns. When she finally paused, Marcy had told her about Consuela Rodriguez. At first, Marcy thought the line had gone dead. "Are you there?" she asked.

She heard a gasp. "Oh no, not another one. Marcy, why am I alive and the others dead?" Kate asked, her voice quavering.

"I don't know."

"I think I'm losing it, Marcy. I don't know how much longer I can hold on."

Marcy's other line buzzed. She looked at caller ID. It was her ex. Should she take it, or talk Kate through her crisis? Her ex was in the military. There could be a problem. "Can you hold for a minute, Kate? I have another incoming call."

"No. I have to hang up. I hear Josh coming." Click.

Marcy moaned as she transferred over. Earl was on the other line with the news that he was about to be deployed to Iraq. This capped the day. The sky was falling.

5:30 PM

Kate's insides were churning, but not because of Josh. Despite all that had happened in the last two days, she was trying her best to put on a cheerful front for her mother. This made it easier to ignore Josh's surreptitious taunts as they sat together in the backseat of the Mercedes on the way home from picking up their mom from Kaiser Hospital.

"Are you two okay?" her mother asked. "You're both so quiet."

"We're fine. But the real question is, how are you?" Kate asked with a gusto she didn't feel.

"Actually, I have terrific news. My lymph nodes were clear of cancer." A smile spread across her mother's pale face. "We caught it early."

"That's the best news we've had all day," her father said.

"Yes!" Josh shouted.

Kate couldn't hold back the tears of joy. She felt a heavy burden lift. "So you're going to be okay?"

"According to my oncologist, I'll receive six weeks of radiation at a clinic right here in Castro Valley."

Josh looked at Kate. Some of the anger he'd directed to her earlier appeared to melt as he turned to face his mother. "But radiation—that doesn't sound good," Josh said.

"I'll be fine. No chemotherapy. No more surgery. No pills."

A flood of emotions spilled over Kate. Visions of her first mother's cancer-ravished face transformed in her mind to bright colors exploding like fireworks over a river. *This mother—my new mother—will live to fight another day.*

With a tear running down her face, Kate lifted her chin high and began singing, "You'll Never Walk Alone." Josh swallowed hard as he glanced at Kate. Then he turned his head and looked out the window. Soon her mother and father added their bass and alto voices, and the car reverberated with melody.

6:00 PM

Jamison studied the autopsy report. Heart Failure. Why? Everything had gone as planned. The recipient had been in better physical shape than the Craig girl, and the procedure had gone without a hitch. No mistakes.

But something was missing. And he was sure that the TULOG protesters would be stronger tomorrow . . . out in force. He had received hundreds of applications for the next brain transplant, and when another match was found, the Stanford team would be ready. But he couldn't afford another fatality. His team must be meticulous, leave no stone unturned. The stakes were too high.

chapter thirty

Thursday, February 14, Valentine's Day, 5:30 PM

Today was a red-letter day. Kate felt optimistic as she stirred the frosting for her birthday cake. The last six weeks had been difficult, but Josh's belligerence had down-shifted to second gear, and going to school offered time away from him along with an opportunity to meet others closer to "her age." In addition, a week ago her parents had taken her to Stanford for tests and resisted Dr. Jamison's efforts to readmit her. He kept emphasizing that she was at risk, pointing to the deaths of the other two transplant patients. They were grateful for his concern but firm—she was doing just fine, they told him, and her place was at home with her family. Best of all, Dr. Jamison's fourth transplant patient, Ruby Nuygen, operated on just three days ago, was alive and breathing on her own. And the protesters at Stanford were losing steam.

"Why are you grinning?" her mother asked as she took the frosting and began spreading it on the cake, a bright red apron protecting her blue and white hounds-tooth pantsuit.

Eyes brimming with tears, Kate said, "Because you look so healthy and today is my birthday." *Twelve years old . . . again.* She planted a kiss on her mother's cheek and noted that she was almost as tall as her new mom, a mere five feet, one inch. "And because Melanie will be here soon to help celebrate."

Her mother nudged her with her forehead. "I know how hard it's been for you to make friends after everything that's happened, but it will only get better. I promise."

Kate blinked rapidly. "I know." With that, she leaned her head on her mother's shoulder and watched as she put the final decorative touches on the chocolate cake.

She wondered at this woman's many talents. Then she swallowed hard, realizing that she had been only half a mother to Mark and Megan. She'd been too young and self-centered to give enough attention and time to her family. When she compared her parenting skills to her new mother's, she didn't measure up.

"By the way, I got a call from Mr. Nankervis," her mom said.

"The choir director?"

"He wants you and Josh to sing a duet two weeks from this coming Sunday."

Kate lifted her head from her mother's shoulder. "I don't have a problem with that, but Josh might not be so crazy about the idea."

"Don't worry about your brother. I'll talk to him. Nothing would make me more proud than to see, and hear, my two musical prodigies up at the podium singing together. The director says we can pick the music to fit the theme—'Make a Joyful Sound.' "

Kate frowned. A duet could provide the opportunity for a breakthrough with Josh. She blinked, pursed her lips, and rolled up the sleeves of her yellow sweater so she could wash the spatula and decorating equipment her mother had used. Glancing out the kitchen window, she spied her dad and Josh, both in jeans and T-shirts, despite the cold, dribbling and shooting hoops with the new basketball Josh had received for Christmas. Josh seemed so happy, so absorbed.

As Kate stood lost in thought, the phone rang. She dried her hands on a paper towel and walked over to the kitchen extension. "Craig residence, Kate speaking."

"Kate, this is Marcy."

Kate could hear panic in Marcy's voice. "What is it?" she asked, glancing quickly at her mother.

"Is any member of your family within earshot?"

"Yes," Kate said, trying to keep a placid face.

"Then brace yourself. There's been a tragedy and you need to know about it before the media invades your place."

Kate blinked rapidly to gather her bearings.

"The last transplant patient, Ruby Nuygen, died an hour ago, just minutes after regaining consciousness—just like Brian Jorgensen. She was fine—vital signs good—until she opened her eyes. Then . . ."

Kate felt a black curtain of depression wrap around her like a shroud.

"Are you still there?" Marcy asked.

"Yes."

"The announcement just went out."

Kate turned her back on her mother so she couldn't read her expression. "Okay. I'll see you at school tomorrow. Thanks for calling, Carly."

"Wait. Don't hang up. I think I know why they died and you didn't."

"Really?" Kate asked, trying to act as though she was talking about something trivial.

"You have a memory. It's the only thing that went wrong with your surgery. Or maybe it was the one thing that went right."

The doorbell rang.

"Why would that matter?" she asked.

"I'm not sure, but . . ."

The doorbell rang again. What if it was Melanie? She had to get Melanie and her parents inside before the reporters arrived.

"Thanks for letting me know," Kate said, cutting her off. "I have to go now."

She put the receiver gently back in its cradle and ran toward the front entrance, trying to make sense of what Marcy had said.

"I think Melanie and her parents are here!" she shouted to her mom as she swung the door open.

"Kate Craig?" asked a vaguely familiar face. "I'm Randall Simms from KNOP. Can I speak to your par—?"

Kate didn't hear the rest of his words. Bright lights flashed, cameras whirred and clicked, and microphones were shoved in her face. The TV vans and newspaper reporters on the front lawn formed a wall of media.

The house phone rang. Her mother's cell phone rang. More lights flashed. A dozen voices shouted questions.

"Get away from here," her mom shouted at the crowd, shoving Kate behind her.

"But, Mrs. Craig, another brain-transplant patient died today. Your daughter is the only successful recipient. How does that make you feel?"

"How do I feel? I feel like slamming this door in your face."

As her mom began to close the door, Kate saw Melanie standing across the street, peering over the team of reporters. "Mom, my friend is out there—and her parents."

"Stay here!" her mother commanded before stepping outside.

"No. You stay here," her dad said as he and Josh converged at the front door. "We'll take care of it."

The two of them went out, closing the door behind them. Kate could hear the angry voices of her father and Josh ordering people off the property and threatening to call the police. But when they came back inside a few minutes later, there was no Melanie, just Josh holding out a package wrapped in white paper with pink balloons on it and a big pink ribbon.

"Melanie and her parents say happy birthday, but they'll visit another day, once things calm down," her father said.

Kate fell to her knees, held her face between her hands, and let out a low moan. She felt the strong, comforting arms of her father as he lifted and cradled her and heard her mother's soft cooing.

"I'm sorry," Josh said. Then he was gone.

6:30 PM

As Charles Rubenstein stood outside the hospital, listening to chants of "Death to the Death Doctor," he was once again relieved that CNN had reassigned him to cover the demonstrations against Stanford Hospital and its chief neurological surgeon, Dr. Jamison. It was a welcome relief to the Middle East assignments. He still broke out in a cold sweat whenever he recalled the many times he had been entrenched in war-torn areas, hiding until he could be whisked away. For weeks they'd moved him from one troubled area to another and, although he wasn't a religious man, he had found himself mumbling excerpts he had recited for his bar mitzvah and asking God for deliverance. When CNN had offered to transfer him back to cover the growing turmoil surrounding the deaths of the brain-transplant patients, he had jumped at the chance. However, the transition hadn't been painless.

The chaos had escalated after the Rodriguez woman's death. But when Ruby Nuygen had died today, pandemonium erupted.

"Stop the Death Squad! Down with Jamison. Stop the Death Squad! Down with Jamison," the protesters shouted as they walked the hospital's perimeter.

"Stanford has had to triple its security forces to deal with the protesters, many of whom have tried to force their way into the operating rooms to search for the chief surgeon," Rubenstein said over the din of voices. He pointed to a light post, and the cameraman panned to the object hanging from the light. "As you can see, the doctor has been hung in effigy. And we've just learned that several patients have been moved to other hospitals to avoid harassment."

Next the camera panned to the enraged faces of the crowd and then back to Rubenstein. "A small opposing demonstration of family members and friends of brain-dead patients are holding hands around the fountain area that leads into the main entrance. They say their only hope is for the transplant surgery—that without it, their loved ones will die."

Approaching the small band and looking for a vantage point where they could talk with one of the anti-demonstrators, Charles and his cameraman, Joe, pushed their way through the crowd. Just as Charles fought the last few steps to the fountain area, his cameraman pointed frantically to something or someone behind Charles. As he turned, he saw a crazed man with a sign attached to a thick board. He ducked in time to avoid being hit by it. Instead, the sign and the man crashed into the camera and sent the expensive equipment, the protestor, and Joe to the ground.

Without thought for his safety, Charles threw his full weight against the sign-wielding protestor. Clenching his hand into a fist, he drove it as hard as he could into the man's face. He was shocked when he saw the man's cheek crack like a broken mirror and blood ooze from his nose. The man drew his arms up around his face and shouted, "No more!"

Charles got up off the ground and brushed himself off. "Are you all right, Joe?"

"I'm okay," Joe said.

"Did you get the guy swinging the sign on camera?"

"I think so."

Charles held his hand to his earplug. "I'm getting feedback from central. We captured the entire attack on video."

And I thought the Middle East was dangerous.

9:15 PM

Bruce muted the sound on the TV and reached for the ringing phone.

"Hi, Bruce, this is Marcy."

Bruce lowered his feet on the recliner and sat up straight. "Marcy. Good to hear from you."

"I was just calling about this coming Saturday."

Bruce could hear something desperate in her voice. "Adriana's birthday. What can I do to help?"

"Everything's set. But it would be nice if you could come an hour earlier than the invitation says. That way we'll have a chance to visit before the rest of the girls arrive."

Bruce twirled his finger around the coiled phone wire. "We'll be there. By the way, I saw on the news that there's quite a ruckus at Stanford. Are you okay?"

"Most of the patients are being transferred to other hospitals, and my outpatients have found other clinics to complete their therapy. I'm on leave, with pay—at least until the administration figures out what to do."

"You must be going through some tough times, what with your ex being sent overseas too."

She sighed. "Well, that hasn't made life any easier. But I'm glad I have you as my email buddy."

"You know, Mark has a soccer match the Saturday after this one. Would you and Adriana like to come? We could go out with the team for pizza afterward—"

"Pizza two Saturdays in a row? How can I resist?" She laughed, the earlier tension gone.

"I'd say we're in a rut."

She laughed again. "Okay, it's a date. Just talking to you makes me feel better. But people might gossip about us."

"Let them talk."

10:30 PM

Donald Jamison paced the floor in the two-room suite he'd rented at the San Francisco Hilton. Inna was in the bedroom, sedated.

He'd paid cash for a week's stay and made special arrangements with management that under no circumstances would they let the media or anyone, except for a list of persons he had given them, know they were there.

His life had become a nightmare: death threats, car tires slashed, his wife harassed and forced to withdraw from her charity work. He was grateful that he hadn't been at Stanford when Ruby died. But as soon as the hospital called him, he and Inna had gathered up a few items of clothing, his laptop, and their cell phone chargers. Then he'd called the hotel, withdrawn $4,000 from the bank, and driven in to the city.

Moving out of the country was looking better and better. But there was no leaving the U.S. until he could find out why the others had died while Kate had lived. He swore to himself that he would never do another brain transplant until he had the answer. It just didn't make sense. He had gone over the charts a thousand times. The procedure was exactly the same, so Kate should have died too. And since she was alive, then they should be alive.

"Donald. Come to bed," a drowsy Inna called from the bedroom.

"In a minute."

Next week, after reviewing the online records, he'd call the Craigs and force them to bring her to an off-campus clinic where he could re-examine the procedure step-by-step and solve the puzzle.

chapter thirty-one

Friday, February 15, 7:25 AM

Kate brushed her fingers through her hair, pushing the short black curls off her forehead. She looked at her face in the mirror. Her eyes were red and swollen, and the rim of her nose was bright pink and tender from blowing. Even though her upper body was warm, her feet were like icebergs.

She shuffled from room to room, avoiding Josh while looking for her mother. Soon the gentle sound of tapping led her to her mother's office. Kate tiptoed in and watched as her mother entered some sort of data into an Excel file. She had overheard some of her parents' conversation and knew that money had become a big concern.

Kate's father had left early that morning, flying back to Portland to finish critical details on one of his road projects. He'd said he'd be gone for at least a week but had promised to call every night. He'd made it clear that he hadn't wanted to go, but he'd already taken off too much time from his job. The economy was taking a nosedive. Mom's accounting business had already lost two clients. On the other hand, contracts for roads and bridges—infrastructure—was getting a boost from the government. Her dad had to be "at the helm" or others would outbid them. And he needed to ensure that all of his current projects were completed at or under bid. There could be no overages. Stricter standards now applied.

Kate moved back to the doorway and watched her mother for a minute. Then she said, "Mom, please don't make me go to school today."

Her mom swiveled her chair around, stood up, and walked over to her.

"Is it the media?" her mom asked.

"The newsmen are driving me crazy." She walked to the front door, with her mother at her heels, and peeked through the stained-glass side panels. Television vans, reporters, and photographers were still gathered on and around their property.

Her mother let out a long sigh and put her arm around Kate's waist. "You don't have to go to school today. I'll call the office and let them know."

Just as Kate was about to turn and walk back to her bedroom, Josh sauntered past, swung his backpack off the marble-top entry table, and onto his shoulder. He mumbled, "See you later." Kate could tell that despite the earlier truce he was once again angry.

"Josh! You got your lunch money?" his mother asked.

"Yes . . . and my books, and my assignments," he said in a tone that meant "Get off my back."

"Okay. Maybe if we ignore the news people they'll go away."

"Right," Josh said as he slammed the door behind him. Kate went into the living room and pulled the drapes back just enough to peek outside. She watched as Josh worked his way through the crowd. Cameras snapped, questions were shouted, and microphones were thrust at his face. "Leave me alone!" he yelled as he began running, one shoulder thrust forward like a football player trying to make his way to the end-field.

Kate turned back and slid down onto the couch. She covered her face with her hands. The short conversation she'd had with Marcy yesterday kept replaying like a stuck record. "Your memory . . . your memory . . ."

Why would memories make me survive while others died?

She wrestled with Marcy's theory. Prior life memories couldn't possibly be the answer, could they?

If Marcy was right, could Dr. Jamison subject her to the memory erasure procedure if he knew? And if he did, would she die? On the other hand, if he concluded that memory was an essential element to a successful transplant, would he let her keep it? Would he tell her parents? And if he did, would they still love her?

The walls of her own deception were collapsing in on her. The secret she'd been keeping, the tapestry she had draped around her, was unraveling. She had to know if her memory was a factor.

"Mom, I need to talk with Dr. Jamison," she blurted out.

Her mother hesitated, then walked over and put her arm around Kate's shoulder and gave it a squeeze. "I'll call the hospital."

8:05 AM

"Mrs. Craig, you don't know how happy I am you called," Jamison said, feeling a glimmer of relief at the sound of her voice.

"We heard about the death of your patient and wanted to extend our condolences," Kate's mother said.

"Yes, of course." Jamison's throat constricted and his words came out high-pitched. He sipped some water, wishing it were wine. "As you know, I very much need to see Kate again, but not at Stanford—that would be impossible under the circumstances. I have a colleague with a clinic in Oakland, not far from where you live."

"And what do you want from my daughter, Dr. Jamison?" she asked.

He could feel a protective barrier going up between him and Kate—a mother lion guarding her cub.

"We've run dozens of tests. I've gone over every step of the last three operations and can find no reason why they weren't successful. It comes down to this: there's something special about Kate. It may have been the encephalitis coupled with some of the earlier treatments. Hers was the only case of slow atrophy whereas the others were comatose from head trauma."

He took another sip of water. "It could even be psychological."

"What do you mean?"

"Almost all my studies and tests have been measuring physical results. Even when Kate met with the child psychiatrist, our emphasis was on measuring her IQ and learning ability. But, I've seen cases where fairly healthy patients give up even before an operation's underway. They get depressed, and their immune systems shut down. I've seen others who shouldn't have survived a week, but something inside them drove them to hang on. Some lived for months, others for years, and a few others are still with us."

He paused in hopes that Mrs. Craig would say something encouraging, but she was silent. "Please understand, I'm at a crossroad. I cannot and will not perform another brain transplant until I know why three physically healthy patients died and your daughter lived. Mrs. Craig, I'm not used to begging, but if that's what it takes, then I'll do it. Please." He realized that his voice was shaking.

"Very well, Dr. Jamison. My daughter wants to meet with you too. Tell me where and when, and I'll bring her. But this time I want to be present for any tests. She's not a guinea pig. She's just a little girl who needs to get on with her life."

11:00 AM

Kate's mother worked out a plan with the city police to help escort their car a short distance to escape the paparazzi. Once they were certain they weren't being followed, she made a beeline onto the MacArthur Freeway and the police escort veered away.

Kate, dressed in jeans and a blue pullover sweater, sat back and took a deep breath. This was the day. Jamison had to be told. She couldn't bear the burden of guilt, the deaths of others, if indeed it was her memories that kept her alive. She hoped to have an opportunity to talk privately with Dr. Jamison.

She nervously fingered her small pink purse, a note inside it. If she couldn't find the opportunity for a one-on-one conversation with the doctor, then giving him the note would be her only option.

Traffic was light and in a little less than twenty minutes they pulled into a small parking lot in the Oakland Lake Park District. A sign read "Lake Merritt Clinic." Kate was surprised to see the simple beige one-story building. Compared to Stanford, it was unimpressive. She glanced at her mother but saw no expression of doubt or fear.

The interior was as simple as the exterior. A few chairs were lined against a white wall, and several feet in front of the chairs was a wall with a pair of sliding opaque glass windows and a one-foot-deep counter. A bell sat on the counter, and a sign instructed patients to ring for service. Another sign taped to the right of the window stated, "Payments and Co-pays Must be Paid in Advance."

The window slid open and a young Asian woman dressed in a medical tunic asked, "How may I help you?"

"We have an appointment with Dr. Jamison," Kate's mother said.

"You must be Mrs. Craig and Kate. We've been expecting you." She stared openly at Kate. After a moment, she seemed to catch herself and closed the window. Seconds later she reappeared, opening a door to the left of the window. "Please follow me," she said, chart tucked under her arm. The woman pointed at an open door. "The doctor will be with you shortly."

Kate sat on the exam table, and her mother sat on the only chair in the small room. It had the requisite counter with multiple drawers and cupboard doors, a sink, a box of sterile gloves, and a round stool on wheels. Kate scanned the posters and charts on the walls as she rubbed her arms. Even with a sweater, she felt chilled. She wondered if keeping medical rooms just above freezing helped prevent the spread of germs. Perhaps it was the profession's way of moving patients quickly.

Five minutes later Dr. Jamison came in. "Sorry I kept you waiting. I just got here myself," he said as he closed the door behind him. Kate noticed dark circles under his eyes, and he seemed shorter, bent over.

"How've you been, Kate?" he asked.

"I'd be better if a thousand reporters weren't camped in front of our house."

Jamison cleared his throat and nodded.

The next two hours were nothing more than a marathon of lies and half-truths. A local psychiatrist, Dr. Marion Berger, and Jamison tried to pry into every corner of Kate's psyche. Several times Dr. Berger raised an eyebrow, as though questioning her response.

At the end of the two hours, Kate felt beaten, and her mother must have sensed it because she said, "Enough!" Then her mother stood and expelled a loud breath. "I'm sorry. But you've asked the same questions over and over again, and Kate has answered you. She's tired and so am I." She turned to Kate and said in a calm voice, "Come on, dear."

Kate had to do it now. Jamison had to know. She opened her purse. What she took from it would finally reveal the truth. "Dr. Jamison, this is just a thank you note to let you know I appreciate everything you've done for me."

He started to open it.

"No," she said in a rush. Her knees felt weak, and her mouth went dry. "Wait until you get home."

He nodded, and she and her mother hurried out.

Kate couldn't remember the ride back. Would Jamison expose her? Would Bruce and her children find out? Would her parents hate her?

Only time will tell.

2:15 PM

Jamison slid the plastic key through the slot and heard a click. Then he opened the door to his hotel suite.

"Is that you, Donald?" Inna asked, her voice coming from the bedroom. Inna appeared barefoot in a terry bathrobe at the doorway between the bedroom and the living quarters. "How'd it go with Kate?" she asked as she entered the room, patting down her hair with a towel.

"Dr. Berger was no help. She felt the girl was withholding something. The only significant difference that I can establish is that the other patients suffered head trauma. But that doesn't make sense to me." He removed the note from his jacket and then laid the jacket across the back of the sofa. "She wrote me a thank you note."

"At least she's grateful. And I'm sure her parents are too. Someday the whole world will be grateful for your contributions," Inna said as she touched Jamison's cheek.

"Maybe." Jamison picked up the envelope. It read "Dr, Jamison. Personal." He chuckled. What could be so personal about a thank-you note? He opened the envelope, unfolded the stationery, and read the letter.

The letter dropped from his hands and floated to the floor. He felt his way to the couch and sat with a thud. He shook his head. "No. No," he moaned.

"What is it?" Inna asked as she came to his side.

"What have I done?"

chapter thirty-two

Saturday, February 23, 8:00 AM

Jamison felt twenty years older than his actual age. His back ached and his joints felt sore. He stared around the room, walked over to the opposite wall, and took down the last placard. Then he wrapped it in white packing paper and placed it in the cardboard box. He ran his hand over the smooth desktop. It was bare now. At least the protesters were gone. They were content with his resignation and the hospital's press release that brain transplants would no longer take place. The people from TULOG were celebrating. But their actions hadn't caused the about-face. No. It was Kate's note.

Now he knew the truth. He hadn't saved a child. Oh no, he had killed the child—killed Kate. And encased the essence of a grown woman into the body of a child. He had performed a "body transplant." Such a procedure would never pass ethical scrutiny. If people knew the truth, very wealthy people might "purchase" comatose bodies from indigent families. No, the ethical world wasn't ready now, and probably never would be, for a body transplant. "Do no harm." He repeated the doctor's oath in his head.

He walked to the sink and washed his hands. Could he ever get the blood off them? For the first time, the smell of the antiseptic soap turned his stomach.

As he dried his hands, his thoughts segued back to all those "successful" animal experiments, a testament to what Kate had written. For indeed, he'd never bothered to erase the dogs' memories. Nine of the last twelve animal brain transplant "patients" were still alive. They had their memories.

His stomach growled. He hadn't eaten dinner last night or breakfast this morning. He tried to comprehend how terrible it must have been for Elizabeth Lindsay to awaken in the body of a child, to learn that she would never again be a wife to the man she had married or a mother to the children she had born.

He rubbed his face. He wanted to confess his sins, but he knew deep down he would never tell the world. It was horrible enough that he and "Kate" would have to live with the awful truth.

The hospital had asked for an explanation. He'd told them Kate was an anomaly. Her special set of circumstances was one in a million: an eleven-year-old girl with years of medical attention; a combination of drugs and surgeries; and a mother who massaged and exercised Kate's limbs. The combination would never be so perfect again.

Like Kate, he lied—lied to keep the dark secret from the world. He would carry it to his grave, just as, he assumed, she would.

Jamison sat for the last time in his worn leather chair. He put his head on the desk and let go a stream of tears—tears for Kate, tears for Elizabeth. He mourned them both along with his medical career.

Primum non nocere.

"Do no harm. Do no harm. Do no harm."

8:30 AM

Marcy watched as Adriana ran ahead of her and rapped on the door. She heard the quick thumping of a child's running footsteps, and within seconds the front door flew open.

"Oh, good, you're here," Megan said, eyes aglow. "We're almost ready to go." Megan grabbed Adriana by the hand, and the two giggled and ran upstairs.

Marcy was pleased at the growing friendship between her daughter and Megan. The birthday sleepover party last weekend had cinched not only the connection between the two girls, but also her blossoming romance with Bruce. She recalled with relish the kisses she'd received from both Mark and Bruce after the pizza party, just as they were leaving. The kiss from Bruce wasn't just a friendly peck. It was a deep, passionate kiss that lingered on her lips all day.

Her heart raced and color rushed to her cheeks as Bruce lumbered into the room, leash in hand, and Algae at his heel. "You look great!"

Marcy laughed. She was in a purple jogging suit, and the only makeup she had applied that morning was light pink lipstick. She wasn't wearing earrings, only a watch.

"I'll wear this outfit more often."

Bruce glanced upstairs and then walked over to her, put an arm around her waist, and drew her against his hard body. He kissed her gently, running his tongue across the front of her lips. She opened her mouth, wanting more of him. But the sound of footsteps interrupted them.

"Okay, let's hit the road," Bruce yelled up. He winked at Marcy, bent down, and attached the leash to Algae's collar. "Game starts in half an hour."

Bruce took Marcy's hand and squeezed it. She pressed his hand in return. At that very moment, another smaller hand clasped her free one.

"Hi, Marcy. I love you," Mark said, looking up at her with pure adoration.

"I love you back," Marcy said.

She swelled with joy. Everything was looking up. The hospital had called her yesterday, telling her that with Jamison's resignation the protesters were gone and she could be back to work next week. Her ex was stationed in Baghdad within the safe zone and was sending emails to Adriana.

But just as she was beginning to feel upbeat, once again an image of Kate—or was it Liz?—knocked her back. She bit the inside of her lip. She couldn't deny that her relationship with Bruce and his kids was built on a lie. But, she reasoned, Kate could never be Bruce's wife or Megan and Mark's mother again. It was time for everyone to move on.

She consciously pushed Kate's face out of the picture and replaced it with the image of that last kiss. *Go away, guilt. I want this man, this family.*

9:30 AM

A chill of excitement ran through Kate. Maybe it was the brisk winter air, but more likely it was the thrill of knowing she might see her husband and children today. She'd gone online two days ago on the pretense of doing homework. But instead she had looked up Mark's soccer team's schedule. Today, here at a park next to the Hayward Plunge, he was scheduled to play on the new soccer field, and Bruce was the assistant coach. Maybe she could catch a glimpse of them.

Although Melissa parked her car on the opposite side of the park from the soccer field, Kate could see the game in progress as soon as she stepped out of the backseat of the car. She instantly recognized Mark's slender body and funny gait as he ran down the field after the ball.

"Josh, Melissa, I want to watch the game for a while," she said, pointing toward the field.

"I thought you told Mom you wanted to go swimming," Josh replied.

"In a minute. You two go ahead."

"Do whatever you want." With that he stomped off toward the indoor pool with Melissa running to keep up.

Kate jogged, tote bag under her arm, toward the soccer field.

From the distance she spied Megan and a young girl sitting next to Marcy. The girl was probably Marcy's daughter, Adriana. Bruce was standing on the opposite side of the field, whistle in his mouth.

Just then, Megan's arm jerked upward as Algae tugged and leaped into the air. Suddenly the dog broke loose and came darting across the field, leash dragging behind him. Algae ran toward Kate, ears flapping.

Within seconds Algae was upon Kate. Her knees buckled and she fell to the ground as the dog licked her face and neck with loud slurps, tail wagging. Kate laughed and hugged the wiggling animal.

Algae knows who I am! He missed me.

"I'm sorry. I don't know what's wrong with him," Megan said, puffing from her run to retrieve Algae. "Bad dog!" she shouted as she pulled at Algae's collar and grabbed for his leash. "Are you okay?"

Kate looked at her daughter. She was taller and sounded more mature. Kate yearned to hold her. Tears welled up and spilled over the rims of her eyes.

"You're hurt, aren't you?" Megan said as she bent over and laid her hand on Kate's shoulder.

Kate reached up and touched her daughter's soft hand. "I'm okay." Then Kate turned her face away so Megan wouldn't see the pain in her eyes.

Kate sat up and brushed herself off. It took everything in her power not to blurt out, "I'm your mother." Instead she said, "I'm sure your dog was just being friendly."

Megan stood up and jerked at Algae's leash again. "Bad, bad, dog," she scolded. Algae lowered his head and his eyes, then emitted a small whining sound.

"No, he's a nice dog." Kate wanted to keep the conversation going. "What's his name?"

Megan was still tugging at the leash and giving Algae the evil eye. "Algae. I'm Megan."

What else can I say to keep her here? "You were sitting with that woman over there—and that girl," Kate said, pointing a shaky finger across the field. "Is that your mom . . . and sister?" She knew the truth, but to Kate, Megan's voice was like the sound of soft raindrops and the perfume of fresh cut lilies.

Megan looked at her with an expression that Kate knew well—that, "'Yeah, so?" look. Then Megan must have thought better of it because she said, "That's my dad's girlfriend and her daughter."

"Girlfriend?" Kate fell back on her haunches. Even though she'd been encouraging Marcy, she wasn't ready to hear it put into words. Or to accept what it meant.

In a conspiratorial whisper, Megan added, "I saw them kissing."

Kate tried to send a mind-message to her daughter: I'm your mother. I'm your mother. But unlike Algae, Megan didn't respond.

"Oh. But where's your mom?" Kate asked.

Megan cocked her head to one side as though trying to determine whether she should answer. Then her mouth turned down and she answered in a small voice, "She's in heaven with my grandma."

Megan bit her lip, as though struggling with the memory. Then she pulled once more on the dog's leash and turned away just as Bruce ran over and bent down to help Kate to her feet.

"Are you all right, little girl?" For a moment, Kate didn't realize he was addressing her.

"Uh . . . I-I'm fine," she stammered.

He pulled her up as though she was weightless. She held onto his hand—never wanted to let go. Thoughts of her last days with him flashed through her mind—the fight they'd had the night before the accident. She'd been selfish, unreasonable. She knew now that a bigger house wasn't the answer to happiness. It was the love of family, the companionship of friends, and good health.

"Are you sure you're all right? Where are your parents?" Bruce asked looking around.

"I-I'm with my brother. He's at the pool," she said.

Bruce frowned and bent closer. "Haven't I seen you somewhere before?"

She wanted to say yes, a thousand nights and a thousand mornings. But instead she merely clenched her jaw. "I don't know. Maybe," she replied in a tone devoid of feeling.

He drew away suddenly, as though afraid of her. "You're sure you're okay?" He backed up but didn't take his eyes off her.

She nodded even though she was dying inside.

He shook his head as if trying to clear it and said, "As long as you're certain you're not hurt."

She watched as Bruce began walking toward the soccer field. Twice he turned and looked at her. Marcy had started toward them but had stopped halfway and was standing there, white-faced, staring at her.

Kate couldn't hear what they were saying, but after a short exchange, Bruce took Marcy's hand and they walked together to the soccer field.

Kate hugged herself and fought back tears. She saw it in their walk. They were a couple. Bruce might have recognized Kate, but not as Liz. He just saw a strange little girl he'd seen once before. And that's how he'd referred to her—"little girl."

Of her entire family, only Algae knew who she was. And the only other person who recognized her was Marcy, and she would never tell anyone because she was now Elizabeth Lindsay's replacement.

Kate stumbled toward the indoor swimming pool, clutching her tote bag to her chest.

9:45 AM

Josh slammed the locker closed, wrapped the towel around his neck, and put the combination lock on the locker door. Okay, so maybe he had been way off base about the whole "possessed" thing, but there was something different about Kate. After everything that had happened with their mom, he'd just started to warm up to Kate when she pulled this. She had begged him to take her to the pool as a "birthday present."

"Idiot," he said out loud.

"What'd you call me?" A burly teenager a few lockers down puffed himself up like a blowfish.

"Not you. My sister," Josh said quickly.

The guy jutted out his bottom lip. "Hey, I know what you mean." He smiled at Josh as though they shared a common bond. "Sisters can be a real pain."

"Got that right."

They exchanged high-fives. Nowadays, more often than not, Melissa seemed to be taking Kate's side. It was probably a girl thing.

Josh showered and then walked out of the men's locker room into the pool area. Through the plate glass windows he saw his sister making her way toward the building. For a moment, he felt guilty for leaving her alone. He was supposed to be responsible for her. If something had happened, he would be blamed. That's the way it was when you were the older brother.

But then he saw her crying and immediately regretted being so mean. He knew she couldn't help the fact that she'd been sick. It was just that everything had always been about her. It was like he had become the invisible child. Even now, with the media circus, he would constantly get hammered with questions about Kate. For once he wanted someone to ask about *his* day, how *his* life was going. Was that too much to ask? He released a pressured sigh and looked around for Melissa.

9:55 AM

Kate's distress soon melted into numbness as she let the cool water of the pool ripple over her. She had always loved the weightlessness of water. Swimming was the closest thing to flying. And for the moment, she was a bird.

She walked across the shallowest end of the pool, making small waves with her hands. Maybe she'd been a marine mammal in a past life—a spinner dolphin or a seal.

Josh and Melissa were swimming close together, splashing water at each other. They were happy, like she had been at one time. She wished that he was as relaxed around her as he was around Melissa.

"Hey, watch this," Josh said to Melissa, climbing out of the pool and then running and jumping close to Melissa, splashing water into her face.

Be careful, Josh. She watched first in fascination, then in horror as her brother scooted out of the pool, hollered at Melissa to watch again, and then dove backward into the mid-section of the pool. In an instant, Kate knew that the area was too shallow for the angle that he entered.

When Josh didn't come up, Melissa screamed. Terrified, Kate dove underwater, her short legs kicking hard and her arms reaching forward in fast, hard strokes. She swam fast like Liz, Hayward High School Swim Champion, not Kate who had spent most of her life as an invalid. Then she saw him, his lifeless body near the bottom. His eyes were open, his face pale, and a ribbon of blood oozed from his head. For a nanosecond she froze. Then she went into automatic. *You know what to do.* She grabbed Josh about the torso and with every ounce of strength pulled him to the surface.

The lifeguard was still several strokes behind her when she brought Josh's head above the water. She pushed him upward as a teenage boy who seemed to know Josh helped pull him from the water. Kate was out of the pool in an instant. She fell to her knees in front of Josh, then opened his mouth and cleared it with a finger. She held his head back and breathed into him. Once. Twice. Three times. As she took in another breath, she whispered, "Don't die."

Others gathered around. The lifeguard tried to pull her off. "No!" she yelled. "I know what I'm doing."

"Josh. Josh, breathe," she commanded between each breath. "We love you. I love you."

Her efforts seemed to be in vain. Several seconds passed. Finally Josh coughed and spat up water.

Kate sobbed for joy as she repeated, "I love you, Josh."

Josh stared into her eyes. His jaw drooped open. Then he reached up and cupped her chin. "I-I love you too."

chapter thirty-three

Friday, July 4, 7:45 PM

Jamison held tight to Inna's arm as they entered the Cal State East Bay stadium. It occurred to him, as they shuffled their way to a seat in the stands, that this would be their last stateside event. He fingered the airline tickets in his inner pocket, checking again for the third time to make sure they were still there. Tomorrow they would fly to Paris for a week of museums and galleries before going to their final destination, Australia. They'd settle in Melbourne. He thought he might take up painting or sculpting.

He hoped that tonight's performance would raise his spirits and release him from his depression. The newspaper headlines had read, "Special Performance—Brain Transplant Survivor and Brother Sing." It drew him like the siren's song. Maybe Kate's future wasn't so bleak. Perhaps he had given her a new beginning. The media referred to her as a potential opera star.

"Are you all right?" Inna asked. "You seem so far away."

"I'm fine, dear," he said. But Inna knew the truth. He had told her everything. He could never keep anything from her. She had turned pale when she learned about Kate, but then she drew herself up and said, "You've always done the right thing. I'm still very proud of you."

He was grateful for his wife. As long as she stood beside him, he would be fine. She was stronger than he would ever be—his pillar.

He looked into the sky. The night was balmy and the stars were out in full force. Even the bright stadium lights couldn't totally dim them. For the first time since he'd learned the truth, he felt a small flicker of hope.

7:50 PM

Charles Rubenstein didn't miss CNN. After Jamison's retirement, they'd tried to assign him to cover the Somali pirates—told him they wanted him to interview the pirates. He just shook his head and said, "No thanks." He'd had enough adventure for a lifetime. He was more than grateful that KROX was willing to take him back. They even gave him a raise. He now had an international name and warranted a higher salary, even though his stint with CNN had been short.

He unwrapped a stick of Juicy Fruit gum, wadded the gum into a ball, and popped it into his mouth. He'd quit smoking, but he couldn't give up the gum—not with his nerves so fried from all the stress.

Tonight's event would be a snap. Having personally interviewed Kate and Josh, as well as their parents, gave him the upper edge. He was back in his element, back with his family. Home.

"Hey, whatcha doin'?" his cameraman asked. "You look so pensive."

"Just wondering how these kids will do. Pretty great, isn't it? Less than a year ago the girl was in a coma, close to death, and tonight she's singing to a crowd of thousands in the stands and millions on their TVs." For a moment, he stared off into the distance and saw the child whose lifeless body he had cradled in his arms as he'd run through the streets of Iraq in search of a story. He blinked back the memories and then turned to Mack. "Life throws us curves, but some people can still hit a homerun. That's what Kate Craig has done—that'll be my spin on tonight."

7:55 PM

Josh looked at his sister, who was standing beside their mother. Kate had put on a little weight and no longer appeared so gaunt.

"You look great!" he told her.

"Thanks," she said, flashing him a dimpled smile.

She was almost pretty. Her short, dark curly hair and plump

pink cheeks stood in stark contrast to his memories of that frail, frightened girl he'd seen ten months ago in the hospital. And the way she looked at him with such adoration and respect filled him with renewed guilt for his past behavior. But that feeling quickly faded, because he knew she had forgiven him.

"Kate, your grandma wants you to wear this," their mom said as she hooked a thin gold chain with a pendant heart around Kate's neck. "It's a good-luck necklace that your great-grandma wore—twenty-four carat. And look closely, there's a rosebud etched into the center. It's a precious family heirloom."

Josh peered over the crowd, spotted his grandparents in the front row at stage right, and waved at them. They had reserved seating for their entire extended family, Melissa, himself, and of course, his sister, Kate, from which to view the fireworks after the concert.

Josh looked over at his sister. "You nervous?"

"A little."

"Me too. Five minutes to showtime. How's my red jacket look?" he asked as he adjusted the lapel. His trousers were white. His tie had red and white stripes and blue stars at the knot. He hated to admit it, but he was just as nervous as Kate.

"Your jacket looks awesome. So do you," she said, her eyes flashing. Her dress was the same red as his jacket.

He gazed at her and smiled. He didn't hate her anymore. Sometimes he still felt twinges of jealousy, but that would soon pass. He felt closest to her when they were singing.

With three minutes to go, he whipped out his cell phone and texted a message to Melissa. "ILU prtty grl. CU after." He pushed the send button and then turned off his phone.

"You're on!" the director cued from the side.

Josh felt adrenalin pumping through his veins.

"Let's go," Kate said and they walked onto the stage.

7:55 PM

Marcy tried to hide her fears as Bruce patted the seat next to him. Bruce had insisted they go, said it was their patriotic duty, and the articles in the newspaper had played this to the hilt.

Bruce said he thought he had met the girl in the paper once and wanted to see the performance. He'd said he "needed to see it."

Marcy worried he was putting the pieces together.

"I'm glad we got here early." He put his arm around her.

Adriana, Mark, and Megan were chatting and laughing, completely oblivious to any deeper significance.

A cramp formed in Marcy's left thigh. She massaged it but felt no relief. She was certain it would be over between her and Bruce if he found out. Surely he would trace it back to her—the lies, the mock friendship between her and "Liz."

Her eyes snapped wide and she gasped aloud as Kate walked onto the stage.

"What's wrong?" Bruce asked.

Marcy shook her head. They were seated just two rows back, and Kate was staring straight at them.

8:00 PM

As Kate climbed the stairs to the stage, her arm tucked under Josh's, she caught a whiff of popcorn and sparklers—a strange mixture. But the thunderous applause they received at their introduction made her forget about the odors as her stomach fluttered and the palms of her hands became moist. She feared she might not be up to the task, but then Josh nudged her. When she looked at him, he smiled down at her, giving her confidence a boost. It also reminded her that tonight wasn't just about her. It was also about him.

At first the stadium lights were so bright that Kate couldn't see the audience, not even in the front row. But as the announcer read the short bio about them, her eyes gradually became accustomed to the glare.

It was as if lightning coursed through her bones when she saw them—her other family. *I can't believe this! They're just a few feet from me.* She stood immobile.

"Kate, what's the first number you and Josh will sing?" the announcer asked, handing her the microphone.

She still couldn't move. Josh must have thought it was stage fright. Gently he reached over and took the mic from her, cleared his throat, and spoke into it. "We have a medley of patriotic songs. The first medley starts with songs written by Woody Guthrie."

Josh nudged her again, causing her to snap out of her stupor. She braced herself. She had to let go—let go of the Lindsays, release them, and set herself free. They had moved on. Now it was her turn.

I am Kate Craig, brain transplant survivor, coloratura soprano, twelve-year-old daughter of Donna and John Craig, and sister to Josh.

As the orchestra began the opening music, she closed her eyes, took in a breath, and poured out her heart—with her voice. Each note sent a message of love—a last message from a wife to a husband and a mother to her children. With each new number she forced the holes in her heart to be mended—by Josh—by her parents. She would always love Bruce and Megan and Mark, but it was time to admit that Liz had died last September.

As their last number ended, the crowd erupted with applause and shouts of "bravo" and "encore." They were on their feet. "More, more!" they shouted.

"Okay, okay," the announcer said over the tumult. "We have a surprise for you—one more number. This one is a solo. Kate will sing her favorite operatic number. Talk about fireworks! Wait 'til you hear our own Kate Craig sing 'Un Bel Di,' from Puccini's Madama Butterfly. One day you can say that you were at the debut performance of a famous opera star, because folks, there's no doubt that this young lady is headed for fame."

Josh gave her a wink and stepped to one side. The orchestra director raised his baton, and the music began to permeate the air. Kate squared her shoulders and took in a deep, cleansing breath that filled her diaphragm. At the director's cue, she opened her mouth and let forth the haunting notes and Italian phrases that had thrilled her for years. But this time it was her voice—her crystal clear soprano voice. As she sang the last stanzas, Kate opened her arms as though embracing the audience. It was a last hug for those special people sitting in the second row. Tears cascaded down her cheeks. After the last note was sung, she nodded at Marcy. It was her way of telling Marcy that she was letting go and letting her "fill in."

Butterfly—that's me. One day a caterpillar, then wrapped in a cocoon of confusion and horror, now free to fly to a dream I never thought possible. Kate had found her niche. She knew now that someday her name would be up there with Maria Callas, Joan Sutherland, and Kathleen Cassello. She would live for the Craig family—and music.

She wiped her face with her sleeve and smiled at the audience.

9:05 PM

The crowd around him rose to their feet, offering another ovation. Bruce was on his feet too, but for a different reason. He stared at the girl onstage. The words kept echoing in his head. "Un Bel Di." It was Elizabeth's favorite. Every time she was upset or moody, she'd play that recording and cry. This was the same girl who'd reached out to him at Kaiser—had called him by name. This was the girl at the park—the one that Algae loved.

Good heavens, this girl had a brain transplant. Elizabeth was a donor—just ten months ago.

Hairs stood up on the back of his neck. The roar of the crowd filled his ears like a faraway echo. He knew. "Elizabeth," he whispered.

He turned and looked at Marcy. She was crying, shaking her head and mumbling, "No, no, no."

Dread grabbed him at the small of his back and extended down his arms and legs. He felt weak. He turned away from Marcy and stared at the curly haired girl with the beautiful blue eyes—Liz's eyes.

He pointed at the girl and tried to say her name—tried to shout out "Elizabeth!" but the name stuck in his throat.

"Daddy, what's wrong?" Megan asked.

Mark frowned. "Do you know her?"

"Why are you pointing at her?" Adriana demanded.

Bruce turned to the children. Their little faces were full of concern. He swallowed and shook his head. *Can't be. Can't be. Liz is dead.*

"No. I don't . . . I—I don't know her," he rasped, the half-lie forming a knot in his gut. Bruce felt tears channeling down his cheeks.

A warm hand grasped his. "I'm so sorry," Marcy muttered. He could see the pain on her face, the fear and pleading in her eyes. For one cold moment he felt numb inside. Then the warmth of the hand holding his and the love of three young children brought feeling back to him. He squeezed Marcy's hand and watched as she turned to the girl onstage. Marcy waved and threw a kiss.

The girl on stage threw a kiss back. Marcy mimed catching it and placed it on her heart.

9:10 PM

Kate pivoted away from her husband and children, bowed to each of the sidelines, and looked over at her new family. As the applause died down, she lovingly caressed the golden heart that hung from her neck, the symbol of a new life . . . a life full of opportunities.

book club questions

- How important is memory to the definition of who we are?
- Does the body have a memory?
- Where does the soul reside? In the heart, brain, or some other place?
- Is age a state of mind or is it controlled by man's calendar?
- How adaptable is the human spirit?
- Could a responsible, loving parent ever truly release his or her children to the care of another and remain in the shadows?

acknowledgments

I deeply appreciate:

- Technical contributions from neurologist Bob Seiling, MD, and my sister-in-law, Phyllis Wilks, a retired physical therapist. They helped make *Becoming Kate* seem authentic and believable;
- Carol Craig, my stepdaughter, who served as my editor;
- My son-in-law Phil Lary for photos of Stanford Hospital to keep the site fresh in my mind and for helping me design the website www.becomingkate.com;
- Cedar Fort Publishing for believing in my story and printing my first novel;
- Medora Nankervis, Medora's Writers Group, and Martha Sells for helping me frame important parts of the novel; and
- Howard, my best friend and husband, for listening attentively as I read and reread each chapter.

about the author

Dixie Owens has a wide variety of interests and talents. For example, she has served as campaign manager and fundraiser for a candidate for the Oregon State House; emceed an international convention with more than 1,100 attendees; sung with a chorus in the Duomo in Florence; and last year, she and her husband won first place in a Charleston contest.

She earned her Associate of Arts from Ohlone College, took marketing courses at UC Davis, and completed a "Women in Management" certification program from the University of Southern California's post-graduate school of business.

Her career with the State of California's Employment Development Department (EDD) spanned more than thirty years. Many of those years were in the fields of marketing, media, job development, and event planning. Since retiring in 2000, Dixie has divided her time between singing, sculpting, painting, dancing, swimming, reading, writing, and filling her calendar with friends and events.

Dixie and her husband have a blended family of seven children, their respective spouses, fifteen grandchildren, and eight great-grandchildren. Dixie also has six siblings, countless nieces and nephews, and a Christmas list of over 200.